THREE FOR ALL

ELIA WINTERS

CECAELIA PRESS

Edited by Tera Cuskaden

Cover design by Zoe York

Cover photography by Taria Reed/The Reed Files

ISBN: 978-1-951589-01-1

First Edition November 2019

For the A-Team

1

L ori looked up from her nearly empty glass of champagne as her best friend, Hannah, held a full bottle aloft, announcing to the party room, "Another toast! Who needs a refill?"

She spotted Lori first, and Lori held out her glass in tacit acceptance of the refill. She was, after all, the guest of honor at this party. She was going to have to drink a metric fuck-ton of water to avoid a headache tomorrow, and she should probably have called it a night an hour ago. Hannah filled glasses of all those who gathered around, emptying one champagne bottle and then accepting another from her boyfriend Mitchell, who was somehow pulling out an endless supply from the fridge behind the bar. Hannah's *other* boyfriend Ben was accepting the refills as fast as Hannah could pour them. Things were going to be fun in that house tonight, with all of them plastered. Lori smiled into her champagne flute and tipped back more of the tart bubbles.

"Attention!" Having refilled all the glasses, Hannah was now holding hers up and calling for quiet. Her eyes sparkled, probably half booze and half happiness. "A toast! To this beautiful woman over here, my best friend, and the newest Doctor of Psychology in Mapleton! Doctor Lori Clark!"

It wasn't her first toast, and they had all been basically the same speech, but Lori couldn't even be annoyed. She'd been in school *forever*, and this degree had taken nearly her entire adult life, and so she was going to get buzzed on champagne and celebrate. When the cheers and drinking returned to normal party conversation, though, she pulled Hannah over. "No more toasts, okay?"

"I'm happy for you, that's all." Hannah squeezed Lori's hand. "Why aren't you wearing the hat?"

Lori's tam hung on the coatrack. She reflexively touched her spiral curls. "And crush all these? Hell no. This"—she gestured around her face, to indicate the whole hair-and-makeup combo—"does not happen by accident." The academic tam was indeed one of the most ridiculous items of clothing ever devised, but damn, she did love it. She was probably going to hang it on her wall at home so she could look at it every day.

A gentle nudge from Hannah alerted Lori that yes, she was grinning across the room at a velvet hat. She let herself keep the grin, allowing tiny filaments of relief to thread through her body. "I did that. I finally finished." She raised her glass and clinked it with Hannah's. "I can't believe it's over." The phrase made her pause. "Or, I guess, just starting."

"Commencement." Hannah fumbled the word, adding a few too many *m* sounds. "It means beginning." She was definitely drunker than Lori, but Lori was well on her way, giddiness starting to bubble up like the champagne.

"I know it means beginning." Lori straightened to her full, slightly above-average height and put her shoulders back. "I have a PhD." She rolled the word around on her tongue. "PhD." It sounded fake still. "Doctor Lori Clark."

"Doctor Lori Clark!" Hannah fairly crowed, raised her own glass in a salute, and then caught the eye of someone across the room and went to see them.

Doctor Lori Clark. Lori hadn't let herself say it aloud before her dissertation defense, not even as practice. Uttering the words had felt too much like a jinx. Not that she was superstitious, but as her mom liked to say, she was a *little*-stitious. But now she had the doctorate, was sitting here on the other side of graduation with all the right signatures and that silly velvet academic tam hanging on the coat hook of the Mapleton Pub of all places, and she could say it out loud.

A wave of dizziness sent her to sit on one of the chairs at the side of the room. Head swimming, she put the champagne glass on a nearby table and pressed a palm to her forehead. Immediately, Mitchell was there, the consummate serious host. "Water?"

"Please." It was the champagne, or maybe just overheating —surely, the room was hot for everyone and not just her. Or maybe it was the sudden paralyzing, overwhelming image of her future stretched out before her like an uncharted road in the fog, the future she'd put off facing for the past eight years of school.

Mitchell reemerged from somewhere with a glass of ice water, and Lori chugged it, the coolness a balm against this damn heat. "Is it hot in here?"

"We've got the air on full blast." Mitchell looked around. "Maybe it's the champagne?"

"Must be. I'm okay. Don't let me keep you." She waved him away.

Hannah came over wearing a concerned expression and

pulled up the chair next to Lori. "You all right? You look a little gray."

For Lori's amber-brown skin to look gray, she must have blanched quite a bit. "I guess it's all hitting me now. The champagne, for one. And the next steps."

"You're a planner. You plan stuff. Surely you've got everything lined up and ready to go." Hannah swept a pale arm out in front of her, indicating a whole untapped future. "You still hoping to move away?"

"I quit the newspaper last week." Lori drank some more of her water, little drops of condensation running icy cold down the side of her hand. "So, that's something."

"Shit, really? You didn't tell me." Hannah had swapped her champagne for water along the way as well and looked a bit more serious than she had a few moments earlier. "What are you doing for work? Are you still with the Relationship Therapy place?"

"I'm still there," Lori confirmed, "but now they've got me in a paid position. It's part-time, giving me a bit of money until I find something permanent." It had been so satisfying to give her notice after all those years working at the *Valley Voice* newspaper, taking on more and more hours with little increase in pay. She finally got to walk away and have some time to herself.

Time to myself.

Hannah was looking at her funny; had she said the last bit out loud? "I want some time to myself," she repeated. "Everything's been 'wait until graduation, wait until graduation,' and now it's here. It's over. It's beginning. Whatever. I need…time to think."

Lori sat back in her chair and scanned the room. Everyone was milling around in normal-conversation party mode, the quiet undertone of upbeat music adding to the vibe of the place. Hannah had done a great job throwing this party, blending all the different social circles of Lori's life. Her most intimate circle was mostly Hannah, but had now expanded to include Hannah's boyfriends, Mitchell and Ben. She had some casual friends from the university, where she worked both as an instructor and—until recently—as a doctoral student. Hannah had ferreted out all her university friends to invite but hadn't stopped there. She'd also invited Lori's friends from the *Valley Voice*, her colleagues from Relationship Therapy Associates, and most of the long-time members of the polyamory discussion group Lori had started last year in the final steps of her dissertation research. What an eclectic group had gathered here to celebrate—of all things—her. This weird network was the found family Lori had created here in the absence of her biological family.

"I wish your family had been able to stay for the party." Hannah's comment came as if she'd been reading Lori's mind.

"I was just thinking about them." Lori's mother and brother had made the trip up from DC for her graduation, but neither could get off work long enough to stay the extra week until the party. It was good to see them, to touch base with the family she'd moved away from in pursuit of her dreams, these dreams that now loomed in front of her and demanded her attention. Mapleton was never supposed to be her forever home; she'd moved here for college and kept returning, even after time away, landing back in her too-small apartment every time she tried something new. Now, though, she had a terminal degree, no more school to attend, and every possibility in front of her.

Hannah took her hand and squeezed, a silent bit of reassurance. "You feeling okay? Want me to kick all these people out? I can do it. Mitchell and Ben own the place."

Lori smiled. It was great to have this event space upstairs at the Mapleton Pub, greater still that she was friends with the owners. "Nah. But I do think I'm going to use the bathroom downstairs." She got to her feet, only a little wobbly.

"Don't run away for good," Hannah called after her. Smiling, Lori headed to the elevator. She probably couldn't handle stairs right now.

MAYBE THE MAPLETON PUB wasn't the fanciest restaurant in town, and maybe it was a little bit routine that he and Patrick were here again for date night, but Geoff could not turn down these fries. Patrick was looking at him with that adorable half smile he sometimes gave when Geoff was being cute, and Geoff paused, fry held in midair. "What?"

"You're making happy noises."

Geoff blushed, his cheeks getting warm even if his brown skin tone hid most of the coloring, and Patrick's widening grin implied he knew. "So? I like these fries."

"I know you like the fries. It's why we come here." Patrick drank some of his beer, his Adam's apple bobbing. That beautiful, peach column of Patrick's neck could draw Geoff's gaze any day, let alone when his husband was dressed impeccably, as he was tonight. Geoff was usually content to throw on his sport coat and go, the one with the tweed patches that Patrick had bought him after Geoff earned his associate professorship. Patrick, though, had this whole "hipster chic" look, with his coiffed dark auburn hair and perfect Viking-red beard. Geoff could eat that up. Probably would, later, when they got home, stumbling over the threshold of their condo, hands all over each other…

Geoff cleared his throat. He couldn't forget to keep eating.

"What?" Patrick put his beer down. "You're giving me a look."

"Am I?" Geoff could play coy. It worked now and then, putting on the "scattered professor" persona when he was thinking dirty thoughts. Patrick fell for it about 30 percent of the time.

Patrick coughed into his hand, and it came out suspiciously like he was hiding a laugh. "Whatever you're thinking, you can't keep giving me that look. We have a whole dinner to make it through."

Caught. Geoff laughed in return. "I can't help it. Those suspenders, that shirt, I just want to…" He paused. No one was around, and he leaned closer. "Rip them all off you."

"When we get home." Patrick was more reserved than Geoff, at least in public, generally preferring to keep an air of decorum. It never failed to surprise Geoff. With Patrick's past, Geoff would expect him to be more sexually daring. Not that Geoff had any standard of comparison, though. Patrick had been his first real relationship, a guy he started dating in college after years of postponing his love life entirely to concentrate on his schooling. Now and then, he had moments like this, when his own desires brought him up short with uncertainty.

Geoff turned back to his fries, a bunch of which had somehow vanished from his plate. He furrowed his brow at the empty space where they had once been. Had he really eaten so many of them while they were talking?

"Yes, you already ate a bunch." Patrick's voice had an

amused air. "I see you looking at them like you don't know what happened."

"Sometimes, I swear it's like you're reading my mind." Geoff drank his beer. The Mapleton Pub had good food, sure, and amazing fries, but their seasonal beers would bring him in no matter what. Whatever was in this summer ale, it inspired his longing for the warm days of July, when he'd be on summer break instead of slogging through the end of this rainy May.

Patrick cocked his head to the side and studied Geoff, really studied him, giving him one of his deep, penetrating gazes. Maybe it was Patrick's eyes—piercing, icy blue—that made Geoff feel like he was under an X-ray. Even after Geoff had grown used to it, back in their earliest days of dating, Patrick could hit him with one of these stares and evoke all kinds of "being watched" feelings that combined his self-consciousness and his kinks at the same time.

"What?" Geoff wasn't used to chafing under that gaze.

Patrick relaxed his stare. "Sometimes I wish I could read your mind."

"It's all sex right now." Geoff winked.

Of course, the server chose that moment to appear at the table, and Geoff tried not to choke on the last of his summer ale with his laughter. He was too old to get shy over talking about sex with his husband, even if his impure thoughts did make him blush.

"How is everything? You all doing well?" The server, John or something, looked between the two of them with his friendly smile, so maybe he hadn't heard Geoff. "You want a couple more beers?"

John disappeared to replace their empty drinks, and Patrick leaned forward to rest his chin on his hand. "I have to say, you're definitely in a mood tonight." He gave Geoff one of the smoky, sultry gazes he usually reserved for the bedroom, or for some seriously deliberate flirting. The thought flashed in Geoff's mind of Patrick giving that look to someone else, a past girlfriend or boyfriend, or maybe both. An unsettled prickle dug under his skin. He'd been having thoughts like that a lot lately. It didn't make any sense. Things with Patrick were great, hotter than ever in some ways, but the "time is running out" undercurrent permeated more and more of his days. It was probably anxiety; his anxiety spiked during periods of transition like this, with the school year yielding soon to summer.

"It's the end of the school year. I always have some weird feelings this time of year."

"So, wanting to fuck my brains out is a weird feeling?" Patrick teased.

Geoff tapped his lips in thought, affecting confusion. "You know, it's totally foreign to anything I've ever experienced before. I'm so new at this."

"Mm-hmm. Just a babe in the woods. I would have thought you'd learned a few things in the last six years, but it looks like you're going to need some reteaching." His blue eyes sparkled.

This playful flirting eased some of the prickly discomfort in Geoff's thoughts. "You'll find I'm a *very* good student."

"Most professors are." Patrick drew his tongue across his lower lip. "Filthy, all of you."

"Oh?" Geoff leaned in. "I don't remember hearing any stories about *professors* in your past."

Patrick gave a low chuckle. "I don't like telling stories about my past."

That wasn't the whole truth; Geoff didn't like *hearing*

stories about Patrick's past, and they both knew it. It wasn't like he thought Patrick was going to leave him...well, not *really*. But Patrick had given up a lot to be with him—an active dating life, with people of all genders—and chosen monogamy with one nerdy, inexperienced guy instead of the polyamorous life he'd been living until that point.

Wasn't it normal to wonder if Patrick had given up too much? And if he'd realize it himself someday?

A cloud of gorgeous black curly hair caught his eye, and Geoff looked up as a familiar woman passed by his table on her way to the bar at the other end of the restaurant. Patrick caught his eye and followed his gaze. "Someone you know?"

"A friend from work, I think." Geoff looked after her, struggling to reconcile his knowledge of Lori from school to this version of Lori wearing a slinky black dress.

"Go say hi." Patrick gestured. "I'll be here."

Geoff was already sliding out of the booth. He never saw Lori outside of the university, even though he knew she lived here in Mapleton. He really should get out more. She was leaning on the bar, her gorgeous golden-brown skin radiant, looking off to the side as if waiting for someone.

"Lori?"

She looked at him like she was coming out of a trance, and her face lit up in a warm grin. "Geoff! Hi!" She held out her arms to him, and he went willingly into the hug, surprised. She'd never hugged him at work, but it wasn't like work was a place you often hugged people. She squeezed him close, then held him at arm's length. "Fancy running into you here." She pointed up at the ceiling. "My best friend threw me a graduation party. I needed to get some air, away from all the people." Her words came out a tiny bit slurred. "You should come up. I can introduce you to some people."

"Oh. Thank you, but I'm here with my husband. For dinner." A twinge of regret caught in his throat. Patrick would like Lori. Geoff didn't talk to Lori too often at work; history and psychology were several buildings apart from each other. But they both taught at Bridge—a program for high school upperclassmen who wanted to develop college skills. They served on overlapping committees, and they frequently took lunch at the same time. The university might be a big place, but Lori circled in most of his orbits. Seeing her at the bar, radiant in this snug black dress, with his mind already mixed up in the hormones and anxiety of wanting to fuck his husband and survive the end of the year, he was a tumble of attraction and confusion.

He must not have been broadcasting any of it, though, because Lori smiled and squeezed his arm. She continued holding it, and maybe he was imagining the warmth of her touch through his sport coat and dress shirt. "You have a good dinner, 'kay? Maybe we can get together this week before Bridge starts up."

"I'd like that. Oh, and congratulations on graduating." He'd done the hectic double duty of teaching while getting a PhD, and it must be a tremendous relief for her to be finished.

"Thank you! Fucking finally." She grinned. His impression of her at work was always composed, professional, funny but quintessentially aloof. Now, with her hair literally down in those perfect curls and her lips a deep burgundy red, Geoff thought inexplicably about kissing her, and mixed up in that same thought, imagined Patrick kissing her. She would be the type of woman Patrick would have gone for, most likely: an intellectual, like Geoff.

The thought didn't bother him as much as other thoughts about Patrick's past partners. When he looked back up, she had already left, heading toward the elevator on impossible heels that highlighted the curved muscles of her calves. When the elevator doors closed and hid her from view, he realized he'd been staring at those calves for a long time.

Patrick was waiting for him at their table, drinking his refilled beer and finishing the last of Geoff's french fries.

"Wait, have you been eating those the whole time?" Geoff snatched his plate back.

Patrick put a hand to his heart. "I would never. But you left these unattended." He went to snatch another, and Geoff gathered the remaining ones—a bit more than a mouthful—and shoved them all into his mouth at once. Patrick laughed uproariously, taking his hand back, eyes twinkling. "Okay. Fine."

"Order your own next time," Geoff managed to say around a mouthful of too-many fries then had to control his own laughter to swallow properly. The cold refreshment of his beer soothed his palate. A weird feeling settled in his stomach, a physical sensation that had nothing to do with the fries. Guilt, probably, but that didn't make any sense. He had no reason to feel guilty. Even if he was imagining scenarios where Patrick would fuck other people.

"You want dessert?" Geoff took the desserts-and-drinks menu from the edge of their table and flipped it to the back.

"Gorgeous, I always want dessert." Patrick licked his lips. "Unless you want to skip it. Seems a little earlier like you were ready to *be* the dessert."

Geoff laughed. He could get behind that. "How about both?"

2

Geoff was a wonder. Patrick never knew what to expect from him, whether he was going to spend the evening buried in an ancient book on Egyptian dynasties or go jogging around their neighborhood, but tonight he seemed single-minded ever since the pub. He wasn't always single-minded. Patrick would hesitate to call his husband "scattered," since more often than not, he was hyperfocused on his particular task. Sometimes, he tended toward distraction. Not now, though. Right now, right inside the condo and with Geoff crowding him up against the wall, Patrick smiled into his husband's insistent kisses. Okay, it was going to be this kind of night. *Hell yes.*

Any of Geoff's problems focusing were gone when he kissed. He kissed with the unrelenting obsession with which he approached his favorite hobbies, like baking or listening to history podcasts. This wasn't a history podcast, though. This was a hot, filthy kiss, his mouth and tongue moving over Patrick's with a possessive insistence. His calm exterior—self-possessed, brilliant, nerdy—belied a passionate, fierce partner whose sexual acumen far surpassed his limited experience.

Geoff pulled back, lips leaving Patrick's with a wet sound, and uncertainty flickered in his eyes. "Are you all right?" he asked. "You seem distracted."

"I was thinking about you." Patrick leaned in to kiss Geoff, who paused in kissing back.

"Thinking what?"

Uncertainty again. He got like this sometimes, more often lately. Patrick ran his hands down Geoff's arms. "How hot you are."

It wasn't a lie, but Geoff raised an eyebrow in disbelief. "Okay."

Laughing, Patrick tried again, gripping Geoff's wrists to bring him in close. His body slotted alongside Patrick's, warm and firm and lean.

Geoff gently pulled his hands from Patrick's, but instead of pulling away, he took the opportunity to remove his glasses. Rank that on the list of "things that shouldn't be sexy but are." Maybe Patrick had a professor kink, or maybe he'd developed one over all these years. He groaned. "I can't wait to get you to bed."

Geoff carefully set the glasses on the end table near them, placid. "Nobody's stopping you, you know."

Fuck. Patrick grabbed him behind the neck and dragged their mouths together, his arousal going from "yes, please" to "*yes, now,*" and the growl low in Geoff's throat ratcheted it up even higher. Geoff's mouth was hot, wet, focused, the kiss rapidly escalating from hot to scalding. Thank goodness their condo was a one-floor deal with no stairs to maneuver once they were inside, because he needed this man naked and on their bed immediately. They left the lights off, each kiss turning into another, breaking their connection only long enough to strip away layers. He loved when Geoff got like this, greedy and sharp. Geoff nipped at his lower lip, then the cut of his shoulder, on to his collarbone, the final layers of clothing tumbling away. Patrick would need to pick those up when they were done. He was never one to let clothing go unfolded.

"Stop thinking about the clothes," Geoff said against his mouth, and Patrick laughed into the kiss.

"It's habit."

"Forget your habits." Geoff dragged him onto the bed.

It was easy to forget when Geoff's greedy hands pulled his boxers down the sharp jut of his hipbone. Freed from the fabric, his cock lay heavy against his stomach, hard already, jumping at Geoff's touch as a flush of pleasure ran through Patrick's body.

Sometimes they took their time, leisurely kisses turning into exploratory touches and slow, rhythmic sex. This was not that. Geoff mouthed down his body, not even pausing for breath, and swallowed Patrick's cock.

"Fuck!" Patrick gasped, arching up, his hips thrusting once before Geoff pinned them down with his strong grip. Even swear words faded away as Geoff worked him over, hot, lavish mouth surrounding every inch of him. His husband was impossibly good at this, disproportionately good, narrowing in on the sensitive underside of Patrick's cock head with his tongue until Patrick was twitching at the sheer overwhelming firing of his nerves. Patrick sucked in a breath. He couldn't get enough air, couldn't ground himself; his body was on fire.

Cold air brushed his sensitive cock as Geoff lifted his head, and Patrick shivered, finally able to get his bearings even if he couldn't find his words yet.

"What do you want tonight?" Geoff asked. He dragged his

tongue lightly up the tender skin, making Patrick twitch again. "You want to fuck me?"

Patrick's brain had settled back to something coherent again, even as his dick ached for more. They liked to switch, sometimes settling into a pattern but always willing to change it up. Lately, Geoff had been bottoming more often. Patrick licked his lips, considering. He'd missed that thick, full feeling of bottoming, watching Geoff's face as he struggled to keep control, the feral look in his eyes. "Fuck me." Patrick spread his legs, reaching down to stroke a fist up and down his cock.

Geoff paused, then smiled, his dark eyes glinting. "You want me in you?"

"Hell yes." Patrick repressed a moan as he twisted a hand around the tip of his cock, his balls heavy and tight. "The other night, when you went to bed early, I fucked myself in the ass and thought about you."

Geoff closed his eyes and shivered. Geoff could talk filthy, *really* filthy, and Patrick loved to catch him off guard and turn the tables whenever he could. Geoff's cock hung thick between his legs. It had been too long since Patrick had felt that inside him. He grabbed the lube off the nightstand. Geoff watched, eyes hungry, as Patrick worked slick fingers inside himself. Patrick's own impatience pressed him to go faster, deeper, until he had to pause and adjust. Geoff leaned down and began to gently, carefully suck Patrick's cock.

"Ohh, I'm not gonna make it if you do that." Patrick's voice came out desperate. The sensations were too much, the pressure of his own fingers and the warm tightness of his husband's mouth, and a few more minutes would make him come.

Geoff didn't stop, though, only slowed down, the barest hint of pressure enough to keep Patrick teetering on the knife-edge of pleasure. Geoff loved to do *this* too. Force Patrick to wait, teasing him and sometimes making him beg. This was intense, too intense, and by the time he had stretched himself open, he was ready to burst.

"Please," he moaned, fucking himself back on his hand.

"Mmm." Geoff lifted his head. "You sure you're ready? That wasn't very long. I think you should keep going." He licked the leaking slit, and Patrick's balls tightened painfully, body begging for release.

Patrick choked out a groan, stroking his fingers deeper, adding lube and then returning, the easy slide and stretch echoing the pleasure throughout his body. He had to go slow if he wanted this to last. The intensity, torturous and blissful in turn, had him shaking when Geoff finally stopped sucking him and let him breathe.

"You're an ass." Patrick laughed, dizzy and breathless, finally able to recover and grab for the tissues.

Geoff only smiled, slicking his palm with more lube before wrapping that hand around his own dick. His eyes slipped half-closed, mouth open, his movements stuttering at the shock of pleasure. Patrick had slept with many people, and this was always his favorite part: watching his partner slowly taken under by the current of firing nerves.

Recovering, Geoff positioned himself between Patrick's knees, pushing his legs back and up—the position they chose when they wanted to see the other's face. Geoff licked his lips, lined up, and slowly began to move inside.

Patrick's body took him in without protest, yielding, the heavy pressure perfect. Geoff didn't stop sliding forward until he was all the way in, balls-deep, watching Patrick's face with his own intense gaze. Patrick's legs and cock twitched, and he reached down to stroke himself once before Geoff batted his hand away.

"No, not yet." Geoff's voice sounded strained. "I don't want this to be over too fast."

And damn, that was hotter than anything, having to wait and watch without touching his own dick while Geoff began fucking him. He couldn't come without being touched, and the sensations scraped razor-sharp across the jagged edge between "yes" and "too much." He dragged Geoff down for a kiss, messy and open. They breathed each other's panting breaths as Geoff's sharp thrusts slammed against Patrick's hips. It was brutal and raw, the kind of fucking that would leave him sore, and the friction between their bodies was enough to slip along his cock and send him climbing that precipice.

"I'm gonna—" Patrick gasped, and Geoff bit his neck *hard*.

"Not yet."

"Geoff, *please*." He knew he sounded desperate. His hips shifted up to get more sensation, changing the angle of penetration, and fireworks lit up all along his spine. He wasn't going to be able to hold out any longer.

Geoff reached between them and gripped Patrick's cock, fierce and firm and so goddamn perfect. "Now." Patrick's mind went blank as pleasure shot through his body and he came across his stomach and Geoff's fist.

Geoff was still driving into him when Patrick started to come down, twitchy and overstimulated and too sensitive, and then Geoff gasped and froze and came hot and wet inside him. Head thrown back, mouth open, eyes closed, Geoff looked like a statue of a god.

Afterward, they lay together in silence, the few moments before they would get up and clean themselves and each other.

Rather than peace, though, the air hung heavy with a tension Patrick couldn't identify. Geoff was restless rather than slack, shifting in a dozen micromovements.

"You want to get in the shower with me?" Patrick touched his husband's short, curly hair.

Geoff made a murmuring noise of assent. "We probably need it."

The tension dissipated during their shower, as it always did. The time touching each other in a nonsexual way, both for cleanliness and comfort, eased the tightness in Patrick's chest that was either something radiating from Geoff or something he was creating on his own. A big selling point of this condo had been the large shower, which the perky young real estate agent had promoted as "big enough for two strong men like yourselves" and followed up with an uncomfortable wink. They'd bought anyway, and gratitude washed over Patrick like the hot water, as it did every time they shared this space.

Afterward, washed and changed into lazy lounging clothes, Patrick broached the "something" that had been cropping up more frequently in their encounters. Geoff was curled against him on the sofa, scrolling through some website on his phone while a show they'd seen a dozen times played quietly on the television. "You want to tell me what's been on your mind lately?"

Geoff paused in the scrolling, his thumb hovering over the screen of his phone, and then clicked the button on the side to put it to sleep. "It's not you. It's me."

Patrick gave a laugh that didn't feel funny. "That's what people say when they're breaking up with someone, you know."

Geoff tensed, and for a split second, Patrick thought he might have accidentally hit on something unexpected. No, that couldn't be. Their relationship was wonderful, loving and intimate and warm, and he'd surely have seen some signs. It was something else.

Geoff still rested against him, not making eye contact, although he turned to stare at the television. In the dim blue light, his profile looked stark. "It's hard for me to think about everything you turned down to be with me."

Hurt and irritation bubbled up in Patrick's chest, and he took a deep breath to quiet it. "What do you mean? I didn't turn down anything."

Geoff pulled away from Patrick so he could sit upright. Patrick pushed himself up as well, not liking the feeling of lounging casually while Geoff looked so serious. "I know you say that every time, but sometimes I think about all the people out there. Are you really happy with monogamy?"

"If I weren't happy with monogamy, I would have told you from the beginning." Where was this even coming from? They'd been together for so long, and Geoff had never mentioned any of this before. Sure, they had their arguments, but Patrick had never seen this kind of insecurity underlying their conversation before. "Why are you bringing this up now?"

Geoff looked away. "We just had our sixth anniversary. So we're going on seven. Somebody at work made a seven-year itch joke last week, and...I don't know. It got me thinking."

"Don't you trust me?"

"Of course I trust you." Now it was Geoff's turn to look taken aback, leaning slightly away from Patrick on the couch. "But we've been married a while, and you might be getting restless. You used to date other people, and now you're just married to me. Forever."

That was hard not to take personally. "I'm happy to be

married to you. Forever." Patrick entwined his fingers with Geoff's. "Is this because I used to be polyamorous, or because I'm bisexual?"

Hurt flashed through Geoff's eyes. "Being bi doesn't mean you need multiple partners. We're *both* bi, Patrick. It's a polyamorous thing."

"Why do you think I need more than just you? Don't you think I took my vows seriously?"

"I don't mean that." Geoff shifted, visibly frustrated. "It's not that I think you'd cheat on me, I just don't want you to resent me. Because you used to have more, and now you have less."

Less. How could Geoff sit here and call himself less? Patrick's mind boggled, mouth falling open, searching for the right words. "Geoff, you're wonderful. You're funny, and smart, and a huge fucking nerd, and you make me a better person. I'm not going to leave you for someone else."

Geoff relaxed, his shoulders losing some of their tension. "But don't you miss it?" Geoff asked. "Being with...other people?"

Did he? Patrick considered, thinking back on all the people he'd slept with and dated in his life. "Do I get attracted to other people? Sure. I think that's pretty normal. But I wouldn't give up what I have for that. I'm committed to you. And that's not changing, no matter what gorgeous people I see. I promise."

Geoff relaxed more, and his next question came out more like curiosity, less like desperation. "What if you suddenly realized you wanted to sleep with someone else? What would you do?"

Patrick leaned back again, rubbing his beard. Maybe he

could joke. "Why, did somebody ask you about me? Are they hot?"

Geoff looked stricken for only a second, then laughed. "You're an asshole. No, I mean, really. You were polyamorous. You used to do that kind of thing, right? Sleep with multiple people at once?"

"Not in the sense of threesomes. But, sure, I dated more than one person at the same time, and everybody knew where they stood. We weren't monogamous with each other. It wasn't cheating." They didn't talk about this often, and Geoff might not know the ins and outs of a polyamorous relationship.

"And what about now? If you wanted to sleep with someone else, would you tell me?"

"I tell you about the people I find hot all the time." They had always checked out strangers together, ever since the beginning of their relationship. "It's not like I'm going to leave you to go fuck some random."

Geoff leaned his head on his hand, slowly rolling one of the tight curls beneath his thumb. "You'd just let yourself want someone, but not do anything about it?"

This whole conversation was feeling more bizarre by the minute. Someone on the TV said something funny, and a laugh track echoed in the silence of their living room. Patrick picked up the remote and muted it. "Is this all hypothetical?"

"Of course."

Hypothetical questions about fidelity and polyamory were not a good idea, and Patrick knew that, but he'd been with Geoff a while. He could probably be open. "If I had someone I really wanted to sleep with, I would tell you about it. And that would be it."

"It wouldn't have to be a big deal." Geoff said it like he

was trying to convince himself. "Sex doesn't have to be a big deal."

Patrick agreed, but also knew this wasn't so cut-and-dry with Geoff. "It can be as big a deal as we want it to be," he said.

It had been weird at first for Patrick, knowing he was Geoff's only serious relationship, after the other man had prioritized school above all else well into his twenties. Geoff had graduated from Harvard, for Christ's sake, and near the top of his class. Not that his delayed sexual experiences reflected any aversion, though. Sex had always been something Patrick enjoyed, but he'd been unprepared for the intensity of having sex with Geoff.

Geoff smiled to himself, something hidden and mischievous and wholly unexpected after this conversation, and Patrick really did wish he could read the other man's mind. "What are you thinking?" he asked.

Geoff shrugged. "Thinking about how you look sometimes when I hold you down and make you take my cock."

"Holy shit." Patrick's cock twitched, and he was a goner if Geoff kept talking dirty. "You're trying to kill me, aren't you?"

Geoff chuckled. "That would be mean. Come on. Let's watch a movie."

Geoff settled back in against Patrick's side again, and Patrick unmuted the television and flipped to their streaming service menu before handing the remote over to Geoff to pick. He'd missed something in this conversation, and damn, it felt significant.

3

L ori didn't hear the tapping at her open office door at first. Whenever she dug into work, she easily lost track of where she was and what was happening around her. The louder knock caught her attention and, shit, he might have been knocking for a while. Geoffrey Robinson stood in the doorway, looking curious, holding a printout of some kind.

"Oh, hey, come on in and have a seat." She gestured to an empty chair. "I'm sorry, I didn't hear you. I get pretty into my work."

"You're here late." He sat in the chair, glancing around her office. He'd never been in here before. She seldom saw him in this building at all, actually; he was in the history department, headquartered two buildings over.

She spun in her chair and leaned back, rocking slightly. "I was getting things set up for the Bridge Program, and then I got into cleaning up my laptop. And time got away from me, I guess." She glanced at the clock; it was after seven.

"This has to be the cleanest office I've ever been in. With

most of the history department, you could do an archaeological dig right in the building and never have to travel." He smiled. He had a nice smile, warm and friendly.

She returned the smile. "I like a neat office. It helps me think. I can't get anything done when things are a mess." She eyed him up and down, trying to gauge his purpose for being here. Not that a visit wasn't nice, but they weren't that close, and he'd never come to her office. "So, what are *you* doing here so late?"

"I often stay late on Wednesdays, catch up on things in the middle of the week." He looked down at the flyer he was still holding, which she couldn't see from her vantage point. "I was cleaning off the bulletin boards on my floor for the end of the semester, and I found this. Thought I'd slip it in your mailbox, but the light was on at the end of the hall, and I figured, what the hell." He handed it over.

Lori skimmed it. Shit, she'd forgotten about these. Back when she'd been searching for research subjects to interview for her polyamory dissertation, she'd hung them up on the various campus bulletin boards, and like anything hung on a campus bulletin board, they were promptly buried under other flyers and slipped her mind. This sheet was indistinguishable from the other flyers from psychology postgrads looking for research subjects, all neutral font and bulleted details, but her subject definitely set her apart.

"Sorry, I forgot to take these down. They're probably everywhere." Lori folded it in half and tossed it into the paper recycling. "You could have thrown it away."

"Didn't know if you were sentimental and wanted to keep one for old times' sake." Geoff adjusted his glasses. While he didn't seem to pay much attention to fashion overall, tending toward the same relaxed tweed jacket and button-down shirts for most of the year, he did wear these awesome Warby Parker-style glasses, the kind with the crisp dark frames. She'd never been much for glasses one way or another, but Geoff made them look good.

"Nah, that's okay. I've got the paper that matters, now." She glanced up to the wall, where she'd already had her new degree framed and mounted alongside her master's and bachelor's.

"Congratulations again. I remember being so relieved when I finally finished."

"Did you go straight through?"

"Kindergarten to PhD, one right after another." He shook his head. "I don't know what I was thinking. I put literally everything else in my life on hold for school. When I finally got a terminal degree, I didn't know what to do with myself."

"You went into teaching, of course." Lori knew others who had done the same. "A career academic."

Geoff inclined his head. "Guilty as charged. What about you? You go straight through?"

Lori smiled, letting a little of her normal flirtation into that smile. "I'm flattered you think I look young enough to have gone straight through. But, no, I took some time off in my midtwenties, did a little traveling. Wanted to make sure this was what I really wanted before I committed to more school. It's not cheap."

"It sure isn't."

"Then I came back, went for my master's and then my doctorate. And now I'm done. The world is my oyster, they tell me. And I do like oysters."

Geoff joined her in another laugh. "I hope you aren't leaving us right away."

What an interesting thing for him to say. Lori checked him

out again, surreptitiously. Why hadn't they hung out before? They certainly saw each other enough, on overlapping committees and working on the same branch of campus, but they never sat and talked like this.

"We'll see," she said, letting her reply be noncommittal. Lots of things were up in the air right now about her future, and she wasn't about to divulge anything.

"Tell me about your dissertation. The flyer had me surprised. I didn't know you were studying sexuality for your PhD." He curled his fingers over the armrests of the chair, and she watched the motion without consciously choosing to do so.

"Relationship structures, more than sexuality itself," she corrected. "The sex is secondary."

He opened his mouth like he was going to say something, then stopped and shook his head, laughing to himself.

"What?" she pressed, smiling despite herself. "What were you going to say?"

"It's inappropriate." He was still grinning to himself, his eyes crinkling at the corners.

She gestured at the empty office. "Go on. I won't tell."

"I was going to say that if sex is secondary, maybe you're doing something wrong."

Lori laughed. "Touché." She crossed her legs at the knee, one over the other, and Geoff's gaze followed the motion. She raised an eyebrow at him, but he didn't look embarrassed. He leaned back slightly, studying her through those glasses. He had that contemplative, thoughtful look, common to many people in academia, like he was analyzing her piece by piece and trying to figure her out.

Instead, he brought the conversation back on topic. "And you studied these relationship structures for your doctorate?"

"Extensively." She glanced to her left where a bound copy of her dissertation still sat, the copy she hadn't submitted to the library's records. She reached over and rested her hand on it, the glossy cover slick beneath her fingers. "My main thesis was about the way polyamory enriches certain relationships, and I wanted to understand why it works for some and not others. The goal wasn't just to understand polyamory better, but to serve my future work as a relationship therapist."

"Interesting." He raised his eyebrows. "Do you think it served that purpose?"

"I hope so." She stroked her thumb along the edge of the binding. "Nothing groundbreaking, but I did some cross-cultural analysis, studying polyamory in conjunction with underrepresented populations. Different races and genders. I wanted to reach beyond cis white triads, which seem to be the default in current research."

"Cis white is the default in everything, it seems."

"Ain't that the truth." Lori would have raised a glass if she had one. "What about you? What did you study for your dissertation?"

"A comparative analysis of a couple of the African dynasties precolonialism." He adjusted his glasses. "It's been a favorite topic of mine since I was a kid."

Geoff must have been an adorable little kid, and she could see him sitting in a library armchair reading books about precolonial Africa, glasses too large for his face. She smiled at the imagined memory. "And now you get to teach it."

"Among other things, yes." He looked up at her bookshelves, scanning the titles in what seemed like an absent-minded way. "It seeps into my other classes, even when that's not the topic. Imperialism is such a fundamental shaping factor in history, it's easy to treat it as inevitable instead of interrogating that assumption." He got to his feet to look more closely at some of the spines on her full bookcase. "When you study something in depth, don't you notice it everywhere?"

Lori watched his body language, the way he leaned forward to read her shelves, his hands clasped behind his back. His body was all lean angles. He was probably thinking about his own research, but in the context of hers, the comment carried different weight.

"All the time," she answered. "Which, in my line of study, has some serious ramifications."

One corner of Geoff's mouth twitched, and he shifted his attention from the bookshelves to her. "Do you want to go get a drink?"

Lori sized him up. He was handsome and brilliant, definitely the type of guy she liked to date. He was also married... but he'd been asking her about her polyamory research. Curiosity alone enticed her to let this play out.

"WERE YOU AN UNDERGRAD HERE?" Geoff asked her as they slid into a booth.

"Smith," she said. "Not far. What about you?"

"Harvard." He learned to just say it matter-of-factly, rather than like he was apologizing for his Ivy League education.

Lori cracked a grin, which wasn't the response he was expecting, her white teeth flashing against her deep-red lipstick. "Of course you went to Harvard." She seemed to be laughing at a joke he didn't get.

He frowned, trying to parse her response, but she waved a hand and explained, "You're a bundle of complexity, you know that? I feel like I'm just scratching the surface. What else don't I know about you? You've been teaching here on a PhD since I *started* my PhD, maybe earlier, and you're not that much older than I am, so I'm starting to think you're some supergenius whiz kid. But you also seem to be pretty socially comfortable, so you didn't live your life inside a library."

Geoff adjusted his glasses. "I did, in a way. Both my parents are academics. I spent more of my childhood in the library than playing sports." He headed her off by adding, "I know that's pretty obvious to look at me."

She sized him up, leaning back to appraise him, that cheeky smile still teasing at the corners of her lips. "I wasn't gonna say that. You look like you work out."

"I do. Thank you," he answered. She was flirting with him.

A server came to their table to take drink orders. He got a glass of their house red and, to his surprise, Lori ordered chilled sipping tequila, neat.

He must have raised his eyebrows, because she shrugged. "I know it's a weeknight, but I don't have to get up early tomorrow."

"Cheers to that." He was also in the in-between period when his spring semester responsibilities were done but he hadn't yet begun to prep for the Bridge Program.

Lori tipped her head to the side, considering him. "Where's your husband tonight?"

It wasn't an accusation, but it was valid, especially considering he was sitting in this bar with a beautiful woman when they both knew he was married.

"Patrick has music every Wednesday night. He plays in a band."

"Cool. What's he play?"

"Rock violin. He's a classically trained violinist, and he plays with a folk-classical fusion group."

Her eyebrows went up more. "Wow. That's amazing, actually. I love music, especially unusual types."

"You'd like Patrick. We should all get together sometime, have you two meet up. I'll bet you would get along great." He wasn't really thinking about the ramifications of anything he was saying, just offering it out there, but a tiny voice in the back of his mind was trying to remind him to take things slowly, that he couldn't know where any of this would lead.

The server returned with their drinks, and Lori took a tiny sip of her cold tequila before sighing. She closed her eyes briefly, lashes black against the golden-brown glow of her cheek. Those lashes would feel like a featherlight touch against his skin, if they were close enough... Geoff dragged himself back to the present and turned his attention to his wineglass.

The wine warmed from his stomach outward, casting a light haze over everything. He didn't drink much, and the alcohol softened his edges a bit. "If you're willing," he began cautiously, "I'd love to hear what interests you about polyamory. At least enough to devote your dissertation to it."

Lori made a soft contemplative noise and ran her tongue across her top lip, chasing a spare drop of tequila. She swirled the glass in lazy spirals, watching the clear-silver liquid glisten in the low light. "The way people choose to be together has always fascinated me. My mom never remarried after my dad died, but she surrounded herself with a group of women who became like aunts to me and my brother."

The question rose to Geoff's lips, but it would be rude and invasive to ask. She answered anyway, as if anticipating. "I don't know the intimate details of their relationships, nor do I want to, but I know she loves them, maybe as much as she loved my dad. Still loves them. They're like the *Golden Girls* down in DC, although a lot younger and, you know, Black. And possibly sleeping together."

Geoff laughed.

"I learned my experience wasn't unusual," she continued. "Most people have 'found families,' but they aren't usually sexual or romantic. So, I started reading up on romantic relationships and family structures, gender identity, sexuality, the whole spectrum. It started as a hobby while I was still at Smith, and I picked up a gender studies minor alongside my double major in English and psychology."

"You went the academic route, then." He drank a little more wine. "The intellectual approach."

"It's how I've always confronted things I want to understand. I read about them, rather than doing them." Lori smiled, that cheeky, flirtatious grin again. "Although I have to admit, I think a practical approach would have saved me a little more time, and a lot of money."

Geoff raised his eyebrows. "You're not with anyone right now?"

"Totally single." Lori sipped the tequila again, a tiny bit, savoring the drink. "It's ironic."

"And would you get into a relationship like that, after all your studies?"

"I don't know." She tipped back a bit more tequila and hissed slightly. "Too much. It's smooth, but it's got a burn on the back end." She set the glass on the table. "The more I talk about it, the more I feel like it's inevitable for me in some ways. I can't see myself settling down with one person forever. I've never seen that. Multiple partners, multiple relationships, I'm drawn to that. But I've studied it so long, I don't know if

I'm drawn to it because of sample bias, or because it's my natural inclination. Or," she hesitated before continuing, "I'm drawn to it because I feel like it's less commitment somehow."

"It seems like more, to me." Geoff couldn't see how being in a relationship with more than one person would protect one's heart; wasn't there more potential for heartbreak?

"I know, that's what the studies show, but maybe it's just because it's still in the abstract, for me." She made a face. "I talk, and I talk, and I don't get invested. It's all academic. I provide a sounding board for all kinds of relationships, helping them communicate and get through their problems, and then I detach and go home alone." Her laugh sounded bitter. "Listen to me. I'm rambling on. What about you?" Raising her glass, she gestured toward him. "You're married. How long? How did you decide this was for you?"

There were so many ways to tell this story. Geoff sped through the timeline, dates and key moments flashing through his mind. "We met almost ten years ago. I was doing my master's degree here at the university, and Patrick was going for his bachelor's. He was actually a little older than me, got started in school late. We were roommates, and then we started dating, and we fell in love. We've been married for six years now. Just had our anniversary last month." That was the shortest version he could imagine, the one that left out the details but covered the gist.

"And he's the one for you. You for him. The two of you for each other." She waved her hand back and forth, like drawing a line between him and imaginary Patrick.

"Yes," he said, but it came out more hesitant than he had expected. And then the words tumbled out as though he'd been planning to say them. "Patrick is polyamorous."

"Oh." Lori blinked, then narrowed her eyes in scrutiny. "And you're not." It was more of a statement than a question.

"I don't know." He tried the words out, leaning forward to fold his arms on the table. "I haven't been." While he was opening up, he might as well open up a bit more. "I've known I was bi since high school, but Patrick was my first real relationship. Pretty focused on school and school alone until well into my twenties."

A little more tequila, another swirl of the glass. Something like suspicion darkened Lori's eyes. "Is he asking you to open your marriage?"

"Definitely not." Geoff knew he was the one pushing, but it was for both their own good. "But I think maybe we'd be better off. If he's polyamorous, I shouldn't be forcing him to be monogamous, right? I should let him be how he is."

Lori let out a long sigh, a little louder than she probably would have without the tequila. "This isn't like keeping a wild tiger in a cage, Geoff. I don't know if polyamory is socialized or innate, people are still debating it, but that wasn't my research focus. The point is, if he's happy with you, then he's happy with you. If nothing's broken, why change it?"

Because there must be something else.

The curiosity, the intangible itch beneath his skin, inside his mind, pushed him in that direction. He didn't understand it, but he knew, looking at Lori across the table, that he wanted something else. He could envision Patrick with her, kissing his way down the long, soft stretch of her stomach, and his body burned hot all over at the mere thought.

"Can't I want something different without anything being broken?"

Lori rested her chin on her hand again. As she sipped the tequila, her movements became lazier, more fluid, and maybe she was a little buzzed by now. "Why did you ask me for this drink, Geoff?"

Geoff didn't shy away. He studied her, from her cloud of black spiral curls to the curve of her cheekbones, her full red lips, her eyes dark and gold-flecked and too smart for him to think he was fooling her one bit. "I think my husband would like you."

Lori smiled, first a thin sliver, and then an openmouthed laugh that echoed in the quiet bar. "Geoffrey Robinson, you goddamned matchmaker."

He blinked. "What?"

"Not even a matchmaker. You're a pimp, is that it? Finding some beautiful woman for your husband to fuck?" She tossed back the last of the tequila and set her glass down hard. Her eyes were sharp, but she was still smiling. "Is that what you're doing? Does he know you're doing this?"

"I'm not." His protest sounded hollow, and he didn't even really understand what he was doing here, but her laughter and irritation combined into something smooth and rich and intoxicating, more of a drug than the wine in his hand. "I'm not doing anything. I would never—I'm not making decisions for you, I just thought maybe, if you were interested in meeting, you might hit it off, get to know each other…" He didn't know where to go with that sentence.

Lori snorted. "Well, if anyone wants to 'get to know' me, in the biblical sense or otherwise, it's going to take more than some tequila in the U-Bar." She tossed some cash on the table and slid out of the booth, steady on her feet. Maybe she wasn't affected by the tequila at all and had just let her guard down, because she seemed completely sober right now. She turned to go, then paused, hovering near the table while her expression flicked from amused to contemplative. Then she turned back, put one hand flat on the table's surface and leaned into him. He leaned back reflexively as she invaded his space.

"It would take at least dinner." With a wink, she turned and left the bar.

4

Oh, fuck, what had she *done*? Lori staggered back to her office in a daze, any residual buzz from the tequila wearing off in the coolness of the spring night and the realization of her own actions. She'd done more than flirt; she'd practically propositioned Geoff in the bar. No, that wasn't right. He had propositioned her. Hadn't he? Her mind was still swimming, and it wasn't the booze. She climbed the darkened stairs to the second floor. The building's emptiness echoed around her the way her thoughts echoed in her head. With the air-conditioning system already off for the night, the stale air pressed against her overheated skin like an itchy blanket. Shoes clicking on the floor, she made her way down the hall to her office at the far end, still trying to make sense of everything.

Geoff definitely wanted to either take her to bed, or have his husband take her to bed. This might be a hotwife thing... Well, except with husbands, but she wasn't sure if there was a specific term for that. The way he looked at her, without any shyness or hesitation, was like he was examining a particularly interesting history book. She did *not* mind that *whatsoever*.

She flicked on the light to her office and closed the door behind her, isolating herself even further. The campus was mostly dark outside her window, the lights turned off in most of the buildings she could see, only amber streetlights illuminating bare sidewalk. Maybe Geoff was still sitting there in the booth, contemplating what she'd said as she left. Maybe he'd gone back to his own office to finish up his work. Maybe he was driving home now to fuck his husband.

A twitch of something like envy closed her throat for a moment as she sank into her desk chair. Was it envy for Patrick, Geoff, or both of them? Or maybe this was something else, that curiosity that always drove her into new adventures, the curiosity that sometimes got her into trouble. After all, what would it hurt?

A lot, her logical brain reminded her, the part of her brain that wasn't suffused with low-grade lust like smoldering coals. It was true. She'd talked to enough people, both in her initial research and through the polyamory discussion group she'd founded, to know that shaking up an established relationship was fraught with complications.

This wasn't necessarily about a relationship, though. For every detailed discussion of polyamory, there was also a happily married couple taking a third person to bed for everyone's fun. Threesomes, foursomes, moresomes, none of these had to involve feelings, the same way two people could fuck for fun without the world coming to an end. And damn, she had certainly gone a long time without having anyone to fuck, for fun or otherwise. Her ridiculous schedule of doctoral research, teaching, writing for the newspaper, and doing clinical hours with a relationship therapist didn't leave much time for anything other than light socializing with friends. But now, she'd earned her degree and quit the newspaper. Maybe she had time for a fling.

She didn't know anything about Patrick, Geoff's husband. Geoff was a stone-cold fox, so Patrick was probably equally beautiful. There was something so appealing about Geoff, that quiet confidence and unashamed nerdiness. Damn, she wanted to see what kind of body lay beneath those unassuming dress shirts and slacks.

Leaning back in her chair, she closed her eyes, letting her hands rub slow circles on her thighs through the light fabric of her dress. Geoff had said Patrick was his first real relationship, and that could mean any number of things. It might mean he'd never taken anyone else to bed before. The thought tantalized, settling into her brain like a small spark of something deliciously dirty. He might never have fucked a woman before, at least. She might be the first.

It wasn't like he was a *virgin;* he had likely been having some very filthy sex with his husband for a decade now, and virginity was a ridiculous concept anyway. Regardless, virgins weren't normally Lori's kink—someone's past sexual experience was far less interesting than the attention they paid to her and to making sure they had a good time together. However, she could not deny the appeal of teaching someone something *new* in bed. Geoff would be an eager student. He would want to learn her body, all its unique folds and dips and angles, learn them with his hands and—*oh*—with his mouth as well.

Her breath came faster. She shouldn't even be thinking this. If anything, this was about Geoff's husband, who was apparently the source of Geoff's questioning. But her thoughts circled back to Geoff, always Geoff. How could he not be involved, if they were headed in this direction? Geoff was an intellectual, an academic for his entire life, and he would want to learn to take her apart with precision. He would approach sex like deciphering an obscure primary source, methodical and meticulous and breathtakingly thorough.

She bit her lip, forcing her eyes open. She was in her office. This was her desk chair, the place where she worked, her perfectly organized sanctuary. Having these kinds of thoughts here was a terrible idea—and a decadent one.

But no one was here. Whatever adrenaline pumped through her system at the idea of getting caught, her logical mind knew no one else was in the building, and the temptation was safe enough for her to reach into her purse and pull out the cloth case she always kept in there. Having a best friend who owned a sex toy shop came in handy when she wanted only the highest quality devices. The Tango was a small, powerful vibrator, quiet and discreet and perfect for moments like this. Lori tucked it up beneath her dress, beneath her panties, nestling the angled tip against her clit. Then, she closed her legs to hold the vibe snugly in place, and pressed the button at the base to turn it on.

Sensation raced through her nerves at the contact, and she gripped the arms of her chair, exhaling hard. Shit, she had forgotten how strong that tiny vibe was. Maybe the whole situation was adding to her arousal, chasing an orgasm in her office at work and hoping no one came by to catch her. Adrenaline was a powerful aphrodisiac. She closed her eyes again, letting her attention drift to the current of pleasure and then back to thoughts of Geoff. His hands, his mouth, his dick pressing inside her. She clenched around nothing, muscles fluttering. Fuck, she was going to come, just like this, the tiny vibe carrying her over the edge. Lori put her head back, throat closing even as her mouth fell open, and gave in to the spasms of climax.

She fumbled the vibe off with shaky hands and looked around in reflex. No one was there. No one had seen her, nor would anyone see her; she was alone with a weirdly pleasant undercurrent of having done something "wrong" and gotten away with it. In the clear light after her arousal, the thoughts of why she should *absolutely not* pursue anything with Geoff and Patrick came seeping back into her mind. This train of thought was ridiculous. She didn't know them, didn't know their marriage stability, didn't know what a threesome—or partner swapping, or whatever this proposition was—would do to their dynamic. She was not about to be the woman who broke hearts over a few moments of pleasure and an orgasm. With a collection of vibrators at her disposal and no shortage of men available if she wanted to start swiping right, she could get off without heartbreak.

Her curiosity, though, would not be sated that way, and she'd never been one to deny her curiosity.

Maybe their marriage really was solid. Maybe she could dip her toe into this pond without anyone getting hurt. People had threesomes all the time, right? Perhaps she could just... see what happened. And maybe these wonderings were moot. Geoff might never bring it up again after their interaction tonight.

Lori shifted in her chair and looked back out her window at the darkened campus. Somewhere out there, Geoff was likely headed home by now. She should head home as well.

∾

SITTING in the expansive front window, morning light spilling across the hardwood floors of their condo, Patrick rested his chin on his violin. He drew his bow across the open strings, long, smooth strokes as he always did to warm up before playing. The fluid movements settled something in his mind, notes vibrating through his body like he was a struck tuning fork. From here, he transitioned into one of his favorite pieces, "Lark Ascending," the notes ringing from memory due to the hundreds—thousands?—of times he'd played it. His gaze went soft, letting muscle memory carry him through the opening sequence that climbed aloft like the bird for which it was named.

Geoff joined him, taking a seat in the corner armchair of their breakfast nook. He carried a cup of coffee and his morning bowl of granola and yogurt. Patrick continued to play, working his way from the solo through the rest of the piece, enjoying their contemplative silence together. Geoff would never interrupt his music for anything short of an emergency, just like Patrick would never interrupt Geoff when he was deep into one of his history podcasts. Their condo filled with warm violin music, notes resonating and lingering in the air. For a moment, he was back at Juilliard, sitting on the steps outside Lincoln Center, playing violin on the first warm day of spring. His heart ached for it sometimes, the youthful exuberance and optimism of his late teens, when he was going to make a living on music and dreams.

He let the final notes fade away along with the memory. Time marched on.

"Good morning." Patrick set the violin down in his lap. "How'd you sleep last night?" Geoff had been out later than usual and had mentioned getting a drink with a colleague but had been pretty quiet on the subject altogether before bed.

"Restless." Geoff nodded to his violin. "How did rehearsal go?"

"Good. We've got a gig coming up soon, so we're mostly focusing on that. It's nice to get some classical in after all folk last night."

Geoff made a thoughtful noise and sipped his coffee. "What's on your schedule for today?"

Patrick listed it off. "I'm giving a lesson at eleven and another at one, then I was going to pick up groceries. What about you?"

"I've got a team meeting at noon, and I'm probably going to go in a little before that and get some work done for my Bridge Program classes. I'm also trying to finish up this paper..." He went on, describing the paper, and Patrick watched his mannerisms as much as he listened to his words. Geoff was more agitated than usual. Something was sharper about his movements, his posture more upright, a tension radiating through his body. Patrick set his violin down in its case with the bow and got to his feet, walking around behind Geoff, who paused midsentence as Patrick began to rub his shoulders.

"What are you doing?" Geoff asked, interrupting himself.

"I'm giving you a massage. You look tense."

Geoff stopped his story and eased into the contact, relaxing only minutely. Patrick brushed a thumb across the back of his husband's neck and then kissed the top of his head gently in his nest of tight curls. "You're good to me," Geoff said at last, as Patrick went back to his chair.

"It's why you keep me around." Patrick gave him a broad smile. "Is there more of that coffee in the kitchen?"

"I'm keeping it warm for you."

Patrick returned a few minutes later to see Geoff still

sitting in his chair, staring out the window. Normally, he'd have moved onto technology of some kind by now: he would either be surfing a website or reading a book on his Kindle, not just sitting and staring.

"What's really going on with you?" Patrick asked. Better to approach these things directly.

Geoff licked his lips. "You know how back when we were at the pub last week, I was telling you about that woman I worked with, who was having a party upstairs? Lori?" When Patrick nodded, he continued. "I went for a drink with her last night."

"Oh, yeah, you said you had a good time." Patrick leaned back in his chair.

"I think you should meet her." Geoff looked over at him. "I think we should have her over for dinner this weekend."

Patrick raised an eyebrow. "Okay." There was more to this story, probably. "Is this me not having enough friends or something? Because we both know that's not true."

"No, you have tons of friends. Way more than me. I just think you would like her. You should get to know her." Geoff hesitated, and then pushed forward. "She did her doctoral dissertation on polyamory."

"So, you think we'd have some things to talk about because I used to be polyam?" Patrick stroked his beard, trying to figure out what was behind these comments. Geoff averted his eyes once, like he did when he felt guilty, and Patrick suddenly understood. "Oh. No." Patrick folded his arms. "Not like that, Geoff."

"Why not?" Geoff turned to face him. "It's perfect. She's your type. She's crazy smart, she's into music, and she's bold, with a great sense of humor. And she's...well, she's gorgeous,

she's got this beautiful soft brown skin and these dark eyes..."
He smiled to himself like he was picturing her.

Patrick had to smile as well. "Geoff, I'm happy with you. I don't need to sleep with someone else. I don't need to meet anyone else. Is that why you went out for drinks with her last night? You sizing her up for me? I don't need a pimp, babe."

Geoff set his lips in a thin line. "I don't know why people keep saying that. She accused me of the same thing last night."

"You fucking told her?" He probably shouldn't laugh, but there were only two ways to respond to this: laughter and anger. "What did she say? I'm surprised she didn't punch you in the face."

"No, she kind of reacted like you did, but then she..." He squinted, like he was trying to reason through something. "She said basically if I wanted to get her into bed, I had to buy her dinner first."

Patrick snorted. He didn't know Lori yet, but secretly, he kind of liked her a little just from that. "I can't believe you. What's gotten into you lately? Haven't I been showing you I love you enough? Have I been acting like I want more?"

"It's not that. You've been great. You're always great to me." Geoff pressed his hands down onto his slacks, rubbing them in small arcs back and forth. "I feel like there should be more for you. It doesn't have to be her, I don't even know if she'd want to, but maybe someone? You shouldn't have to settle for just me."

"It's not—" Patrick began, but Geoff pushed on.

"I know it's not settling, but isn't it? When you go from as many people as you want to one, don't you wonder what you're missing out on? Don't you feel like you're narrowing your options down in a completely ridiculous way?"

Patrick was about to argue back, but the words dried up. Geoff's passion, the shine in his eyes, they didn't match what he was saying. An alternate possibility occurred to him. "You're into her."

Geoff froze, his mouth turning down, and then he shook his head. "No, that's ridiculous. I wanted you to have more opportunities. You're the one who's polyamorous."

"Are you sure about that?" This was clicking into place, all the pieces aligning like tumblers in a lock ready to open. "Listen to yourself. You're smitten with this woman." He was smiling, but hopefully Geoff wouldn't think he was being mocked. That wasn't his intent. Geoff was still shaking his head, but he'd gone quiet. "It's okay, Geoff. This is normal. You've only been with me, and you see this beautiful woman you work with all the time. It's okay to be curious."

Geoff got to his feet, agitated. "That doesn't make any sense. I thought of Lori because of the polyam thing, and I thought you and her might like each other. It isn't about *my* feelings for her. I don't—I wasn't—" He twisted his hands together, then fumbled with his glasses, trying to adjust them and knocking them askew.

Patrick got to his feet and gently righted them, then cupped Geoff's face. Geoff put his hands over Patrick's, holding himself steady, and his dark brown eyes were wild and confused and frightened. He wasn't like this; Geoff was always in control of what he wanted and how he was going to get it. This panic, so out of character, drove Patrick's nurturing instinct.

"It's okay," he said again.

"It's not okay." Geoff pushed Patrick's hands away. "I can't believe you think that about me."

"Think what?"

"That I want someone else. That I want someone other than you."

"Isn't that what you think about me, though? You think I want to sleep with this other woman because I'm not happy with you?"

"I know you're happy with me. I thought you'd want more. I thought you wouldn't want to be limited." He started to pace. "I didn't think you were going to try and put all this on me."

"If you want to sleep with her, and she's interested, it's not out of the question," Patrick said, his voice calm. This was perfectly reasonable, after all. "We can talk about it."

"You're missing the point." Geoff shook his head. He grabbed his keys off the hook near the front door. "I need to go for a walk." He pushed out the front door and into the stairwell before Patrick could say anything more.

Patrick watched him go, and a gentle sadness settled inside him. Geoff needed to reach this realization on his own. Now that he'd figured out what was beneath Geoff's feelings, they were hard to interpret any other way. Hopefully, he wouldn't stay in denial for long.

5

Geoff walked briskly away from the building, his mind flashing angrily through his last conversation with Patrick. How dare he? Patrick was usually so astute, and to completely misread the situation like this was out of character for him. They understood each other intimately, more than he'd ever understood another person in his life—or been understood by someone else, as far as he knew—and this felt like more than just a misread. It felt like... He searched for ways to describe it. Like a breach of trust. Yes, like that. Having the right association for the feeling settled him a bit.

Their condo building was an old converted mill abutting a river, and the banks of that river were his favorite place to sit and think. He'd taken graduate texts there, and student papers, and fantasy novels, and sometimes his camera, but now, he climbed through the pine trees down toward the waterline with only his irritation to keep him company.

A mammoth boulder formed part of the barrier between river and land, worn down at the water's edge by lifetimes of current carving away the stone underneath. Geoffrey climbed out onto its surface and hung his feet over the edge, the late-spring river still higher than it would be in just a few months when it slowed to a pleasant, swimmable flow. So many things settled down in the summer, pace lagging in the heat. Spring, though, was a time of upheaval and transition.

Growth, change, discovery, these spring feelings were...a giant pain the ass, honestly. He'd done so well with Patrick's polyamory all these years. It had felt comforting: here was a man who wouldn't hesitate to go after what he wanted, and who wouldn't be confined by society's rules. He wasn't put off by Geoff's lack of sexual experience. They wanted each other, and that's all they needed to get started together.

The water beneath him tumbled along, heading downstream with single-minded intensity. It must be nice not to have this kind of doubt, to know what you were doing and what your purpose was. It must be nice not to feel scared or anxious or uncertain. It must be nice not to have to *feel*.

Patrick was right about his feelings for Lori, and that was the most terrifying thing of all.

He hadn't realized he wanted to sleep with Lori, but, of course, that made the most sense. How fitting Patrick would realize it before Geoff did. Fitting and pretty damn irritating too. He hated not knowing himself. Trying Patrick's interpretation on, though, made a frightening amount of sense. He couldn't ignore a logical conclusion, even when he didn't like it—he was an academic. He'd been spending a lot of time thinking about Lori, seeing her with Patrick, but his fantasies easily spun out beyond that. He wanted her as well. He wanted to kiss her, to feel her in his arms, to know what she sounded like when she came. He'd probably been crushing on her for a while now without admitting it to himself. What a goddamn fool.

He flopped back on the rock, the cold stone pressing against his back, and stared up at the sky through the branches of trees reaching out over the bank. He had so much to do today. There wasn't time for an existential crisis.

When Geoff walked back into the condo a little while later, Patrick was in the kitchen mixing up some kind of marinade for dinner that night. He looked up briefly as Geoff entered the kitchen, his expression neutral, then back to the marinade. Geoff leaned on the doorjamb while Patrick finished up the process. Chicken in the fridge, hands washed, Patrick finally turned to face his husband.

"You going to say something, or just watch me like the Food Network?" He leaned back against the counter, bracing himself with his hands on the edge.

"I think you're right about me and Lori." Geoff stayed leaning against the doorframe, mostly because his legs were unsteady. "I think I've been projecting."

To his credit, Patrick didn't tell him, "Yeah, obviously," or any of the other rude comments he was probably considering in that quick-moving mind of his. He just let Geoff keep talking.

"I feel like a bisexual stereotype," Geoff blurted.

Patrick blinked, pushing up from the counter to stand upright. "What do you mean?"

Geoff waved a hand, like that could possibly explain any of this embarrassing shit. "I'm happy with you. I love you. I *choose you.* I shouldn't need to sleep with someone else just because she's a woman."

Patrick rubbed his beard. "Do you want to sleep with her because she's a woman? Would *any* woman do?"

"No, it's definitely because it's *her*." Geoff couldn't picture anyone else bringing out these conflicting feelings, turning his stomach inside out. "But people say this about us. That bi people cheat. That we can't be trusted. That we're always going to want something else. How am I supposed to feel like that isn't *true*?"

"Do you think that about me because I'm polyamorous?" Patrick didn't sound worried in the least, and damn, his *kingdom* for an ounce of Patrick's nonchalance.

"No."

Patrick walked over to him where he stood in the doorway. "There are polyamorous straight people and gay people. There are monogamous bi people and pan people." Patrick cupped the side of his face. "This doesn't have to be a big deal."

If only Geoff could believe that. "It's a big deal to me."

Patrick nodded. "Of course. I don't mean to minimize that." He leaned in and brushed his lips over Geoff's, a sweet kiss that settled Geoff's nerves slightly. "Listen. Invite her over for dinner this weekend. Let's get to know her."

"Get to know her?" Geoff usually could tell if Patrick was using a euphemism or not, but this could mean anything.

Patrick smiled. "Really. Just get to know her. You said you think I'd like her. And I definitely want to meet the woman who's tempting my sweet, monogamous husband into bed."

Geoff pursed his lips, irritated. "That's not funny." But he had to laugh when Patrick did, pressing their foreheads together. "I don't even know if she's interested."

"Go to work," Patrick said, stepping back and releasing him. "It's all going to be fine."

If only he had Patrick's self-assurance.

LORI COULD NORMALLY DO mundane tasks without much focus, but this was the third time in an hour she'd caught herself staring at the barcode of a package without doing anything about it, scanner gun held uselessly aloft. She'd volunteered to help Hannah with inventory tonight at her sex shop, Yes, Please, but probably hadn't been much help at all since getting here. She scanned the rest of the row of hanging packages of cock rings.

"You doing all right?" Hannah asked.

"I keep spacing out." Lori pulled the "to be scanned" tag off the current display and moved to the next. "I'm probably not much help."

"It's helpful that I don't have to pay you." Hannah finished scanning a rack on the other side of the room and tossed the tag into the trash. "And I don't have to be here until three in the morning like usual."

"You might, if I can't get my shit together." Lori hadn't been planning on helping with inventory, but she wanted to talk to Hannah anyway, so it didn't hurt to help a friend. Providing she was actually being somewhat helpful.

"Yeah, you gonna tell me what's going on? You mentioned, and I quote, 'some bullshit,' but you didn't elaborate." Hannah was moving steadily through the racks while she spoke, methodically repeating a process she'd probably done dozens of times in her life as a business owner.

Lori grimaced at the rack of toys, turning her back to Hannah to continue scanning. "It's weird for me to ask advice about this. I feel like I'm the one usually giving advice."

"You're not wrong."

Lori started in on the enormous rack of lubes, turning each small bottle to scan the barcode. "A friend of mine from work invited me over to have dinner Saturday night with him and his husband. And it's...complicated."

"Complicated how? Do I know this friend?"

"I don't think so. His name's Geoff. We've worked together for a couple of years now, but not really closely. We went out for a drink last night, and this afternoon he emailed and asked if I wanted to have dinner with him and his husband."

Hannah's scanner continued to beep as she worked her way through her task. She didn't comment, probably waiting for Lori to finish answering the rest of her question.

"I think he's propositioning me," Lori added.

"Oooh." Hannah stopped scanning. "Him *and* his husband?"

"Yeah." Lori tried to describe their previous encounter, the discussion in her office and the bar, attempting to get the nuance right. The evening's propositioning had been mostly subtext, so it was incredibly difficult to explain. She skipped the part about going back to her office to rub one out, but tried to give justice to the rest of the evening. Hannah's eyebrows went up and down at various points, and she completely stopped scanning to listen. As soon as Lori finished, Hannah went back to her task with a thoughtful frown.

"If he's inviting you to dinner after that conversation, he's got to be at least a little polyamorous." Hannah checked the screen on her scanner. "He knows what he's asking."

"But do I go?" That was the crux of Lori's question, the battle waging inside her. "I've been studying this topic for years, and I'm not sure what he wants is actually polyamory."

"I seem to remember," Hannah said slowly, "you having a conversation with me last year about how labels didn't really matter that much, but what mattered was everyone being on the same page, and there being lots of ways to have a relation-ship. Or am I misremembering?"

Lori scanned the next few lube bottles with slightly more aggression. "I don't recall that exact conversation."

"Sure." Hannah's smile was audible. "It's just dinner, Lori."

"It might not be just dinner."

"You don't have to sleep with either of them if you don't want to."

Even the possibility of sex with Geoff ignited a fire inside Lori that she didn't want to interrogate. "I might want to. I don't know if it's him, specifically, or just an unspecified horniness because I haven't been sleeping with anyone in way too long and I might just want to get some dick."

"That's fine."

"I know that's fine." Lori appreciated Hannah's sex-posi-tivity, but she wasn't questioning that aspect of her decision. "I don't want to go fucking up their marriage if this isn't what they really want. Geoff's new to this. His husband, Patrick, apparently isn't, but if Geoff's gonna get his heart broken, hell, I don't want anything to do with that." Privately, the thought of Geoff getting his heart broken made her feel all soft and sensitive, but that was just because of her underlying sentimentality. He was a good guy. She would hate for him to be sad.

"You are three grown adults." Hannah had finished her side of the store and moved over to the rack of display harnesses near Lori's lube station. "We've been having these polyam discussion groups for months now, and doesn't it pretty much always come down to 'you're grown adults, decide what you want and how to make it work'?"

"Yeah, but it feels different when it's in the abstract versus in my actual life."

Hannah laughed. "Welcome to my world, girl."

Lori had been witness to everything Hannah had gone through regarding her own personal development to be able to have the relationship she had now, this beautiful triad between her and Ben and Mitchell. Her relationship hadn't been earned easily; she'd suffered through a lot of sleepless nights and long conversations with Lori as well as with her relationship partners.

"Okay, yeah, I don't want any of that." Lori set down her gun. "I love you, and I'm so happy you've got this relationship, but I don't want to get mixed up in this whole tangle of multiple partners right now."

Hannah laughed once, harsh and surprised. "You've been studying this for years. You've been telling me you think monogamy is fundamentally flawed. But now you're saying you don't want multiple partners?"

"I don't want a relationship," Lori specified. "I can't get mixed up with one guy, let alone two, not *right now*. I'm gonna move, Hannah. I'm moving away."

Hannah nodded slowly, her expression going wistful. "I know. I want you to stay, but I know you're starting to look."

She had been looking for jobs only casually, but a serious job search was in her plans. Any day now, she was going to start applying. "I suppose it's just dinner."

Hannah's mouth turned up in a half smile. "Unless you *do* want more."

"But even then, just sex." Lori felt the painful irony of having had a similar conversation with Hannah last year, about "just sex" versus a relationship, back when Hannah was in denial about the path of her encounters with Mitchell and Ben. "And probably nothing at all."

"Right." Hannah didn't look like she believed Lori. "You getting déjà vu, here?"

"It's different than it was with you, though. Geoff and Patrick are married. Together. Happy. I'm a third wheel. You and Ben and Mitchell were just doing your own things back then. It wasn't like they were a couple already."

"Not technically, no."

Lori knew the "technically" part, but she stuck by her distinction. "Plus, I'm moving away. Even if I go to dinner, and something else happens, there's an expiration date. I'll be gone in months. Maybe sooner."

"Go to dinner." Hannah finished the harnesses and set her gun in the cradle to download the next patch of inventory data. "It can't hurt."

Lori handed her the other scanner gun. Hannah was right; dinner was just a way to get to know Patrick and Geoff better, not anything more. "I guess not."

Hannah grabbed her phone. "Let's order a pizza before we do the back room. I'm starved."

6

The old mill buildings just south of Mapleton had long since been converted to offices, apartments, and condos, but Lori had never been inside any of them. When she'd finally written back to Geoff and told him that yes, she'd like to join them for dinner, he'd given her some lengthy instructions on where to park, which entrance to use, and which elevators to look for. It had seemed way too detailed, but after driving through the expansive converted industrial complex, with a dozen buildings and as many entrances, she'd been glad for the specificity. She'd found the right elevator and pressed the call button for the fourth floor, the top floor, and Geoff's familiar voice had invited her up.

Riding up in the achingly slow elevator, Lori stared at her warped reflection in its metallic surface, getting her bearings, her heart beating its nervous tattoo against her ribs. She repeated the mantra she'd been echoing since Thursday night. *This is just dinner. It doesn't have to be a big deal.* She couldn't lie to herself about wanting to impress, though. She'd dressed cute, in one of her favorite springtime dresses in a light yellow color that brought out the golden undertones of her skin. Plus, she'd done a full twist-out on her hair, and her shiny black curls framed her face in a bouncy cloud.

The elevator doors dinged open right into Patrick and Geoff's condo, and she stepped out, shouldering her messenger bag. Her first impressions were of space and light: the condo had high, lofted ceilings with exposed wood beams and brick walls, and the wall to her left was filled with giant floor-to-ceiling windows.

"Hi! You must be Lori."

The gorgeous guy leaving the kitchen and wiping his hands on his apron was definitely not Geoff. He was white, first of all, and okay, maybe she'd been picturing someone different. But damn, different wasn't always bad; he had a hipster vibe, with styled auburn hair and a full, neatly trimmed red beard and mustache, and he was dressed in slim-fitting jeans and a short-sleeved Henley stretched across his chest. He extended a hand. "I'm Patrick."

His hand was large and warm, dwarfing hers. "It's nice to finally meet you," she said. "I've heard so much about you."

"It's all lies." He chuckled and let her hand go. Her nerves settled a bit. Patrick was undeniably gorgeous, but if that joke was any indication, he was also a bit of a dork.

She liked dorks.

"Lori! Hi." Geoff emerged from what was probably their bedroom and came up to take her hand in both of his. "I'm so glad you came."

"Couldn't turn down the opportunity for some free food and conversation, right?" Hopefully, that sounded noncommittal enough. "You have a place I should set my bag?"

Geoff directed her to the coat hooks on the wall near the elevator. She stepped back to look at him again. "I don't think

I've ever seen you in something other than work clothes." He was always wearing dress slacks and a button-down shirt, usually accompanied by that same tweed jacket with its elbow patches. Now, though, he wore jeans and a polo shirt, and damn, that man had beautiful forearms. Forearms had never been something she'd considered sexy before, but he moved his hand a certain way and the muscles rippled, and she had to pull her gaze away. Shit, this wasn't a good indicator of her ability to keep her wits about her tonight.

"Your hair looks beautiful." Geoff adjusted his glasses, like he wanted to see it better. "Those curls are...wow."

"I know you know better than to try and touch them," she said, and he pressed a hand to his chest.

"I would never! You think my mom raised me in a barn?"

They laughed together, and he gestured to the condo at large. "You want the full tour?"

Patrick, who had gone back to the kitchen, called after them, "Take your time! I've still got about ten minutes to go in here."

"It's not that big of a condo, Patrick." Geoff led her over to the windows first. They were open, letting in the late-spring breeze. "We've got a great view of the river, as long as you don't get vertigo."

"Not a big fan of heights, but I'm okay indoors." Lori peered at the water rushing four stories below. Geoff started to tell her about the paper mill that had been here before the building had been converted, and, of course, he knew its whole history. He walked her around the living room like he was giving a formal tour, full of facts and statistics, and she absorbed it like his students probably did: half with an interest in the subject, and half captivated by his sheer depth of knowledge and passion. The living room was bright and

airy with its large windows and high ceilings. Geoff continued
the tour in the back of the condo, opening the door to the
bedroom, then stopping abruptly in the doorway as if realizing
where he was taking her. It wouldn't have been weird if he
hadn't stopped short and then tried to regain his words.

"It's just the one bedroom," he said, like he was apologizing.

She peered past him. "It's nice. Lots of room. I like how
you've decorated." She wasn't kidding either. The room was
resplendent in shades of light blue and purple, spacious with
plenty of room to walk around and even a sitting area in the
corner. She couldn't resist teasing Geoff. "Nice bed."

Rather than getting flustered, though, he smiled. Every
time she thought she might embarrass him, he smoothly
leaned into her teasing. "Thanks. We could never tolerate
something smaller than a king. A person needs room to move
around, don't you think?"

"Of course." She paused. "I'm doing all right with a queen,
but I don't have to share."

"But sharing's the fun part." Geoff licked his lips, adjusted
his glasses, and led her out of the bedroom. "And here's
Patrick, just finishing dinner."

Patrick was indeed wrapping up, setting everything out. He
moved naturally around the kitchen. Every couple had the one
who cooked more, and that seemed to be Patrick.

She joined them both at the table for build-your-own soft
tacos, which was a pretty smart way to have someone over for
dinner, since nobody got anything they didn't like. Geoff poured
wine for them, and Lori settled into the meal and some conversation about wine and how she didn't know much about it.

"I always feel like a poser," Patrick said. "My musician

friends all go on wine tours, and one of them, his dad even owns a vineyard down in Connecticut. And here I am, and I'm like, 'I like the fruity ones.' If it weren't for Geoff, I'd be a complete rube."

"Who says rube?" Geoff rolled his eyes. "I only started learning about wine because of the history element."

"How many podcasts do you listen to about wine?"

Geoff paused, clearly counting in his head, and Lori started laughing. Geoff threw her an indignant look. "Fewer than five."

"Fewer than five!" Lori chortled.

"And what about you?" Geoff turned to his husband. "How many YouTube channels are you subscribed to that are about not just music but specifically stringed instruments?"

"Leave my YouTube out of this." Patrick joined their laughter and added some guacamole to his taco. "What about you, Lori? What are you a giant nerd about? Because don't tell me you're not a giant nerd. I can tell these things about a person."

"Well..." Lori considered how to answer. "Relationships, for one. From my PhD research. And my best friend owns a sex shop, so I've become a nerd about sex toys, but more nerd-adjacent. Although that isn't really proper dinner conversation."

"We are nothing if not proper." Patrick's eyes sparkled, teasing, and something warm curled inside Lori's belly that made her want more. This was going to be trouble, for sure.

"But in a less scandalous bent, I'm fascinated by text production. Old printing presses, typewriters, bookmaking, all that stuff. I seek it out. There's this bookbinding museum in New York..." she began.

"I've been there." Patrick's eyes lit up. "The Center for Book Arts. Right near Koreatown, right?"

Lori gaped. "You know about it?"

"Yeah! I went to one of their workshops with this woman I was dating back when I was in school."

"You're from New York?" Lori was about to add, "I'm thinking of moving there," but didn't, for some reason. She hadn't even applied for any jobs yet.

"Not originally," Patrick explained. "I'm from Boston, but I went to school in New York."

"Juilliard," Geoff added, with a fair amount of pride in his tone.

"Juilliard. Wow." Lori had known at least one person who had applied to Juilliard but no one who had gotten in. "Geoff was telling me you're a violinist."

"I do what I can." Patrick shrugged, but Geoff nudged him.

"He's just being modest. He's amazing. He won the National Youth Music Competition." Geoff fairly glowed when bragging about his husband, and the love between them would be evident to anyone watching this interaction. A single point of tension eased inside Lori. She wasn't going to destroy this relationship by joining them for dinner, or anything else.

Not that they'd reached that point, but Lori couldn't deny the shift in her thoughts about the evening's potential. These men were fine as hell, clearly in love, and—so far, at least—fun to talk with. They'd probably be amazing in bed.

She forced her attention back to the present, because that wasn't a line of thought to entertain while sitting at their dining room table and eating tacos. "You're from Boston, and you moved to New York for Juilliard. What brought you back to Mapleton?"

Patrick seemed to take a long time chewing before answering. "I moved back to Boston to take care of my mom, halfway through my junior year. She had breast cancer, and it progressed a lot faster than the doctors were expecting. She was okay on her own until she wasn't, and so I came home."

"I'm sorry. That must have been difficult." Lori couldn't imagine dealing with that now, let alone in her early twenties.

"Thank you. She really wanted me to finish school, but I didn't have it in me to move back to New York after she died." He refilled all of their wineglasses, which had been rapidly dwindling. "I came out to Mapleton and began taking classes at the university, and I met Geoff. So I stayed." He smiled at his husband, crookedly. "Right, babe?"

"You met out here, but you're both from Boston." Lori sipped her wine.

"Ironic, right? But we love western Mass," Patrick added quickly. "It's beautiful. Even if the music options are kind of limited."

Geoff built another taco with careful, methodical precision as he spoke. "Patrick's never going to have the music scene here that he had back in New York. Or the social scene."

"The social scene is overrated. We've both got friends here. But Geoff's got something more important than friends." Patrick glanced over at his husband. "A tenure-track professorship."

Ah, so that explained a few things. If Patrick had been one of Lori's therapy patients, she would have dug into that more, tried to figure out whether he was really happy here in Mapleton or just convincing himself for Geoff's sake. But she wasn't his therapist, and she barely knew him, and she had enough sense to keep her mouth shut and focus instead on dinner.

"Tell me about you, Lori." Patrick leaned forward, examining her. He had gorgeous blue eyes, like they could stare right into her soul. He hadn't locked onto her with their full power before. "Geoff told me about your thesis, but I don't know much about your story other than that. How did you come to Mapleton? Or are you from here?"

Lori settled for the condensed version of the story, skimming through growing up in Baltimore and wanting to be a lawyer, but changing her mind while at Smith. She mentioned her year abroad in England, couch-surfing and working odd jobs while deciding what to do with the rest of her life. Finally, she shared her return to academia, a semester at Oxford before returning to the States for good. Geoff asked her about her hobbies, and the three of them spent the rest of dinner discussing the best running and biking routes in Mapleton, shows they were watching, and Geoff's attempts to find and recreate ancient pastries from around the world.

After dinner came dessert, a lemon meringue pie Geoff had made from scratch. "I thought we were having some ancient Moroccan delicacy," Lori teased, fork biting through flaky pastry crust.

"I almost made baklava." He smiled. "But I didn't know if you were allergic to nuts."

"I am not," Lori replied. "Despite the way my dating life right now would make it seem."

After a second of silence, Patrick cracked up laughing, and Geoff just shook his head in amusement. "See, Patrick, I told you she was your type—of person." His hesitation gave him away, a moment's pause that Lori locked onto. "His type" meant something different than "type of person."

"What do you mean by that?" Lori asked, washing down her pie with some coffee Geoff had brewed. "What's your type of person, Patrick?"

Patrick stroked his beard, pie abandoned for a moment as he considered her. "I like a good sense of humor. Someone comfortable with themselves. Someone smart, at least smart about some things. Who'll dig into their interests."

"I'm smart about some things." Lori's pie was disappearing at an alarming rate. "Geoff, this pie is criminal."

"Do you want more?" He went to get up, but she waved him down.

"I'll explode. Seriously, have you thought of becoming a baker?"

Geoff made a face, and Patrick laughed. "Geoff will sleep until noon if he doesn't have to go to work. He would never keep baker's hours."

She wouldn't have expected that about Geoff, but he was nodding his agreement to Patrick's statement. "And you?" she asked Patrick. "Are you a night owl or a...morning person? Is there a bird for that?"

"A lark," Geoff answered. "A night owl or a morning lark."

"Whatever's in the middle." Patrick shrugged and finished his pie as well. "Hon, you would know that."

"A hummingbird," Geoff answered. "A little morning lark, a little night owl."

"Then that's me." He made little fluttering motions with his hands. "I'll get up on the early side, and I'll stay up late too. I peak in the midday hours. That's when I do most of my work."

"I'm more of a night owl, like Geoff. Who is apparently only sharing delicious desserts with friends."

"I'm pretty selective with my—desserts." Geoff's lips turned up as he closed them around a forkful of pie. Was that an innuendo? He'd paused a bit right before "desserts," but this time it appeared deliberate. Geoff had never seemed like an innuendo kind of guy, but she was gaining a whole new perspective on him this week.

"Don't lie. Geoff is a slut with his desserts." Patrick winked, and they all laughed.

"It's true." Geoff sighed. "I can't resist. I bake something delicious, I want everyone to be able to enjoy it. Our neighbors downstairs get a lot of it, and the rest of our game night group, and I bring sweets into work all the time."

"Maybe I need to come by your building more often and cash in on this." Lori smiled and set her fork down on her plate. "What about you, Patrick? Are you giving your gifts away as well?"

Patrick raised an eyebrow with mock affront, but the twinkle in his eye indicated he was enjoying their game. "I beg your pardon?"

"Geoff said you play in a band. Do you have any concerts coming up? CDs for sale?"

"Yes to all of that." Patrick played with his fork. "If you're interested, we've got some gigs on the calendar. Maybe you'd like to come along."

"Maybe." The possibility was intriguing. She'd come over for dinner to get to know them better, and with their flirtatious banter building throughout the evening, she could see the possibility of something much riskier to her heart than a one-night stand: an actual, ongoing friendship.

She got to her feet, as unsettled by that realization as she was interested in seeing where the evening took them. "Can I help with the dishes?"

Geoff let her load the dishwasher amid protestations that it was unnecessary, and finally succeeded in shooing her away so he could put the rest of the leftovers in the fridge. When she returned to the living room, Patrick was sitting in an armchair watching her like an attentive predator, gaze following her every move. Damn, it had been a long time since anyone had looked at her like that, like he wanted to devour her. Geoff sat on the couch, leaving room for her to join him.

The breeze blowing in through the windows was cool, but Lori felt a lot warmer. Both men were focused on her with clear interest. The atmosphere pressed heavily against her with a different type of energy. She could get used to this kind of attention, and suddenly, her hopes for the evening shifted toward far more physical desires. Crossing her legs at the knee, she leaned back and stretched one arm along the back of the sofa as Patrick changed the topic to where she thought they might eventually end up.

"Geoff tells me you did a whole doctoral dissertation on polyamory."

"I did." She hesitated, then went for it. "Geoff tells *me* you're polyamorous."

Patrick smiled. "I'm not surprised." His gaze flicked over to his husband, then back to her. "I'd love to hear about your research."

Sometimes, people asked her that like she was going to tell them a list of sordid details from orgies, even though that wasn't what polyamory was about. From Patrick, though, it sounded like both: a genuine invitation and a come-on. His tone was soft, sultry, and a bit playful.

She wanted to give in, flirt back, but it felt wrong to do disservice to her topic. So, she went for the honest route. "The first part of it was pretty dry. Lots of books, most of which said the same things over and over. A fair share of academic journals on human sexuality and psychology. But the later research was better. A lot of interviews with polyam people. Most in person, some by Skype."

"Most in person," Geoff repeated. "Are there that many polyamorous people in Mapleton?"

"More than you'd think." Lori was always surprised by the way small liberal college towns attracted nontraditional relationship structures. "But I traveled as well, across New England. More cities than towns. A good amount in Boston and a bunch down in New York."

Patrick stroked his beard. "Do you think we're all a bunch of kinky degenerates?"

Lori shrugged one shoulder. "I'm sure some of you are." She smiled, eyeing Geoff near her on the couch. He was more than she'd expected: flirty, confident, driven. Although he was pure "buttoned-up professor" at work, he unbuttoned quite a bit at home...and she wanted more. "But I like the kinky degenerates, so I'm probably not the best person to ask."

Geoff laughed. "I think everyone's a weirdo of some kind, when you get down to it."

"Yeah?" Lori shifted, watching Geoff's gaze follow the slide of her hem above her knee. Perfect. "What's your perversion of choice?"

"There are lots of people who would call me a pervert just for being a queer man, let alone a Black queer man." Geoff moved as well, turning to face Lori more directly. Several feet of couch still separated them, but he *seemed* much closer like this. "But I'm a Harvard graduate and I have a PhD, so it is my highly educated perspective that those people can fuck off to hell."

Surprised, Lori laughed like it was punched out of her. Geoff raised his eyebrows, then smiled broadly, as if tickled by her unexpected laughter. "Beyond that, though," he continued, "I'm afraid I don't have a lot of experience being a—what was the phrase?"

"Kinky degenerate," Patrick answered from the armchair.

"Right. I told you before, Patrick was my first real relationship. I haven't had the opportunity to branch out very far." Geoff removed his glasses, folding them neatly and setting them on the coffee table. Without them, he seemed more open, his dark brown eyes locked onto Lori.

Lori nodded to the glasses he'd just removed. "How far can you see without those?"

"You're a bit blurry, but not much."

Lori got up and moved over on the couch, closing the distance between them. "How's that?"

Geoff blinked, lips twitching slightly. "Not so blurry now."

Her heart thudded against her ribs. She'd had reasons why she shouldn't do this tonight, but she'd thrown those aside the moment she saw Patrick and Geoff together at dinner. Geoff's hand moved from the couch to the outside of her knee, his fingertips skimming her skin and raising goose bumps. He hadn't looked away from her face since removing his glasses.

The arm Lori had draped over the back of the couch brought her so close to him, and she let herself lightly touch the back of his neck. She wanted to be even closer, so she drew her knees up onto the couch, kneeling instead of sitting. "Have you ever kissed a girl?" she asked.

Geoff smiled. "I've kissed a few girls."

"How long has it been?"

He tipped his head to the side. "A long time." He looked over past Lori's shoulder, probably at Patrick, with sudden uncertainty.

Lori didn't turn around. "Hey, Patrick?"

Patrick's smile was evident in his voice. "Yeah, Lori?"

She began to trace circles on the back of Geoff's neck. "I want to kiss your husband."

Geoff shivered, his eyes falling half-closed, and he licked his bottom lip in reflex. Fuck, Lori wanted to taste him, her body hot like she had a fever. "And I think your husband wants to kiss me back."

Patrick's chuckle sounded low and filthy behind her. "I think so too. What do you think, Geoff?"

Geoff didn't say anything, focused on Lori's mouth, his body fairly vibrating with tension. Her skin tingled, leg hot where Geoff's hand now pressed. His other hand slid up to cup the back of her neck, just as she held his, and for a few heartbeats, they stayed frozen, neither ready to make the next move.

Patrick's voice broke the silence. "Oh, for god's sake, Geoff. Fucking kiss her already."

Smiling, Geoff pulled Lori's mouth down to his.

7

Holy hell, it had been a long time since Geoff had kissed anyone other than Patrick. The press of Lori's mouth against his ignited his nerve endings, all of them firing at once, sending conflicting messages of *yes, this, more* and *wrong, something is wrong*. The combination exhilarated and terrified at once, stealing his breath, overwhelming his senses. She smelled gorgeous, fruity and earthy like pears, and her smooth skin brushed against his, her lips unbearably soft. He wanted her closer; he slid his arm up from her leg to her back, pulling her down against him. She went easily, body slotting against his, her breasts pressing into his chest. A little hitch in her breath made his cock twitch in interest. When her lips parted, tongue tangling with his, he grew hard in seconds.

Lori broke the kiss first, her eyes dark and wide. Her soft, wet lips parted for her to catch her breath, and he nearly pulled her against him once more but held back. "Oh," she breathed, as if realizing something.

The sound of movement on the armchair brought Geoff's attention past Lori to Patrick, watching them both with undisguised hunger on his face. Patrick looked at him like this when he was about to devour him, when they were going to tumble into bed and not come up for air until morning. Jesus, Geoff wanted more, his throat paralyzed with an inability to ask for it. That wasn't like him; he could talk dirty with the best of them, could bring Patrick to a keening mess with just his words, but this woman shook him to his core.

Lori licked her lips, still sitting up on her knees and looking down at him, like she was trying to make up her mind about something. Then she shifted to look back over her shoulder at Patrick. "You know, there's room on this couch."

Patrick crossed his legs, ankle over knee, and tipped his head to the side in thought. "There's more room in the bedroom."

Geoff's heart skipped, and he swallowed the sudden desire for more that bubbled up inside him like a tangible force. Lori looked between Geoff and Patrick. "I think the couch is a better next step." She ran a thumb across Geoff's lower lip, and his arousal jumped like she'd stroked his cock. "You don't seem ready for the bedroom."

He found words. "Hell yes, I am."

Lori blinked, then laughed in surprise, eyebrows raised. "Yeah? Already?"

Geoff slid his hand down her back, knuckles trailing lightly over her spine, and cupped her ass. She made a soft noise of pleasure as he dragged her closer, flush against him, and began to kiss his way down her neck. Patrick liked roughness, but Lori was unknown, so he teased at her responses with varying sensation. He nipped lightly, felt her indrawn breath, and so sucked hard at the skin above her collarbone. Her hips stuttered, rocking reflexively. Oh, yeah, she liked that. He wanted to lay her out on the bed and devour her, figure out all those places that made her moan and gasp, explore her in ways he'd never done with any woman's body.

A shiver of guilt brought him up short, and he drew back. Patrick was there on the couch, sitting on Lori's other side, and Geoff hadn't even felt him join them. He looked intrigued, not nervous or resentful. Lori pulled back slowly, out of Geoff's arms, watching his face. She moved to straddle Patrick's hips, her skirt riding up as she settled onto his thighs. Geoff's heart raced, a mixture of feelings rising up inside him, but the predominant one was desire.

Lori draped her arms over Patrick's shoulders, over the back of the couch, studying him like she was trying to figure him out. But then she looked over at Geoff. "This okay?" she asked, barely above a whisper.

Geoff nodded, curiosity urging him onward. "I want to see."

Patrick kissed Lori delicately, his lips brushing hers like a tease, one hand cupping her face to bring her down to him while the other rested between them on the couch. Something tight squeezed Geoff's heart, an emotion he couldn't put words to—it was a little bit of fear, yes, but also lust and longing and hope, an emotion that built in concurrence with his growing desire for more. Patrick drew back, glanced over at Geoff, and read everything he needed to on Geoff's face. He pulled Lori close again and devoured her mouth. She gasped, a soft noise that turned into a moan as Patrick skimmed one hand down her side and cupped her breast. Again, she rocked her hips.

Geoff hesitated only a moment, because he couldn't resist any longer, and moved closer to both of them. He cupped her other breast, rubbing his thumb across the nipple through the thin fabric covering. She was so *soft*, her body impossibly curved everywhere his hands longed to touch, and he felt dizzy with the newness. Her nipple hardened beneath his touch, and he twisted the nub gently between his thumb and forefinger.

Lori broke the kiss with a quiet noise of pleasure and turned to him, smiling, her eyes dark. Still straddling Patrick's hips, she leaned over to kiss Geoff again, mouth soft and wet, and his cock throbbed inside his pants. God, he wanted her, wanted Patrick, wanted her *and* Patrick, need overwhelming him.

Lori caught her breath, one hand on each of their shoulders. "I think you were saying something about a bedroom?"

Patrick scooped her off him and stood, taking Geoff's hand. "You want this?" he asked. He pulled Geoff against him, all hard lines and firm muscles, one hand sliding down to press against Geoff's cock. Lori's gaze felt like a touch on the side of Geoff's face as he leaned into his husband for a kiss. It was all he could do not to thrust into Patrick's hand. This was familiar, and Lori was totally unfamiliar, and the combination spiked his adrenaline.

"Yeah." He eyed Lori up and down, his body pulsing with need. "Yes. Absolutely. Let's go."

In the bedroom, Lori moved to Geoff first, skimming her hands down the front of his shirt. "Do you know," she said, rubbing her palms against the fabric, "I've never done this before?"

"What?" She could mean nearly anything by that.

Her palms grazed his nipples, and they tightened. "This." She looked between him and Patrick. "Two guys at once. Two anybody at once. This is new."

Patrick smiled. "Then it's a night of firsts. This is new to us too." He moved in behind her, so she was sandwiched between them, bending to nuzzle at the back of her neck through her cloud of spiral curls. "We should talk safety."

"Mmm." Lori tipped her head to the side, giving him more room. "I like you already."

"We got tested when we first started dating." Geoff couldn't stop touching Lori, didn't want to stop, her curves soft and yielding beneath his hands. "We're both negative."

"Me too." Lori licked her lips, then leaned up to kiss him, murmuring against his mouth. "I've got condoms."

Patrick laughed. "Ulterior motives?"

Lori smiled against Geoff's mouth, then paused to nibble his lower lip, sending a jolt straight to his groin. "I always have condoms. It's called being smart." She shifted her hips back against Patrick, and his sudden intake of breath caught Geoff's attention. Patrick was very much into this, just like him and Lori. "And," she added, "I might have hoped we'd all want this."

Geoff groaned, because she'd wanted it too, wanted to end up here in their arms. Relief and arousal flooded through him. This was too much talking, not enough moving forward, and Geoff was a man of action. He slid his hands up her sides and onto her breasts, fumbling slightly.

"Show me," he whispered. "Teach me to touch you."

Lori turned in his arms, lining up her back to his front, and wrapped his arms around her from behind. Covering his hands with hers, she placed them over her breasts.

"Like this," she said. She guided him, caressing, squeezing, rolling the nipples between her fingers, until Geoff took over and she let her hands drop away. Lori smiled and sighed, leaning back against him. "You're a quick study."

"I've been told that." Geoff nipped her earlobe, then her neck again, then turned her around in his arms so he could kiss her again. He wanted to get his mouth and hands all over her as soon as possible. She ran her fingers up under his shirt, her light touch sending shivers down his spine. He pulled his shirt over his head and let it fall. Lori looked him up and down, licked her lips in unmistakable desire, and dragged her palms across his tight nipples and over his chest. He was so damn hard, and they had barely started taking their clothes off.

Patrick bit down on Lori's shoulder, nuzzling up behind her, and she closed her eyes. Geoff traced her curves and reached behind her for the zipper of her dress. She opened her eyes again to watch his face as he slowly dragged the zipper down. The dress slipped off her narrow shoulders and pooled on the ground around her feet. Oh, she was beautiful, all glowing brown skin radiant in the golden light of sunset. Beneath her sundress, she wore a matching set of bra and panties in lacy pink fabric—sheer gauze that did little to conceal what lay beneath. The sudden emotion of this moment closed his throat, and he had to touch, to taste, to move forward *now*.

She swerved away from his approach, deftly ducking out from under his arm with a mischievous smile, backing toward the bed. She climbed up onto the wide, soft king-sized mattress and knelt in the middle, looking between the two men still standing at the foot of the bed. Without speaking, she reached behind her back and unclasped her bra. Geoff's cock twitched again at the sight of her full breasts and dark nipples, her nearly naked body and that flirtatious, inviting grin.

"Fuck. Me." Patrick shook his head in wonder, and he began pulling off his clothes. Geoff watched him disrobe—the rose-white skin of his back and chest, his auburn chest hair, the freckles dusting his shoulders as he carefully folded his clothes and set them aside. His husband stopped when he got down to his boxers and gave Geoff a crooked smile. "You coming, or just want to watch?"

Geoff hadn't realized he'd frozen midmotion, hands lingering at his waistband. He had to laugh as he pulled off his jeans. But then Lori lay back on the bed, propped up on her elbows, and the need to laugh dissolved into pure desire.

They stretched out on either side of her, and Lori dragged Geoff down to kiss her. He propped himself up half over her, wanting more, wanting everything, wanting to rush forward with this and also not wanting it to be over too quickly. He was already getting used to the softness of her mouth against his, her delicate skin beneath his fingers, a contrast to Patrick. Geoff lifted his head to watch her face as he pinched a nipple. She moaned, biting her lower lip, eyes still closed. He tested what she liked: softer, then harder, a strong pinch that made her jerk her hips up in shock.

"Oh," she gasped, eyes flying open. "Yes. Do that again."

He did, pinching the other nipple this time, and she let her head fall back against the pillow with a low groan. Beside her, Patrick lay propped up on his side, resting his head on his hand, watching all of this with his other hand lightly grazing his cock through his boxers. Geoff felt his husband's gaze on him as he lowered his head to take Lori's nipple into his mouth.

She dug her fingers into his scalp and moaned. The nub, tight beneath his tongue, seemed to tighten even more as he sucked harder on it. He switched between her breasts, leaning over her body. Damn, this was incredible, the soft fullness of her breasts beneath his hands and mouth. He moved back to the first breast and Patrick leaned in to mirror him on the other side.

"Fuck." Lori's curse sounded broken, a note of need and surprise, and she twisted beneath them. No, he wasn't done with her. Geoff put a hand flat on her stomach to hold her still, and her hips lifted against him. He wasn't thinking consciously about it, moving his hand on instinct until his fingers brushed the juncture of her thighs and he lifted his head. His hand was right there, and his breath stuttered as she parted her legs.

"Do you want to see me?" Lori asked, breathless.

Geoff nodded. He sat up, sliding down the bed, moving to get a better vantage point. Her lacy panties clung wetly to her skin, outlining soft folds, and he was overcome with the desire for more. Slowly, he brushed his fingers over the damp fabric.

Lori hooked her fingers in the waistband of her panties and lifted her hips, bringing her body up toward his face, and god, he could *smell* her. Then she slid the underwear down and off, tossing it aside, and let him look at her gorgeous pussy.

Geoff brushed his fingers against her again, this time without fabric in the way, and she grabbed for his wrist to bring it to her folds. "More."

Patrick was watching him touch her, his expression rapt, but Geoff's focus was drawn to Lori and her responses. She guided him at first, reaching down to part her folds and bring his fingers to her clit. He let her use his hand as her own, rubbing her clit in small circles. Her head fell back, mouth open, all her words gone, and she let her arms fall to the sides so he could continue on his own. He worked her steadily at the pace she'd set, neither speeding up nor slowing down. The tightness in her body told him all he needed to know. She was getting close, muscles tensing, her hands gripping at the sheets...so he stopped.

She lifted her head immediately, breathless. "What? Why'd you stop?"

He loved that breathless whine in her voice. Geoff hadn't planned on this ahead of time, but he couldn't resist this kind of teasing. "I don't want to rush."

"I can come more than once, you know." She smiled, eyes twinkling.

Patrick leaned in to nuzzle her ear. "You know how you asked about Geoff's kink before? He likes to make you wait."

Lori raised an eyebrow, her breath quickening. "Oh, do you? That's pretty sexy."

Geoff began to rub her clit again, slower this time, and Lori fell against the pillows. "Waiting draws things out. It prolongs the pleasure. Maybe I want to keep doing this for a while."

Lori shivered.

"He's lying." Patrick's hand skimmed across Lori's body, fingers dancing over her skin. "He wants to tease. He wants to make you beg."

Lori smiled, clearly interested, and Geoff wanted her to *moan*. He pressed a finger downward, sliding it into her body, and she made a soft "ooh" noise. Two fingers made her breath catch. She was so hot and tight around his fingers, muscles fluttering, and he needed more of her right now.

He stretched out along the foot of the bed, between her legs. Lori opened her eyes, a question on her lips, until he lifted one of her legs over him and pillowed his head on her thigh. She was beautiful, her folds open like a flower, wet and inviting. This close, her clit pulsed lightly in front of him, begging for his touch, and so he leaned in and drew his tongue across the tight, swollen skin.

Lori clamped her legs together around his head, arching up before he could still her with a hand on her hip. He looked up the length of her body and Patrick was watching him, undisguised lust in his expression. Patrick nodded at him, slowly, dragging his tongue across his upper lip. Then Patrick leaned in and kissed Lori.

Patrick's kisses muffled Lori's cries as Geoff returned to her clit. He licked it, trying to circle it the way he'd done with his fingers, and then sucked it directly into his mouth. It was intuitive; her body responded to each motion, guiding him. She twitched and thrust against his face. She was holding Patrick's hand with one of hers, so Geoff reached up to take her other hand, gripping it as he focused his attention right where she wanted it. She clung to him like a lifeline. He caught his breath and dipped his tongue lower, into her pussy, her tangy taste like heaven on his tongue. His erection was bordering on painful, so he reached down into his boxers with his free hand to give himself a few gentle strokes for some relief.

"My clit," Lori said, voice muffled and strung out, like a plea. "Please, suck on my clit."

How could he deny her anything, when she sounded like that?

He teased her first, licking the tiny bud once, twice, three times, and then pulled it between his lips and sucked. Her hand twitched in his, hips starting to shift on the bed, and this time, he wasn't going to stop. He was going to make her come in his mouth. He looked up the length of her body as Patrick took her nipple into his mouth again, and her cries rang out unmuffled—keening, desperate noises that drove him to distraction. He could focus on a task when it mattered, though, and he gave all his attention to the sweet, throbbing button of her clit until finally, finally, she squeezed his head between her thighs and came beneath his tongue with a loud, broken cry.

Her orgasm went on forever. He didn't stop, even as her fingernails dug into the back of his hand, even as she thrust against his face. Her pleasure ran through him like a current, a direct line to his cock.

"Geoff, please..." she cried, and finally got out the word, "Please, enough!"

Geoff released Lori's clit, and her legs dropped, her body sagging, wobbly and weak. He caught his breath and sat up, face wet, dizzy with his own neglected arousal and lack of air. Patrick was looking at him like he'd seen the face of god, and before he could do much else, Patrick was dragging Geoff up the bed to kiss him on the mouth.

"That was incredible," Patrick murmured.

Then it was Lori's turn to kiss Geoff, tugging him down to her. "Are you sure," she breathed when he at last pulled away, "that you've never done that before?"

Geoff smiled. "Swear to god."

"You are a natural." She let her head flop back again. "I'm gonna need a minute."

Patrick pulled Geoff over to him, hands skimming over the muscles of his back, down to his ass. "Get these off." He tugged at Geoff's boxers.

"You too." Geoff did the same to Patrick. The blood pounding in his cock was making it seriously difficult to think right now.

When they were both naked, Geoff somehow ended up on his back in the middle of the bed, Patrick half on top of him and Lori stretched out along his other side, still recovering. Patrick's mouth pressed hot and wet against his, hand stroking Geoff's cock in slow, light strokes...

No, that wasn't right. The hand touching him was too slender, too soft. Geoff groaned into Patrick's mouth, his erection twitching in Lori's hand. She was perfect at this, rolling her thumb across the head, squeezing the length, spreading his slickness along the surface. He had to catch his breath. Patrick kissed his jaw, his ear, and then drew back to watch the scene before him.

Geoff's arousal burned in his veins like hot wax, searing him from the inside. Lori was watching his face with interest as she stroked his aching cock. A few more strokes and she released him, eyes dark as she licked the wetness on her thumb. She winked at him.

"How do you feel about fucking me?" she asked.

Yes, holy shit, yes, he wanted that. He looked to Patrick, who nodded, back to stroking his own cock this time. "What about you?" he asked Patrick, who shouldn't be left out of all this.

Patrick smiled lazily. "I'm happy to watch for now, but I would also be happy to fuck Geoff at the same time."

Lori swore breathlessly as Geoff groaned, the thought of it alone making his balls tighten. He had barely started to nod before Lori was pulling him onto his side to face her. "Here." She slapped a condom into his hand, then Patrick's, and finally dragged Geoff's mouth to hers.

Jesus, the woman knew how to kiss. She knew what she wanted, and she knew how to get it, and Geoff vacillated between wanting to take charge like usual and happy to be along for the ride. He slid the condom down over his erection, pulling away from her long enough to make sure it was properly seated. Then, without further preamble, she lined herself up with him, draped her leg over his hip, and carefully guided his cock into her pussy.

Geoff's breath caught as the head slipped inside. Even through the condom, she was all tightness and heat, wet and soft and gripping him perfectly. They faced each other on their sides, the position unexpectedly intimate, and Lori rocked her hips gently to pull him in deeper. Geoff's hand trembled as he gripped the leg swung over his, using it to shift their bodies until he was finally, mercifully deep inside her. She felt incredible wrapped around him, and her breath came in short pants as she gripped his upper arm to steady herself. "Are you okay?" he asked, and his voice came out gravelly.

Lori laughed once, and the laugh made her pussy squeeze his dick. "God, yeah, I'm great. You feel fantastic."

Geoff slid his top leg between hers, changing their angle and giving himself some leverage to rock his hips against her. He couldn't drive deep like this, no pounding thrusts, just the rhythmic in and out of their bodies sliding against each other.

The heat of Patrick's body along Geoff's back made him jump, as did the sudden pressure of Patrick's lubed fingers against his exposed ass. Patrick circled his hole, waiting for permission, and Geoff nodded. "Yeah."

Patrick slipped one, then two very slick fingers into him, and Geoff froze up, overwhelmed. Lori's lips on his made him open his eyes. He hadn't realized he'd closed them. She was watching his face, like she had before, watching the way he reacted to the pressure inside him. Her lips were parted, expression captivated.

Patrick was opening him up with steady, confident pressure now, and Geoff wanted to thrust back onto his hand, but he stayed motionless inside Lori. "You all right?" Patrick asked, curling his fingers to press against Geoff's prostate.

Geoff gasped, hips jerking and driving him reflexively into Lori, who squeezed around him. "God. Yes." He wanted to be composed, but this was hitting his senses faster than he could process. More lube, another finger, a deeper stretch that threatened to soften him.

He shifted, and the wet slickness around his cock had him fully hard again in seconds. It was perfect, it was too much, it wasn't enough, it was nothing like what he had been prepared to experience. He heard a condom wrapper, and then Patrick was pressing his blunt, thick cock slowly inside Geoff.

"Fuck," Lori swore, watching the two of them. "You're gorgeous."

Every time Geoff bottomed, he lost himself in the deep, thick push of a dick inside him, that pressure and fullness hitting all of his hot spots. That was nothing next to having this combined with a slick, wet grip around his cock at the same time. He was going to lose his goddamn mind, right here. Finally—*finally*—Patrick bottomed out, and he exhaled, long and shaky, against Geoff's cheek.

"You feel incredible." He gripped Geoff's arm, and then began to rock his hips. The pressure drove Geoff deeper inside Lori, who groaned and tightened around him. Geoff caught his bearings and focused on fucking the gorgeous woman in his arms. Lori clung to him, making low, sexy noises with each movement of his cock. Careful not to touch her delicate twists, he cupped the side of her face to look into her eyes. She kept her gaze locked on him as he moved within her. He wanted to say something, to tease, to talk dirty, to capture some of that control from before, but he was utterly lost in her beauty and the sweet grip of her body around his.

Behind him, Patrick was moving in sync with him. Each rock backward pushed him farther onto Patrick's cock, and each shift forward pushed him deeper into Lori. Patrick gripped his upper arm, his lips against Geoff's ear. "I love you," he murmured. "You're so damn hot, spread open on my cock, filling her up at the same time. I could watch you like this forever. I can't wait to feel you come. Can't wait to feel you squeezing all around me."

Geoff swore under his breath. His balls tightened against his body, the deep tingle of arousal shifting into the steady climb to orgasm. He wasn't ready to come yet. "I want you to come again," he said to Lori, words halting as he rocked into her.

She nodded frantically. "I want that." Sliding her hand down between their bodies, she found her clit, fingertips brushing against the base of his cock where it moved inside her. Her muscles *squeezed* around him, tight as a vise, tight enough to make him groan and pause so he didn't come too quickly. But she was shifting, pressing against him, gripping his arm with her free hand, eyes going wide as she reached the edge.

"That's it." Patrick began to fuck him harder, driving him deeper. "Come for us."

He might have been talking to Lori, or to Geoff, but Lori was the first to yield. She gasped, going motionless, and then exhaled in a cry as her muscles rippled along his length. That was too much for Geoff to resist, the deep pull of climax bearing down on him, and he cried out as he emptied himself inside her. He clamped down on Patrick, the pressure and fullness driving him higher and higher, extending his pleasure as he fell apart.

Patrick was moving inside Geoff as he recovered, and the

rippling aftershocks kept Geoff twitching throughout. He was still inside Lori, and she was watching Patrick over Geoff's shoulder with her jaw slack. Patrick thrust once, twice, and then came with a groan.

They remained entwined together for a few moments, breathing shallowly and unevenly into the silence. Then someone moved, and they shifted into untangling limbs, taking care of condoms, cleaning up, the general aftermath of sex. Finally, they settled back into a sprawl on the bed, naked and content to lie quietly. Geoff stared up at the high ceiling of their loft. His body tingled all over, worn out from sex and adrenaline.

Already, though, his mind raced with possibilities. Lori was incredible. Tonight was incredible. If she was ever interested in doing this again, maybe they could try something else. They'd both clearly focused on him, but they could make things more equitable next time.

Shit, he shouldn't hope for a next time. A next time was too much to ask for. This was the kind of once-in-a-lifetime experience most people never got, and wanting it again was selfish. He could be content with this memory. He looked over at the two people next to him. Lori was idly running her fingers through Patrick's auburn hair while he smiled, eyes closed.

"That feels amazing," Patrick said quietly. He blinked his eyes open. "Do you want to spend the night?"

Lori paused, then sat up, scooting back to rest against their headboard. She looked over past Geoff at the clock on the nightstand. "I wasn't planning on it." She laughed. "I wasn't really 'planning' on any of this, to tell you the truth."

"You can stay," Geoff added. She should know how he felt as well. "The bed's big enough for all of us."

Lori bit her lip, visibly tempted. Geoff didn't want to look too closely at his desires to have her stay, to extend this as long as possible. Eventually, she shook her head. "I should go."

Geoff's disappointment washed through him like cold water, but he forced a smile anyway.

8

Patrick insisted on walking Lori to her car, and it wasn't just to enjoy a few more minutes of her company. Lori smiled up at Patrick as they hit the elevator button to go downstairs and the doors slid shut on them. Aside from a bit more wildness in her beautiful curly hair, she might have just come from dinner that ended with light conversation and nothing more.

"That was really fun." She leaned into him, a gentle weight against his side. "I don't know if Geoff is going to recover anytime soon."

Patrick chuckled. "He's a pretty resilient guy. He can stand it."

"And what about you?" She nudged him with an elbow. "You do all right, watching your man with someone else?"

Patrick shrugged. "It's all right by me. You heard him. My polyamory goes way back."

"And what about now?" She brushed some curls back out of her face, uncertainty only visible in the tightness of her smile. "What happens now?"

The elevator door dinged open, and they stepped out into the lobby, then into the cool May night. Visitor parking was off to one end, and he walked with her along the sidewalk, thinking about her question. Lori was definitely the kind of person he would want to be friends with, even if Geoff hadn't introduced them. "I like you. I know Geoff likes you. We should get together again sometime."

"What, for more of this?" Lori gestured between the two of them, then up toward the window of the condo, and he knew what she meant.

"Maybe." He rubbed his beard. "If you're up for it."

Lori laughed. "Not sure. I'm not really looking to get mixed up in a relationship right now." Her smile dimmed. "I wasn't even really looking to get mixed up in tonight, to tell you the truth."

"Some regrets?" He would never want that for her.

Lori paused, head tipped to the side. "No." She glanced back up at him. "No regrets. Just surprises. I don't usually do this kind of thing."

The idea that she might drive off tonight and not see them again felt suddenly overwhelming. What a loss to let her friendship slip away, right when they were on the verge of something great. "I would like to get together with you again, regardless." Patrick resisted the urge to take her hand, like he might with Geoff when they were walking together. "Not for sex. For friendship." He paused. "Unless you want sex?"

Lori laughed again. "I see why Geoff likes you. You're a pretty good guy." She looked him up and down. "And I have to admit, I didn't get nearly as much of you as I'd have wanted if we'd gone for round two."

Patrick's too-tired cock nevertheless perked up in interest

at that. "Don't do that to me, Lori. I'm gonna be thinking about it all night."

They reached her car, and she put her palm flat on his chest. "Okay. If Geoff isn't totally freaked out after tonight, maybe we can get together again. As friends. Go get drinks or go see a show or something. Lord knows it looks like we have enough common interests."

"Are you on social media?" Patrick asked.

Lori grimaced. "Unfortunately, yes. But it's better to text me. Got your phone on you?"

Patrick handed over his phone, and Lori added her number to his contacts before handing it back. "There," she said. "No excuses now."

She had the best smile, all flirtatious charm and mischief, the same kind of mischief he liked when Geoff got on a tear about something. He wanted to kiss her. The urge welled up inside him out of nowhere, like Geoff wasn't right upstairs waiting for him, like this was a date instead of a friends-with-benefits one-night stand, or whatever the hell it was.

She seemed to read the expression in his face, because something shifted in the way she looked at him. He wanted it to be desire, the way her eyes got wider in the glow of the streetlamp, the soft touch of her tongue to her lip in thought. But then it was gone. She turned away and got her car keys out of her bag. "Have a good night, Patrick. Stay in touch."

He took a step backward, out of her personal space, away from the intoxicating aroma of fruity sweetness and sex that still clung to her body. "You too. Thanks for coming."

She opened the car door and spared him a wink. "Twice." Then, laughing at her own joke, she got in the car and drove away.

Geoff was sitting on the couch when Patrick returned,

wearing baggy gym shorts and an old T-shirt. "She doing all right?"

"She's fine." Patrick sat next to him and slung an arm around Geoff's shoulders. "How are you feeling?"

"Fucked out and sore, but I think I'll live." Geoff rested his head back on Patrick's arm. "You?"

"I'm fine. But I didn't mean physically. How are you doing, you know, with all this?" Patrick gestured to them, a gesture that hopefully encompassed everything they'd just done.

Geoff tutted. "I'm an academic, Patrick. There's no reason for me not to be fine. I wanted to try something, and I got to try it. I think that makes me pretty lucky." He leaned in to kiss Patrick on the lips, careful and deliberate. Patrick kissed him back. They had this, still. More than anything, he valued this marriage. Even if he wanted more, even if he could imagine a world where Lori shared their bed regularly, Geoff had been clear about his desires and fulfilling them. His monogamous husband had already pushed himself quite a lot tonight. Thinking of more was unfair to both of them.

Geoff broke the kiss to slap Patrick, playful but firm. "Stop getting lost in your head."

Patrick smiled. "How do you always know?"

"Your lips stop moving."

Patrick rolled his eyes. "Fine. It's why I can't ever lie to you. You'd see right through me."

Geoff nodded. "It's mutual. Now come on." He tugged Patrick to his feet. "Let's go to bed before I pass out here in the living room."

Patrick let Geoff lead him into the bedroom, because going to bed was easier than talking further. Maybe there was nothing more that needed to be said.

GOD, she'd wanted to stay.

The whole way back to her apartment, Lori had to force herself not to turn around and go back. She'd been invited to stay the night, and she'd been sorely tempted, but going home was the *right decision*. Just because it was the right decision, though, didn't mean she was happy about it.

Tonight had been incredible. Beyond words. She hesitated to use the words "life-changing" about some really good dick, because she was a practical woman who hated hyperbole, but tonight had been at least *near* life-changing dick. Sure, sleeping with Geoff was amazing, especially considering he'd never had sex with a woman before, but this wasn't strictly amazing sex. Having both men there, seeing Geoff and Patrick together while they each took turns doting on her as well, feeling Geoff get fucked while also fucking her, it was like the most over-the-top porn she'd ever imagined.

She wanted to stay the night. She wanted to wake them up in the morning and go for another round. And that was why she had to get home.

Her apartment was cool, dark, and silent. She never liked that kind of silence, so she turned on music as soon as she walked in the door. As classic rock echoed through the space, she hung up her bag and kicked off her shoes. She could still feel Geoff's and Patrick's hands on her skin, phantom brushes of their fingers, and she kept touching her own arms in reflex. Being in her own space should have shaken these desires. Instead, her mind kept circling back to reliving the night. A hot shower might help.

A hot shower didn't help, although she stood in there for a while, letting the steam invigorate her hair while cursing her lack of impulse control. What was she thinking, fucking them on what was essentially a first date? This wasn't just fucking a random stranger; she'd slept with a married man *from work* and his husband.

It was their first threesome, all of them, and she'd just jumped right into it without much prior conversation or negotiation. She knew better, damn it. She had a whole doctorate about doing better. If one of her therapy clients had come to her with this story, she'd have pressed them with gentle but probing questions. *What do you think sparked this decision? You said you felt impulsive. Have you been feeling out of control in any aspects of your life?*

Lori made a face at the blue tile of her bathroom wall. It was a bitch to psychoanalyze herself. Yeah, of course she'd been feeling out of control. Of course she'd been acting a little irrationally. Not to mention her sex drought. Plus, could *anyone* attracted to men look at Geoff and Patrick and *not* want to fuck them senseless?

Patrick had been so deliberate when fucking Geoff. He'd worked him steadily, holding him tight. She'd only gotten to fuck Geoff, and it would be fun to fuck each of them, maybe at the same time…

Apparently, she was incorrigible. She shut off the hot water and let the air raise goose bumps on her skin before drying off. She needed to cool off, for crying out loud. Two orgasms and she was still thirsty for more. She pulled on a light nightshirt and sleep shorts and tried to focus on the process of evening hair care. Maybe the methodical, mindless repetition could settle her antsy nerves.

Like the shower, the nightly hair routine didn't do anything for her pent-up feelings, and she was just as worked up as ever when she finished. Fucking fine. Her brain wanted to work? She'd put it to some good use.

Her computer was still showing an open spreadsheet when she logged on. She'd kept that spreadsheet open for two weeks now, listing all the jobs she'd spotted online that she might want to apply for but wasn't quite ready to move forward on. That ended tonight. She had already updated her resume, which was saved as a PDF waiting to be sent into the ether of the internet. With a deep, cleansing breath, Lori clicked the top spreadsheet link and began to reread the job specifics.

She might have made some impulsive decisions tonight, but that didn't mean she was scared to pursue her dreams. Her life was in her hands. She wouldn't let a detour dissuade her from her true path.

Lori clicked open a new document and began to type a cover letter.

9

Geoff didn't visit Lori's building very often, but this was the second time in a very short stretch that he'd found himself walking down the corridor toward her office. Not that it was accidental, obviously; he'd meant to go see her both times. Last time it was impulse, brought on by seeing her flyer buried beneath layers of paper detritus on the bulletin board. This time, though, he had a purpose.

Her door was open, and she sat at her desk, frowning at her computer screen. Geoff hadn't seen her since this past weekend, and the cognitive dissonance made his brain misfire. She was simultaneously his brilliant colleague who was a consummate professional, and the gorgeous temptress who had come on his tongue and his cock.

Just as he was raising his fist to knock at the open door, she spoke up. "Come on in, Geoff. Don't just stand there." Her welcoming smile lingered as she focused on the screen. "Just let me finish this email." Tongue between her teeth, she typed rapidly, her look of concentration fading to a frown that made him wonder about the content of the email. Geoff took the chance to scan the bookshelves in her room, the actual reason he was here. It wasn't just to see her, even if seeing her buoyed his spirits.

"Okay." She sighed, pushing back from her desk and wheeling around. "Sorry about that. I said I'd handle this round of emails for the Bridge Program, and it's been nothing but bullshit." She got up and took a step toward him, then paused. "Can we hug? Is this a hugging friendship now?"

Geoff glanced behind him to make sure the hallway was clear. "It's more than a hugging friendship, I think."

Lori's answering chuckle eased something tight he'd been carrying in his chest. She smelled good, bringing back a collection of sense memories from their night together. It wouldn't do to relive those memories here, in his workplace, and definitely not in this vague "after" context they'd failed to define. He held her a bit longer than was probably necessary, and she stayed, her body pressed against his. "I'm sorry I couldn't stay the other night," she began.

He stepped back to put some distance between them. "Don't worry about it. It was presumptuous to ask."

"I would have liked to stay, though." She hesitated, like she was going to explain further, but then didn't. "What can I help you with? Is this a work thing?"

"Not really." He rested a hand on one of the bookshelves. "I was hoping you might recommend some books to me?"

Lori scanned the spines. "What kind of books?"

"Polyamory books."

Lori clasped her hands behind her back, her attention turning from the bookcase back to him. "What's on your mind?"

Geoff had to laugh. "Everything's on my mind, Lori. Come on."

Her answering smile was kind. "Okay. Well, let me ask a better question. What do you want to learn? There are a lot of books. Most of them say the same things."

"I'm curious about polyamory and how people make it work. Patrick is chill with everything. And I..." He shrugged. "I am not chill."

Lori's smile faded. "Are you feeling okay, after this weekend? I was worried about it, I have to be honest. The last thing I want to do is mess stuff up with you and Patrick."

"Of course. Yeah. Everything's fine." He waved a hand to try and dismiss her concerns. He wasn't lying either; things were fine at home. "Maybe too fine? If that's a thing."

"Too fine?" Lori raised an eyebrow. "Is that bad?"

"You know me, Lori. It's not like me to rush into something without researching it."

She leaned against a bookshelf and crossed her arms. "Did you research anything before Saturday night?"

Geoff couldn't help but grin. "No."

"And see? That turned out all right." She nudged his shoulder. "Better than all right, by my accounts."

Geoff didn't want to unload his inner monologue here, not to this woman he was just getting to know, this woman who had been flitting in and out of his mind in guilty daydreams all weekend. "I just feel like I should know what I'm getting into, if this is something we want to do again."

Lori paused, her hand on one of the books, and she glanced over her shoulder. "Is it something you want to do again?"

Geoff hesitated. *Yes*, he wanted to say. *Yes, of course, I want it again, I want it right now, I want it more than I've wanted anything in a long time.* "It's too soon for me to know," he said instead.

Was that disappointment on her face? Her expression moved too rapidly to read. "Of course. Well, here are a few classics." She pulled a couple of books off the shelves, scanning the titles. "A few terms in this book might be a little outdated. Lots of people say 'poly' instead of 'polyam' or 'polya,' for example, but Polynesian people have asked us to stop co-opting their term for themselves, and we've started listening." She grabbed another book from the third shelf down. "I don't know how much repetition you'll find in these, but they're still considered key texts. I'd recommend starting here." She set the books in his hands. "And if you want, I help facilitate a polyam discussion group here in Mapleton every few weeks. It started out with my thesis research and took on a life of its own. We haven't met in a while, but we might do another soon."

"Can I read your thesis?"

Lori shrugged. "If you want to. It's kind of dry in places."

"I have a history doctorate, Lori. I'm used to dry academic texts."

"Knock yourself out, then." She sat back in her chair. "Want me to send it to your work email, or—"

"My personal." He leaned over her shoulder and dictated the address to her as she typed. "Thanks."

"Of course." She turned her chair, bringing them very close together again, and Geoff pulled back in reflex. Being too close to Lori when he was feeling so drawn to her was a bad idea.

"I'll take these to start." He held up the pile and took a step toward the door as Lori got back to her feet. Before he was really conscious of it, he found himself adding, "Maybe we can get together again soon."

"Yeah, didn't Patrick tell you?" Lori leaned back in her chair. "He invited me to his gig Friday night."

"Um, no, he didn't mention that." And Geoff felt all kinds of ways about that.

"He just texted me last night. I'm sure he was going to bring it up to you today. You're going too, right?"

"Of course." He went to most of Patrick's gigs.

Maybe he was broadcasting his inner monologue more than he wanted to, because Lori frowned. "You're not upset about that, right? It's literally just a friend thing. I like that kind of music. I assumed he would have told you."

"It's not a problem." Geoff forced an air of nonchalance. It shouldn't be a problem. He shouldn't feel this mixture of jealous and embarrassed—the sensation of being left out of an important conversation. The conversation, after all, wasn't important. "I'll see you there, then. Plus, I mean, probably around the building. And at the Bridge meeting tomorrow."

Lori grimaced. "Oh, hell, don't remind me. Another five parents have probably just emailed me afraid of their teenager spending time in a dorm."

Geoff laughed, more genuinely this time. "Thanks for the heads-up to never volunteer for email duty."

"Save yourself." She moved in for another hug, and he held the books out to the side to wrap his free arm around her. "It's good to see you."

"Yeah, you too." He inhaled the sweet scent of her hair and forced himself to step back before he extended the hug. "I guess I'll see you on Friday."

Back in his office, Geoff flipped through the books while an unsettled feeling persisted in his stomach. Logically, he shouldn't care at all that Lori was coming to Patrick's gig on Friday night, since he was the one who said they should get together again soon. This wasn't jealousy. Jealousy was some-thing ugly and dark, and these feelings were…mild, question-ing, unsettled. Like no matter how he shifted in his chair, he couldn't get comfortable.

He should just go home; he was done with his work for the day and didn't have any meetings or other obligations today, but Patrick would be home by now and he wasn't quite ready to be reading polyamory books in front of his husband. He would do what he always did: study, research, and come to his own conclusions independently before bringing someone else into the situation. That strategy had worked well until this point, and it would continue working well in the future, obviously.

Frowning, he chose one of the three books at random and skimmed the table of contents for a place to begin.

THE SOUND of the elevator dinging jolted Patrick out of a light doze. Fuck, Geoff was home already? He rubbed his eyes and glanced at the clock. Usually, Geoff liked to work until the middle of the afternoon before coming home, but it was only —oh, shit, it was after four. He hadn't intended to doze off; he'd taught two lessons and practiced for an hour or so on his own, but the couch had looked so inviting, and he'd appar-ently conked out without intending to do so. Whoops.

Geoff came in, carrying his leather satchel and wearing a frown.

"Hey! How was your day?" Patrick asked, standing on wobbly legs and having to catch himself on the armrest. "Whoa. I fell asleep."

Geoff raised his eyebrows, but at least he looked more

amused than irritated. "Apparently. You all right?" He looked Patrick up and down. "You haven't been sleeping all day, have you?"

"Nah. Been out of the house for most of it." He stifled a yawn behind his hand. "Two lessons this morning, then some practice. And I got groceries."

"Groceries. Nice." Geoff walked past him toward the bedroom, tossing his satchel onto the table as he went. Patrick followed him into the bedroom as he got changed out of his work clothes.

"You have a good day?" Patrick asked.

Geoff shrugged, bending to untie his shoes and toe them off, along with his socks. "It was all right. Intersession time is always a little loose." He unbuttoned his shirt and slipped it off, revealing a snug white T-shirt.

"You should take a day off this week. Stay home with me." Patrick stepped closer and ran his hands down his husband's arms. "We could play hooky together."

Geoff made a noncommittal noise, stepping out of Patrick's arms to pull off his T-shirt as well. Bare-chested, he unfastened his belt. Damn, that was a gorgeous sight, his husband stripping in front of him. He would never get tired of that.

Patrick licked his lips, and Geoff stopped, his lips twitching. "Are you checking me out?"

"Yup." Patrick stepped back in again, tugging the belt slowly from Geoff's belt loops. "Can't help it. You're sexy."

Geoff rolled his eyes. "You're impossible. Didn't you get enough last weekend?"

"Last weekend? It's been days. And you go walking around hot as fuck and expecting me not to want to climb all over you."

"Maybe you need more hobbies." Geoff turned away,

leaving Patrick holding just the belt. He pulled off his pants and set them on the bed.

Patrick snapped the belt, and Geoff froze, then turned slowly to face Patrick, one eyebrow raised. "I'll take that, thank you." He pulled the belt slowly out of Patrick's grip, the leather dragging along Patrick's palms as it slipped away. Patrick was still grinning. Whatever funk Geoff was in, he should snap out of it and play along.

"What's wrong?" Patrick cupped Geoff's ass through the thin fabric of his boxers. "You're grumpy."

"I'm not grumpy. I'm just thinking about some things." Geoff seemed to consider Patrick, tapping the looped belt against his palm. The rhythmic motion held Patrick's attention. *Tap. Tap. Tap.* Then, without further preamble, he moved fast and looped the belt behind Patrick's neck, using it to drag Patrick down to his knees.

Holy fuck. Patrick fell hard, gasping in surprise, and his cock stiffened immediately. Geoff held each end of the belt in his hands, looking down at his husband, a merciless intensity in his stare. They played power games, sure, but Geoff looked downright dangerous like this, and Patrick couldn't describe how much it fucking turned him *on* to be down on his knees in front of his husband with a belt behind his neck.

Geoff's boxers didn't hide his erection, so apparently Patrick wasn't the only one turned on by this. He leaned forward, daring, and mouthed at the outline of Geoff's cock through the material.

Geoff sucked in a breath but didn't stop him. Patrick carefully pulled down the waistband of the boxers, and Geoff let him release his erection, keeping the pressure of the belt at the back of Patrick's neck. That tiny reminder of control ran right to Patrick's groin, making him even harder. He should have undressed himself before getting mixed up in this, but it was too late to remedy that now, and he pressed his lips to the head of Geoff's cock before opening his mouth to suck him down.

He wasn't expecting the belt pressure again, pulling him forward a bit before letting him go. Patrick looked up to meet Geoff's eyes, mouth wrapped just around Geoff's cock head.

"Do you want me to fuck your face?" Geoff asked in a whisper.

Patrick nodded, and then the belt pulled him flush with Geoff's groin, forcing him to swallow the full length of the hard dick in his mouth. Jesus Christ. Geoff knew Patrick could deep throat, knew he could tap out if he wanted to, but Patrick *definitely* did not want to. Patrick moaned, his erection nearly painful now, as the pressure on the back of his neck slackened and he drew back. He sucked the tip, focusing his attention there, relaxing his jaw. Geoff tasted salty, like skin and sweat, and sucking his cock always turned Patrick on more than nearly anything else. Geoff pulled the belt tight again, and Patrick groaned in surprise as his mouth was filled once more, Geoff thrusting all the way into his throat. He set up a rhythm, letting Patrick pull back but then dragging him forward again, never freeing his mouth of Geoff's cock. Patrick could end this anytime, but the most fun part was pretending he couldn't. This helplessness, arms hanging slack by his side as he let Geoff fuck his mouth, had him achingly hard and desperate. Geoff's motions were growing uneven, and Patrick sucked in breaths through his nose as he swallowed around the erection in his mouth. Geoff wasn't pulling back anymore, wasn't thrusting, was holding his cock as far as Patrick could take him and shuddering on the verge of orgasm. Patrick sucked, laving the bottom of the shaft with his tongue, and god, Patrick wanted to taste him. He wanted to *serve*. He wanted this consuming, helpless arousal, and the belt held him willingly prisoner. Finally, Geoff came, emptying himself down Patrick's throat with a low groan, and Patrick drank him down with a desperate, needy noise.

Geoff released the belt and staggered back, his knees hitting the bed, sitting hard on the edge. He pressed a hand to his forehead, like he was just coming out of a dizzy spell, the belt falling to the hardwood floor. Patrick caught his breath, sitting back on his heels.

"Fuck." Geoff shook his head and closed his eyes. "I don't know. I wasn't planning on doing that."

"Shh." Patrick shook his head. "It's okay. It's all right. It was—"

Geoff slid his fingers into Patrick's auburn hair, his dark eyes wild with something Patrick had never seen, and the words died in Patrick's throat. "Touch yourself," he commanded.

Patrick fumbled his dick out of his jeans, anything to relieve this aching pressure, and began to stroke in fast, furious motions. Geoff wouldn't stop staring into his eyes, his grip on Patrick's hair keeping him down on his knees, and Patrick was on the edge in no time at all. He hadn't realized how close he was, and now holding back was a painful type of pleasure.

"Please?" Patrick asked, gasping, and he didn't usually ask, but it felt right in this moment. "Please let me come."

"Yes. Come." Geoff tugged his hair, painfully tight, and Patrick spilled all over his own fist with a harsh cry rasping through his throat. The orgasm left him weak, nerves firing like a web of electrical sparks. Geoff released him, and Patrick collapsed backward.

They cleaned up in silence. Geoff pulled on new boxers and shorts, and Patrick washed up in the bathroom with hands that wouldn't stop trembling. When he returned to the bedroom, Geoff was sitting on the bed, still a little wide-eyed, like he couldn't reconcile his expectations to his own actions. Patrick sat beside him and pulled him in for a kiss. Sometimes, Geoff needed to be reassured everything was okay, especially when he got aggressive in bed.

As soon as Geoff opened his mouth, Patrick pressed his fingers to it. "No apologizing."

"I wasn't going to apologize," Geoff murmured against Patrick's fingers, and Patrick put his hands in his lap. "I wanted to say thanks. I think I needed that."

Patrick nodded. "Bad day at work?"

"No…" Geoff's voice trailed off, and his brow furrowed. "I guess a thoughtful day." He turned to face Patrick. "You invited Lori to your gig on Friday night."

Oh, fuck, he'd been meaning to talk to Geoff about that today. "Yeah, we were chatting last night. I meant to tell you."

"How long have you two been chatting?"

"Since she came over. We've been texting. Why?" He blinked. "Are you upset about this? I thought you were fine with friendship. You're friends with her already. You could be texting her too, you know."

"Yes, of course, it's fine." Geoff shook his head like he was brushing the thought away. "It took me by surprise, though. I didn't know we were seeing her again so soon."

Patrick rubbed his beard. "We're getting to be friends. That's what friendship is. We see each other."

Geoff's back straightened. "Are you going to sleep with her?"

"What? No, of course not." Why would Geoff even think that? "That's not what this is. She wants to hear my music. I don't want to fuck her." He stopped, and Geoff looked over with a raised eyebrow, prompting Patrick to amend. "Okay, yes, I do want to fuck her. Saturday was incredible. We already went over this, right? We've talked about it. But I'm not going to push you like that."

"It's fine if you want to. It's why I first wanted you to meet her. I knew you two would hit it off." Geoff's voice sounded closed-off, resigned, and Patrick tried to put these pieces together.

"If it bothers you that I invited her, I can tell her I changed my mind." He put a hand on Geoff's. "But I hope you don't feel that way. This is about all three of us, together. A friendship. It doesn't have to be anything else."

Geoff hesitated. He opened his mouth a bit, then closed it again, looking at the bedroom wall as he seemed to frame a response. "I don't mean to overreact. It just surprised me, and it made me think about what I want out of this. What a friendship with her would mean. After Saturday, I feel mixed up about things."

"Do you want me to tell her to stay home?"

"No." He shook his head. "Not just because it would be rude, but because I also would like to see her."

This was treading into delicate territory, and Patrick framed his next words carefully. "We're just texting. There's nothing else. I'm not cheating on you. I would never cheat on you."

Geoff rubbed the back of his neck, looking away for a moment before turning back to his husband. "I know. I trust you. I'm not accusing you of anything. I guess…" He paused. "I guess I am still trying to figure out what I want." There was more, judging by the way his lips hovered open, forming the start of words that he didn't say, but then he closed his mouth.

"Okay. Okay, that's fine. Just talk to me." Patrick kissed his cheek. "Or, fuck my face. You know, that's all right too."

10

Patrick dragged his bow across the strings of his violin a few times, as he always did, the familiar motion settling him into his body. Around him, the other members of the band were doing their own similar warm-up routines: Theo and Dixie tuning the electric and bass guitars and fiddling with amp settings, Dean riffing on drums. Russell the cellist was finagling his pickup. On vocals, Maddy was doing some weird buzzing and *whooshing* noises that she'd once tried to explain to the group as Linklater-something, but nobody remembered the specifics. Patrick paused to look out at the Rusty Carousel, their currently empty venue. The place would start to fill up in an hour or so as folks arrived for the opening acts and then, finally, for their band: Nine Possum Thursday, often affectionately called NPT. The Rusty Carousel wasn't much, but it was their home, and the worn wooden stage and wide-open dance floor had replaced formal concert halls and theaters in the shifting spectrum of his musical life. If he didn't think about it too much, he didn't even miss the way things used to be.

"Knock knock!"

The door to the green room opened, and a familiar face popped his head through the opening.

"Harrison!" Maddy was the first to greet their old friend and former bandmate, blond hair bounding as she ran and threw her arms around him. Similar greetings went up from the rest of the band, including Patrick.

Harrison stepped farther into the green room, looking around like he wanted to memorize the place. "Shit, it's been a while. Thought I'd swing by and say hi to you all before heading out. I'm moving to New York."

"New York?" Theo, tuning his guitar, stopped and set it aside. "What are you gonna do there?"

Harrison scrubbed at the back of his curly light-brown hair. Although he was in his thirties, like all of them, the freckles across his pale skin made him look a lot younger. "I got a spot doing sound design for a TV studio. It's not a lot, but it'll pay the bills, and leave me my evenings free to do music in the city."

"Good for you." Dean tapped his drumsticks on his legs, his normal habit. "Glad to see a guy doing what he loves."

Patrick forced a smile despite his muddle of emotions. No one could deny the pull of the big city, least of all him. But hadn't he been through this already? He'd made his peace with Mapleton. Leaving New York let him take care of his mother when she needed him. Leaving New York had brought him Geoff. Geoff made enough money that Patrick could pursue his music as a hobby, rather than risk everything to make it work as a business. He should be grateful for how things had turned out.

"Good thing I've already left the band, right?" Harrison shrugged. "I'd hate to fuck you over."

Maddy waved him off. "Nah, man, you know the deal. We're adults. Shit happens and people move on. The band stays." She smiled, her teeth white against the startling red of her lipstick. Nine Possum Thursday was more than the sum of its parts. They'd always been clear with one another that when people moved on, the band would remain, and they'd fill the spot. Maddy was around since the beginning, and she kept everything running. It wasn't much, but as local bands went, they had a good time together.

They pressed Harrison with more questions, about where he'd be staying, when he made the decision, his time frame for moving, the usual stuff.

When the questions eased, Harrison shifted his attention to Patrick. "Okay, what should I know about living in New York?" They knew Patrick's background and where he'd gotten his start, although people didn't tend to ask him much about it.

Patrick stroked his beard. He wanted to say something cynical, like, *Get ready to live with three roommates,* or *Don't let someone piss in your bag,* but the cynicism wasn't genuine. Days like this, seeing someone else ready to go off and pursue their dreams made his heart twinge—just a little bit—for what might have been. "It's great," he said truthfully. "It's expensive and tough and sometimes ridiculous, but there's nothing like New York. You're gonna kill it."

Harrison smiled. "Thanks, man."

"Okay, you fuckers, we gotta warm up." Maddy gave Harrison another hug, then shoved him away affectionately. "Get outta here." The rest of the band members got up to also wish him luck. Patrick was last, throwing an arm around his former bandmate and clapping him on the back. With a flurry of goodbyes, Harrison was gone, leaving them alone again in the green room. In his absence, the group felt smaller than before, even though the band was the same size as it had been for months.

Dixie fingered a fast bass line, breaking the somber feeling in the room. "Maddy, what do you want to go over first?"

Maddy cracked her knuckles and shook her head from side to side. "Let's do a run through of 'Void Light' and see how we feel."

Patrick checked his pickup and adjusted his violin back onto his shoulder. Tonight, he could lose himself in the music and remember all the wonderful things he had in his life. He had so many reasons to be grateful, and this band was one of them. Whatever possibilities he'd left behind were gone. The future lay ahead of him, and the future was stable. He couldn't let stable go for the pie-in-the-sky dreams he'd chased as a teenager. He was Patrick Walsh, and he was a grown-ass adult.

Dean counted them in on the drumsticks, and they began to play.

LORI WASN'T REALLY PREPARED for Nine Possum Thursday in concert. She had heard some of their songs after Patrick sent her the link to their site, but listening online was a different experience than rocking out with a crowd of strangers all dancing and jumping around. The music was supremely danceable, and she loved to dance.

And Patrick? Fuck, the man could *play*. His violin work was somewhere between "classical" and "fiddle," and his fast finger work looked effortless. It was hard not to watch him, even with the rest of the band as talented as they were. She knew why he'd dropped out of Juilliard, and she couldn't say she was a music expert or anything, but it seemed a crying shame to have a guy with this much talent playing in a rock violin band in Nowhere, Massachusetts. But she couldn't think about that for long, because dancing was too much fun.

Geoff was the biggest surprise. He'd met her here in slim-cut jeans and a snug navy-blue T-shirt, and he fucking *danced*. A couple of times, she stopped dancing to watch him, but before long, she was too caught up in the music to stay still. Somewhere in the middle of the set, they'd shifted from dancing near each other to dancing together. He spun and whirled her around to the music until both of them were breathless and laughing. After one particularly rousing song, they fought the crowd for a seat at the bar to catch their breath.

"What do you think?" Geoff asked, leaning toward her to be heard over the din while the bartender made her way over.

"It's great! He's fucking fantastic." She looked back toward the stage where Patrick was smiling as he wove his bow across the strings. "How do you keep everyone's hands off him?"

She wasn't thinking about the ramifications of that last line, intending it as a compliment, until Geoff paused. His smile seemed tight. "Apparently, I don't." He turned to the bartender and ordered a beer, an order which Lori echoed.

"I'm not trying to steal your man, you know." She took a long drag from the bottle as soon as it was handed to her. "I couldn't even if I wanted to."

Geoff smiled more easily. "I don't know about that."

"It's true. Anybody could see how much he loves you from a mile away."

Geoff's lips curled around the mouth of the bottle, and Lori suddenly wanted to be that bottle. Whoa. They hadn't discussed a repeat occurrence from the other night. She leaned back away from him and looked for a subject change. "You read those books yet?"

"A little. Not too much." He stepped away from the bar. "Come on. Let's go dance again."

"You could just say you don't want to talk," she said, but she let him take her hand and drag her back into the crowd, holding her beer aloft. Another song picked up. Talking was hard, and dancing was easy, and she could lose herself here without having to think about these guys, and the possibilities they presented, and the terrifying and wonderful future she wanted away from Mapleton.

They were both in that overtired-but-energized state when Patrick found them after the set. He leaned in to kiss Geoff, holding his husband close for a long moment, and then reached over to pull Lori in for a hug that he stopped at the last second. "Oh, shit, I'm so sweaty. You probably want to stay away."

"It's okay. We've been dancing." She leaned in to hug him anyway, indulgently, because there was something decadent about the press of a gorgeous, sweaty man against her. "You killed it up there. I had no idea you were that good."

"Thanks." Patrick beamed. "You all want to go grab a drink somewhere? Night Owl?"

"Actually." Geoff laughed, kind of to himself. "Do you want to get some ice cream?"

They found themselves sitting on the grass of the small street-side park across from the ice cream parlor as late-night wanderers passed by, the town streets alive on a Friday night in spring.

"This is better," Patrick observed, taking a lick from his cone of black raspberry. Geoff had chosen butter pecan, which seemed to suit him somehow, and Lori had ended up with a sundae after being unable to choose between a few different flavors. The streetlights overhead buzzed with electricity, and the first moths of the season hovered around them.

"So, tell me about your band. First off. Your name." Lori had been meaning to ask ever since they first started talking. "Why are you called Nine Possum Thursday?"

Patrick laughed, more to himself than to her. "Maddy named us. Her husband is in animal control, and as part of that, they clean up roadkill. Apparently, one day he came home and announced it was a nine possum Thursday."

Lori stared, agape, as both Geoff and Patrick laughed. "That's horrifying," she said. "I wish I hadn't asked."

"He usually tells people not to ask," Geoff said, grinning. He seemed much more relaxed tonight. Maybe it was all the dancing, or the ice cream.

Patrick winked at her. "Lori deserves the truth."

"I'm starting to wonder if that's true." She scraped some ice cream onto her spoon and savored the rich flavor. Though it wasn't summer yet, she could taste the season ahead of her. "Tell me how you all got started. More about your music."

Patrick told the band's origin story, with Geoff interjecting a few fun details now and then. She listened to him, of course, but also watched him and Geoff. They were beautiful together. Geoff leaned toward Patrick subconsciously when Patrick spoke, and Patrick did the same to Geoff. They ended up on a tangent about some concert they'd gone to see up in Portland, Maine, and they moved into each other's spaces as gracefully and naturally as only long-term couples did. Something ached in her stomach watching them, and it had nothing to do with too much ice cream.

She'd hoped to be invited back to their apartment after the concert. She'd even put an overnight bag in her car, just in case. Watching them like this, though, her desires had been foolish. They were settled. They didn't want her complicating their relationship with anything other than friendship, and she had been silly to think otherwise. Not that it was bad. She was planning to move away...eventually, anyway. She'd sent out those resumes and cover letters days ago.

She could deal with friendship, though. If she felt a little remorse at not having something else, those feelings were normal, and they didn't mean anyone was doing anything wrong. She could be happy like this, dancing at a concert, then sitting and eating ice cream at the park. Patrick leaned into Geoff, the two of them laughing together, and she smiled.

When they'd long since finished their ice cream, and as the conversation reached a natural lull, Lori checked the time on her phone. "It's late."

Patrick made an unconcerned noise. "It's a weekend. We all get to sleep in."

He wrapped Lori up in their "we all," like she was going to sleep in with them. The thought tempted her. If she asked to go home with them tonight, they'd probably say yes.

She wanted to ask.

But she was just getting to know Patrick, still, despite texting with him this week. And whatever friendship she was cultivating with Geoff was new as well, unformed and shifting. She liked them. They were fun to hang out with. Jumping right into bed with them again was going to send a message that she was only looking for sex.

"I'm gonna head home." She went to stand, but Geoff's hand on her leg made her pause.

"Just like that, without saying goodbye?"

Lori sized him up: the sparkle in his eyes, his close proximity, the way his hand burned hot through her jeans. "Oh, I'd hate to leave without saying goodbye."

This might not be what he meant, but what the hell. She leaned toward him, cupping the side of his face, and kissed him on the mouth. Geoff's hand tightened on her leg, and he parted his lips, kissing her back with deliberate focus that immediately returned her to the previous weekend. Next to them, Patrick sucked in a breath, the noise beautiful in Lori's ear. She released Geoff and then leaned across his lap to kiss Patrick as well. His lips turned up in a smile against hers, and he kissed her back, sweet and light and perfect.

Lori sat back on her heels, lips tingling. "Okay. Goodbye."

11

Patrick watched Lori walk away, heading back to her car, her ass shifting side to side in those tight jeans. Next to him, Geoff watched as well. Patrick nudged him. "I see that."

Geoff returned his smile. They sat next to each other on the grass, and Geoff leaned back on his hands to stare up at the sky. Patrick followed his gaze. Even with the streetlight glowing near them, the stars shone crisp through the darkness. The park had long since been abandoned, and they should probably leave too. Gigs ramped up Patrick's adrenaline, though, and he certainly wasn't going to fall asleep anytime soon. Maybe they could stay a little longer.

"I saw you dancing together." Patrick traced the long line of Geoff's back with his palm. "You looked good." He'd lost his rhythm once at the sight of them twirling together, both laughing in what seemed like sheer joy.

"She's a good dancer. It was fun."

"I liked watching."

Geoff laughed softly. "Apparently."

Patrick leaned over to kiss him. He tasted like ice cream, sweet and rich, and what started as a gentle, affectionate kiss grew into something more intense as Geoff opened his mouth and tangled their tongues together. Geoff's fingers slid into his hair. Something desperate and needy came through in his kisses, the possessive way he gripped Patrick's hair, the aggressive press of his mouth. Geoff was an assertive kisser, but this was harder, rougher, sharper. Patrick let Geoff overpower him, pushing him onto his back until he was lying flush on the ground with Geoff half on top of him. Blades of grass tickled Patrick's ear as Geoff devoured his mouth.

When his hand slid down to Patrick's cock, though, Patrick broke away. "Hey, easy." He caught his breath, pushing Geoff gently up away from him. "We're in the *park*, Geoff."

Geoff seemed to come to that realization at the same time, his eyebrows going up as he glanced around. He sat up and brushed a few strands of grass off his sleeve while Patrick got his bearings. As Patrick composed himself—except for his partial erection, which was not going away anytime soon—Geoff got to his feet all in one fast motion. "We should get home."

Patrick was still dazed from the kisses, first Lori and now Geoff, from the energy crackling between them. "Or we could slip into those trees back there." He gestured to the dark line of thicker forest at the back border of the park.

Geoff gave him a tight smile, stepping into his space. "I'm not interested in getting caught by the cops with my mouth on my husband's cock, thank you."

"Fuck." The mental image did *not* help Patrick's persistent arousal. "Yeah. Let's get home."

As soon as they got to the car, though, Geoff was on him

again. Geoff leaned across to the passenger seat and kissed him hard, one hand dangerously high up on Patrick's thigh. Patrick inhaled sharply, and Geoff bit his lower lip, teeth holding him close by a tender bit of skin that sent sharp pangs of arousal through his body. Geoff released Patrick's mouth as he cupped Patrick's dick through his jeans.

"Jesus." Patrick threw his head back against the headrest, going from half-hard to fully erect in a few brief heartbeats. "What's gotten into you?"

"Not Jesus." Geoff grinned. "I guess I'm just in a mood." He leaned in for another bruising kiss. Geoff's bedroom assertiveness didn't usually extend to PDA. Not that an abandoned parking garage at midnight really counted as "public" for a public display of affection, and the possessive way he gripped Patrick's erection wasn't "affection" as much as "staking claim." He released Patrick enough to pop the buttons on his button-fly jeans with one sharp yank, and Patrick's cock bobbed against the fabric of his boxers before Geoff slipped one hot hand through the opening and found his length.

The car was already warm, and they were going to steam up the windows if this continued, but Patrick was not going to ask him to stop. Fuck, he was already worked up, and this steady grip on his erection pushed all the buttons inside him begging for more.

But then, just as suddenly as he had started, Geoff pulled his hand away. Patrick opened his eyes to his husband still incredibly close, his deep brown eyes intently focused on Patrick's face.

"Touch yourself on the drive home." Geoff's tone did not invite argument, even if Patrick had wanted to argue, which he did not. "But don't get too close. I just want you to stay interested."

"I'm interested," Patrick said through a tight throat, fumbling into his seat belt as Geoff slid back to the driver's side to buckle up and start the car.

Geoff paused, key in the ignition, and looked pointedly over at Patrick. "Well?"

His face suddenly warm, Patrick began to lightly stroke his cock. Geoff could always do this, shift the power dynamic in ways that stole Patrick's breath and made him achingly hard. Thank god for machine-operated parking garages and the emptiness of Mapleton after midnight.

They sat in silence as Geoff drove home. Patrick couldn't stop his heavy breathing as he touched himself, the chance of being seen a turn-on he hadn't expected. Already, his dick was leaking, and he rubbed the slickness across the head with his thumb. Patrick didn't want to get too turned on, or this drive was going to be torture, but the effort *not* to get turned on was turning him on. Whatever fucking catch-22 of arousal this was had him all messed up in a way that scrambled his brain.

Instead of going the direct way home, Geoff turned down a side street to make it an even longer trip. The roads were deserted at this hour, but now their ten-minute drive had turned into twenty, and Patrick might explode. Geoff wasn't immune either. His cock was a hard line against his tight jeans, and he had to be suffering as much as Patrick was. That gave Patrick an idea. He slipped the shoulder strap of his seat belt behind him.

With his free hand, he reached across the center console and unfastened Geoff's zipper. It took some deft fingering, and Geoff glanced down briefly. "What are you doing?" There was an added edge to his voice, ragged with arousal.

Patrick eased Geoff's cock through the fly of his jeans. "Don't crash the car." And then he leaned across the console and took Geoff's cock in his mouth.

"Fuck!" Geoff swore loudly, hips twitching. "Patrick—Patrick, this is unsafe—"

"Only if you crash." He sucked the tip, pretty much all he could reach, his other hand still working his own erection. "Don't crash."

Geoff's hand left the steering wheel to tangle in Patrick's hair. "You'd better be—*ohh*—stroking yourself."

Patrick made an affirmative noise, mouth currently full. His efforts on Geoff's cock were making it easier to ignore his own mounting desire to come, his balls already tight against his body. Geoff tasted like salt from sweat, and he smelled like sex, and Patrick wanted to rip his clothes off right now and climb on top of that fantastic cock. But they were driving, and home was too far away.

Geoff's groan sounded strangled, and he tugged at Patrick's hair. "Fuck, Patrick, you've—you've gotta stop—"

Patrick could do what Geoff always did to him, make him wait, take him to the edge and hold him there, but he had some mercy and let Geoff's cock slide out of his mouth. Geoff was breathing heavily, cock glistening and pulsing with his heartbeat. He gave Patrick a quick, indignant glare and then pulled his T-shirt down over his erection. "You're gonna pay for that."

"You like it."

Geoff smiled despite what seemed to be an effort not to, turning his attention back to the road. "Stroke faster, you whore."

Patrick kept his touch light, and the knowledge that now Geoff was as needy as he was helped ease the desperation pulsing in his veins. What had gotten into both of them tonight? Geoff was driving as fast as he safely could through these back roads, both hands gripping the steering wheel, his mouth set in a thin line. This had to be Lori's doing, charging them both up like some kind of sex battery and then leaving them to fend for themselves.

Patrick's balls ached by the time they got home. They both dressed themselves in the parking lot, tucking everything away and zipping their pants. Back in the elevator, though, as soon as Geoff swiped their key card and the doors slid shut, Patrick slammed him up against the wall for a kiss. He was stronger than Geoff, although not by much, and they were usually physically well-matched. Geoff grabbed him by the lapels of his button-down and kissed back, giving as good as he got.

"You want me?" Patrick breathed against his mouth.

"Yeah. I want you." Geoff gripped Patrick's hair, enough to pull, and Patrick growled in response. Geoff knew how much he loved having his hair pulled. The doors slid open, and Geoff shoved Patrick out into their condo, catching him off-balance. He stumbled, and Geoff was there, pushing him backward until they both toppled onto the sofa. Geoff's eyes flashed, and Patrick would be a little bit scared if he weren't already so fucking turned on.

Geoff pinned Patrick down by the length of his body, and their cocks rubbed together through the stiff fabric of their jeans. They needed to be naked now, and Patrick pulled at Geoff's shirt and then his own. Geoff took the hint, and they both stripped down as fast as possible before falling together on the couch again. Their cocks slotted together between their sandwiched bodies. This felt urgent, wildly urgent, maybe because Patrick had been touching himself for what seemed like ages now without any sign of relief.

"I like you like this," Geoff said, fast and a little breathless. "Desperate for me."

"I'm desperate?" Patrick ground up against him, pressing their hips together, watching Geoff's breath catch. "We both are."

"Sure. Maybe." Geoff pulled Patrick's hair again, lying full on top of him, rutting against him like he just couldn't resist. "But you're a cock slut and you know it."

The words went right to Patrick's erection, and he bucked up in response, trying to catch his breath and find his words. "Seeing Lori—get you all worked up?"

Geoff stilled, drawing back, his eyes narrowing. "What?"

"Lori." Patrick reached between them, wrapping his fist around both their cocks and making Geoff groan. "You get turned on, dancing with her tonight?"

"I just— I'm with you. Now." Geoff pressed their mouths together again. Patrick didn't have much room in this position, but he managed to stroke them roughly, using the pressure of their bodies as much as the grip of his hand. Patrick pulled back to breathe, their mouths only inches apart.

"I know. But do you think about her? Here with us. Now."

Geoff licked his lips, their mouths so close that his tongue brushed Patrick's lips. "Again?"

"Yeah. Again. Don't you want her?"

Geoff hesitated. His hips were still moving, thrusting into Patrick's fist, like he couldn't control it. "Fuck. I don't know. Yes." He dropped his head to Patrick's shoulder. "I want *you*."

"You want us both?"

"I want you...to shut up." He leaned up to free one hand

and pressed it over Patrick's mouth, his eyes flashing. "And get to the bedroom."

That look in Geoff's eyes was dangerous and hot, and Patrick knew when he was pushing Geoff too much, so he wasted no time at all getting out from under him on the couch. He went to gather their clothes, only for Geoff's voice —amused, now—to stop him. "Leave the clothes. They can wait."

Geoff got him on the bed in no time, stretched out on his back, cock lying flat on his belly and dying for release. Patrick couldn't resist stroking himself, even though it would just make his need worse. Every stroke felt so damn good. Geoff climbed onto the bed with him and pulled his hands away. "Hands above your head. Cross your wrists. Keep them there."

Patrick was not about to resist being told what to do in bed, and he obeyed, crossing one hand over the other. This definitely pinged some kind of exposure kink as Geoff ran his hands down Patrick's body, settling around his cock for a few light strokes. Then he grabbed the lube off the nightstand and drizzled it liberally over Patrick's erection, the cool liquid stinging his hot skin. In that position, Geoff straddled his thighs and lined up their cocks to wrap his fist around them both like Patrick had done on the couch. But he had leverage and lube and a merciless grip and *oh*, Patrick throbbed in his touch.

"You like that?" Geoff said, voice sounding tight. "Don't you move those hands. We do this at my pace. Understood?"

"Fuck, yes, whatever you want." Patrick groaned, rocking his hips into the touch. With his arms above his head, he didn't have as much leverage, and that added to this sense of helplessness that left him dizzy with arousal.

"Look at you." Geoff's tone was filled with awe. "If I'd known you liked this so much, I'd have tied you to the bed years ago."

"Ah, shit." Patrick laughed, because his cock gave a hard twitch at the thought. "Never thought I'd be into that."

"Surprises." Geoff's demeanor had softened since they left the other room. "Like me with Lori."

Patrick lifted his head. Was he really bringing Lori up, unprovoked? Geoff seemed to try it out. "Maybe we could both tie you to the bed and have our way with you," Geoff teased. "Let her see how desperate you are."

The heavy, thick pleasure of climax was building fast inside Patrick's body, his balls hard and tight, his cock pulsing with every heartbeat, and that mental image nearly sent him over the edge. He whimpered—he couldn't deny it was a whimper—imagining being helpless for Geoff and Lori together. Geoff was stroking them harder now, faster, hand whipping across their lengths. Patrick closed his eyes. He wasn't going to last; his climax was already building, only a few strokes from the point of no return. He tried to hold back, but he couldn't, muscles tensing until the pleasure exploded outward and he came. His cock twitched and jerked, emptying all over his own stomach and Geoff's fist, and Geoff kept stroking. God, he didn't stop, chasing his climax, the pleasure for Patrick too sharp and raw and bordering on pain. Geoff milked every drop out of him, past the point where he thought he could no longer come, his body still twitching and spasming as finally, Geoff groaned in his own release.

Patrick remembered that he could move his arms. He took them down, his shoulders twinging from how tightly he'd pressed his wrists into the bed, and tried to relax. Holy shit.

Geoff flopped onto his back beside him, shaking and trying to catch his breath.

When Patrick could find his voice again, he touched Geoff's shoulder. "Hey."

Geoff looked over, tiredness in his heavy eyelids and lazy smile. "Hi."

Patrick looked down at his come-covered body. "I'm a mess."

Geoff laughed, putting one arm over his forehead. "We're both a mess."

Patrick gestured to the bathroom. "Shower?"

"Shower."

They were halfway through washing themselves and each other before Geoff cleared his throat. "So. Uh." He looked up from the tile floor to find Patrick's eyes. "You been thinking about Lori?"

There were a lot of ways he could respond to that, but Patrick wasn't about to play games, and Geoff deserved to know where he stood. "Yeah. I like her. I'd like to see her again. Either as a friend, or…"

"A friend with benefits?" Geoff supplied.

That was really what they were talking about, wasn't it? "Yeah. But it's not…crucial. If you don't want to invite her to bed again, I'm fine with that. No matter what, though, I think I'd like to keep getting to know her."

Geoff looked over to the side, to the tile wall, frowning in thought. "I might want to sleep with her again. With you." He met Patrick's gaze again. "I still don't know how to feel about that."

"It's okay." If only he could make Geoff feel the same confidence he felt. Sex didn't have to mean anything more than sex. "It's just sex. You and me?" He gestured between the two of them. "We're fine. We're solid. Bringing someone else to bed doesn't affect anything you and I do together."

Geoff didn't look convinced, but after a pause, he nodded. "Okay." He tried out a smile. "Okay. Maybe we can just keep seeing her without making it about sex and see where things lead."

"That's great." Patrick grabbed the handheld showerhead to rinse them both off. "Don't worry. It's gonna be fine."

12

"Ahh, damn, it's good to be here." Lori turned a full circle near the big clock in the middle of Grand Central terminal, taking in the details: the metallic library smell, the sweeping constellation mural on the ceiling, the mix of old and new fixtures announcing train times and track numbers.

Hannah walked up beside her, glancing around at the space. "Nothing like New York, huh?"

"Like no place on earth." Lori wrapped both hands around her backpack straps, anchoring herself. No matter how long since her last visit, something here always felt like home, her spirit recognizing some intangible element of the city and yearning for more. "You mind if we get a car? I don't feel like dealing with the trains right now."

Hannah brushed a strand of hair back behind her ear. She'd tied her hair up, but a few bits had come loose. "You're the expert here. Point the way."

They ordered a rideshare to their hotel in Midtown with a driver who was fortunately not much for conversation, leaving

Lori the chance to take in the sights with Hannah. "I can't believe we've never been to New York together," Lori said as their driver deftly swapped lanes in the middle of an intersection.

"I've been here," Hannah reminded her. "But just a couple of times, and not in...geez, probably at least five years. Maybe more. I might have been in college last time I was here. How long did you live here, again?"

"Just one summer." Lori tried to see to the tops of the tallest buildings without rolling down her window. "After junior year. My roommate at Smith was doing a summer internship in Manhattan and invited me to come stay with her in her sublet in Brooklyn." The apartment had been ridiculously tiny, especially by Mapleton standards, but Lori hadn't minded.

Hannah made a thoughtful "mmm" noise. "It's not for me. Too fast. Too much going on."

"That's what I like about it. You can do anything, see anything, eat whatever you want. It's all a train ride away. So many opportunities." She'd made a home in Mapleton, but the more time passed, the less content she felt there.

Their driver dropped them off at the hotel, and after checking in, Lori was grateful to take off her backpack and flop down on her hotel bed. "So good." She kicked off her sneakers while Hannah stretched out on the other bed. "Hotel indulgence is the best."

"Damn straight." Hannah's voice sounded muffled in the duvet, and she rolled onto her side, facing Lori. "I know you've got a whole timeline for this trip. What's the plan?"

Lori had indeed lured Hannah away from work with a promise of "I'll take care of everything, just schedule yourself a weekend off and tell me your budget and I'll make it happen." Hannah did enough planning in the rest of her life; she was not likely to want to plan their getaway as well. "Well," Lori said, wiggling her feet off the end of the bed, "I have a menu of options to choose from, depending on your priorities. But there are a couple of must-dos."

"Okay." Hannah sounded cautious.

"I know you're going to want to check out at least one kink shop, so I put a few on the map."

Hannah nodded. "Seems like a good start."

"Also, a show. I thought we'd check discount rush tickets for something tomorrow night."

Hannah's face lit up. "*Hamilton*?"

"On our budget? Hell no." Lori shook her head. "But there's a ton of other stuff playing, and we might get lucky. I've also got a half-dozen restaurants on the list for you to choose from. And, if you're game, I'd like to walk you by the places where I applied for jobs."

Hannah shot up to sitting. "What? You already applied?"

"Almost two weeks ago." Lori bit her lip. "No word yet."

"Still. I didn't know you'd applied anywhere." Hannah frowned, folding one leg up beneath her on the bed. "I kind of thought you were putting the 'moving away' thing on pause while you were hanging out with Geoff and Patrick."

"What?" Lori rolled onto her side to face Hannah across the space between their beds. "It's not that serious. I went over for dinner two weeks ago, and last weekend was the concert." She hesitated. "And Geoff and I have had lunch a few times this week. And we all went out to dinner at the pub last night. And we've been texting." Saying it all out loud made her realize how much time she'd started spending with them. "But we're friends! I'm getting to know them as friends. I'm certainly not making decisions about my future with them in mind."

Hannah shook her head. "Of course. It's too soon for that."

"They're fun." Lori examined her fingernails, because it was easier than making eye contact with Hannah right now, for some reason. "I have a lot in common with both of them."

As if on cue, Lori's phone buzzed, and she pulled it over to check it. It was Geoff, texting her a picture of a cherry pie he presumably had just finished baking. She smiled at the screen before she felt Hannah looking at her. "What?"

"Funny text?"

"Geoff's sending me pictures of the things he's baking." She tossed the phone aside. "He makes a really good pie."

Her phone buzzed again, and under Hannah's amused stare, she dragged the phone back over. Patrick had sent her a picture of the same pie, only he had written "PIE!!!" across the screen using the in-phone editing app. "It's Patrick. He sent me a picture of the same pie." She shook her head and put the phone away again.

"You're not on a group text yet?" Hannah tipped her head to the side, lips still twitching in amusement.

"I don't think we're at 'group text' level." Their blossoming friendship didn't count as dating, not really, no matter what Hannah might be insinuating.

"When the group texts start, that's when things get serious." Hannah nodded sagely. "I'm surprised that didn't come up in your polyamory research. That, and the magical moment you create a shared Google Calendar."

Lori chucked a pillow across the divide, and Hannah caught it, laughing. "Seriously," Lori said. "I only slept with them the one time. I'm pretty sure Geoff just had to get it out of his system."

"Okay." Hannah didn't sound convinced. "But you know, your objections kind of sound like me last year."

Ugh, it would figure she'd bring this up. Lori had hoped Hannah wasn't going to try and draw parallels. She stayed quiet, and Hannah added a little more. "If they want to sleep with you again, will you?"

Lori rolled onto her back again to stare up at the ceiling. "Probably. Sex is sex." She propped herself up on her elbows to look over at Hannah, who was opening her mouth to add something. Lori jumped in before she could. "It's not the same as you and the guys. Geoff and Patrick are married. They've got each other already. They're committed. If anything, I'm a third wheel. Mitchell and Ben, they needed to both fall in love with you to figure out their shit with each other. But Geoff and Patrick don't have that shit. They're together for good, and even if they want to fool around with somebody else sometimes, that's all it's going to be." She sat up the rest of the way, remembering Geoff borrowing polyamory books from her. "Sometimes polyamory isn't a closed triad in a happily-ever-after like you and Ben and Mitchell. Sometimes it's a married couple who take a third to bed now and then." She sighed and scrubbed a hand over her face. "Enough about Geoff and Patrick, okay?"

"Okay, no problem." Hannah held up her hands in surrender, then clasped them in her lap. "Now tell me about these *jobs*."

That was a much better topic, even if it brought up some general low-grade anxiety. "They're all relationship therapy positions. I don't want to try to open my own practice, not yet, not in a place like New York where there's so much competition." She had priced out a variety of options back when she first decided to move to a city. "But there are agencies and organizations that are often looking to take on new people, and with my expertise in nontraditional relationship structures, I would hope to fill a niche." She wouldn't be the only one with that kind of expertise, obviously, but New York was a big city. Surely someone had need of her.

Hannah had taken her hair out of its twist, and the waves spilled across her shoulders as she leaned forward. "What's your dream? If you could design your perfect position, what would it be?"

Lori had already thought about this. "I would love to work with an organization that supports people of color and LGBTQ folx in nontraditional relationships: polyamory, kink, that sort of thing. I'd like to offer classes and workshops while also taking on clients for relationship therapy."

"Do any of the jobs you applied for fall into that category?"

Lori hesitated. "One." Even saying it out loud felt too big, too risky, that "little-stitious" quality rearing up again. "It's a practice that works in conjunction with a few community organizations and does outreach and education along with therapy. It's top of my list, but I think it's a long shot."

"Still. It's exciting to think about," Hannah said encouragingly. "You're so practical. It must be nice to dream a little."

Lori snorted. "I'm eminently practical, Hannah. That's why I don't want to hope for something in case I don't get it." When Hannah opened her mouth, Lori waved her away. "Trust me, I'm working it all out with my therapist. It's our favorite topic lately, the topic of 'why Lori thinks she won't get good things.'" She smiled, so Hannah knew she wasn't upset. "But yeah. That's my top hope. My long shot."

"Did you only apply in New York?"

"And Boston. But I'm hoping for New York, even though it's farther away. There's something about this city." She got up and walked to the window, looking out at the obstructed skyline. "It gets in your blood, I think. I wasn't here long, but I feel like I've always been kind of working my way back here."

Behind her, Hannah laughed softly. "All I remember is traffic. And the subway's confusing."

"It's not so bad. I can teach you." Lori could imagine Hannah coming here to visit, getting to know her way around. Patrick popped into her mind suddenly. He had lived here for years as a student at Juilliard. Did he, too, miss the city the way she did? Or was he happy to have left the hecticness and crowds behind him? Maybe she could find a way to ask him sometime. If they stayed friends.

She should probably tell them she was leaving. It hadn't seemed relevant at first, because everything was up in the air, but she was applying for jobs now. And they were becoming friends. If she was going to move away, or even seriously considering it—and she was—then she should come clean.

"Penny for your thoughts."

Hannah's voice made Lori turn. She'd been standing at the window for a while in silence, hadn't she? She pushed her worries aside. "All right. Let's pick a restaurant to start with. I'm starving."

HANNAH FELL ASLEEP that night pretty much the moment she climbed into her hotel bed, but Lori stayed restless. Normally, the amount of walking New York demanded, plus an endless string of activities, would leave her as exhausted as Hannah. Tonight, though, sleep was elusive. After an hour of tossing and turning, she sat up against the padded headboard and pulled her phone off the nightstand. She'd received a message from Geoff a little while ago: a psychology meme. This week, he'd been sending her jokes that apparently reminded him of her. It was sweet. She responded with a laughing emoji.

You're up late. Geoff's answering text arrived immediately.

So are you.

I'm always up late. I hate going to bed.

She could picture him texting her in bed, the blue glow of his phone illuminating his face. She'd learned over the last week that he was the kind of guy who texted in complete sentences, and she naturally fell into the same pattern while they wrote.

I can't sleep, she wrote back. *I'm all worked up.* That sounded more sexual than she intended, so she added, *The city's a hectic place.*

Fun though, right?

She stared at Geoff's reply. *It sure isn't Mapleton.*

LOL. Mapleton isn't anyone's idea of a metropolis.

Geoff was probably the only person Lori knew who would use the word "metropolis" in a text, and she liked that. *Do you miss Boston?* she asked.

The phone was quiet for a while without his reply, and she was starting to think he had dozed off on the other end. Right before she went to check her social media, though, his reply popped up in a block of text.

Not really. I liked Boston, and I like Mapleton. I'm less concerned with where I'm living and more with what I'm doing. I've got a career headed right where I want to go.

Geoff was a pretty straightforward guy, so that shouldn't surprise her, but she couldn't relate. She typed, *If you've already met all your goals, it lets you relax, yeah?* With a PhD and a professorship with tenure on the way, as well as a lengthy list of publications, Geoff had reached a level of achievement in his field that others only dreamed about.

I haven't met all my goals.

Of course, he would be a stickler for the details. *Besides tenure, I mean.*

I have more goals than just tenure, he replied.

She waited for him to reply, and when he didn't, she pressed. *Well? What are they?*

I know we're lucky: financial stability, health, happiness. But I'd like to travel more. And find some way for Patrick to pursue his dreams.

Patrick was in a band and also teaching music, able to live full-time as a musician with the support of Geoff's more stable career. *What are Patrick's dreams?* she asked.

You'll have to ask him that. :)

That was fair. *Anything else?*

Maybe a family someday. We aren't sure if we want to have kids or not.

Again, the sense of getting in the middle of something profound and special settled over Lori like a heavy weight. Geoff and Patrick were considering having kids someday. They had a healthy relationship with financial stability. Whatever she was starting to build with them, it could never be on the same level as their marriage.

What about you? Geoff asked.

And just like that, she was telling him. *I want to move here to New York.* She started typing out the job she was looking for, the description she'd shared with Hannah earlier that day, unloading all of her hopes for a perfect position that she had sent out into the universe. Before sending it, she hesitated, finger hovering above the send button. By telling Geoff, she was essentially telling both of them. Telling them would send the message that she wasn't interested in anything permanent, and that was the right thing to do. She pressed send.

The phone was silent for a few minutes. This agonizing wait was the worst, when her message was received but no one had responded. She kept staring at the chat thread until finally, his reply popped up.

Cool. :) Good luck!

It was such a banal response, something eased inside her. Then Geoff added more.

Do you want to get together this week sometime? I'd love to spend more time with you.

They'd been getting together more frequently all week, and she had just assumed it would continue. What did "spend more time with you" mean? Was this another dinner? Was he hinting about sex? She paused long enough that he added another text.

I'm sure Patrick would too.

She was always counseling others to be direct. She could be direct too. *I'd love to keep seeing you both. But I want to be clear. Are you asking me to hang out, or are you asking me to bed again?*

This time, she hit send before she could let herself hesitate. Her heart thumped against her chest, and the phone revealed nothing, holding her in this state of uncertainty until his response finally (fucking finally) came through.

We're both open to that if you are. But it's okay if you just want to hang out as friends.

Relief washed away the temporary anxiety, but she wanted to be clear where things stood. *It's still hanging out as friends, no matter what. :)* Now, when to schedule? Her week was filled with the Bridge Program during the day and her part-time therapy work. *How about Friday night? Patrick have a gig or anything?*

We've got game night Friday night. A few friends are coming over, but the more the merrier. Do you want to join us, and then maybe stay a little later? Or overnight?

Lori loved board games. *Sure. Sounds fun.*

Great. We can figure out times and stuff later this week. Lunch this week again?

I'd like that. Her lunches with Geoff made her days more pleasant, even if they mostly talked shop.

Lori glanced over at Hannah again, then back at her phone. It was after midnight, she wasn't quite ready to get off the phone, and her boundaries were beginning to blur. *Are you in bed?* she asked.

Yeah.

She was typing the next question before she thought too much about it. *What are you wearing?*

Haha. I'm wearing boxers. You?

Lori looked down at herself. *A tank top and sleep shorts. And a very sexy silk sleep bonnet.*

Love a cute sleep bonnet. And your legs.

Lori smiled at the phone. *Geoffrey Robinson, are you flirting with me?* They were just words on a screen, but he was on the other end, writing to her, thinking of her.

I think I am. Don't tell my husband.

Lori frowned, but before she could reply with any kind of admonishment, Geoff added, *Because then he'll start flirting with you too.*

Smiling like an idiot again, Lori snuggled back under the covers. How long had it been since she was chatting with any guy after midnight? *I don't know if I can handle both of you at once.*

We should find out.

Ah, fuck, she hadn't meant her comment like that, but his

response went straight to her groin. *Careful. You'll get me all worked up and I'm not alone here.*

I like you worked up, Geoff replied.

This wasn't just flirting, this was full-on teasing, and Lori couldn't help the way her body responded to the mere idea of it. *You're a tease.*

Do you like it?

She hesitated. *Maybe.*

I like teasing you. I'm getting worked up myself, though. I might have to wake Patrick up so I have someone here to play with.

Lori pressed her lips together, and damn, she could *picture* that, and it was hot as hell. *I'd love to see that,* she replied.

Maybe you can sometime.

She let out a shaky breath. Geoff was not making it easy for her to stay detached from this whole thing. Good sex was good sex, and they'd had *great* sex. It was only natural for her to want it again. She'd had meaningless sex before, and sex with friends, and she could do it again. *I'd like that,* she typed. If this continued, she was going to start sexting with Geoff, and that wasn't anything she should get into while Hannah slept one bed over. *I should go to sleep before I get carried away. Have a good night, Geoff.*

You too. I'll talk to you this week.

She set the phone aside on the nightstand and stared up at the ceiling.

13

L abyrinthine, smelling intensely of dust and old books, the university library provided an essential retreat when Lori's office attracted too much foot traffic for her to get a lot done. Sometimes, she enjoyed the nice change of pace of taking her laptop into the stacks for paperwork, even if her office was perfectly suitable. This evening, she'd retreated to one of the upper floors of the library to sit near one of the large windows and work on Bridge Program interim reports. She'd tried and failed to work on these in her office all morning. Hopefully a new location would be sufficient to shake her distractions.

Lori was deep into compiling program data at her computer screen when her phone vibrated. So much for a distraction-free workspace. She glanced at her clock first, and wow, she'd been working steadily for almost two hours. Never underestimate the power of a new location. The text was from Patrick, which wasn't surprising, since she'd continued texting back and forth with him and Geoff since coming back from New York a couple of days ago. He'd sent her a picture of his violin alongside a new set of strings. He'd captioned it: "unending maintenance."

She got up to frame a picture of her work space in return, getting the laptop in frame as well as a bit of the window overlooking the campus. She captioned it: "unending reports" and sent it back before sliding into her seat again.

Working hard? he replied.

Doing my best. Been at it pretty steadily for a couple of hours. She didn't have too much left to do, hopefully. She added, *No rehearsal tonight?* She didn't have his schedule in her mind yet.

Tomorrow, Patrick responded. *Wednesdays are for Nine Possum Thursday. Ironically, not Thursdays. Hang on, let me send you something.*

A moment later, an invitation to a Google Calendar popped up in her inbox. She frowned.

What's this?

Shared calendar. To keep track of our schedules. I never know when you're free.

Lori set her phone down and stared up at the ceiling of the library. It was helpful, sure, but she could hear Hannah laughing in her head.

Thanks, she texted back, and added the shared calendar to her phone.

You want a break? he asked. *You're a quick drive from here.*

Lori couldn't deny that she wanted to see them. She'd had lunch with Geoff today, but things were different with the two of them together. *I'm seeing you Friday night,* she reminded him. Maybe he'd forgotten.

So? There a law against a midweek visit? We had fun at the pub last week.

Lori rubbed her mouth. Before she could respond, he sent

another text. *It's okay if you're busy, just thought you might want a distraction. We could bring you takeout.*

I'm tempted, she admitted. *Woo me with your takeout plans.*

The BBQ place. Picnic Package. Brisket, pork, ribs, chicken, all the sides. Cornbread. I'm drooling from here.

He definitely knew how to be tempting. *Okay, I'll let you woo me away. But there's no way you can bring that into the library.* The thought of Patrick with a sack of ribs being chased by some underpaid front desk clerk had Lori giggling.

Picnic on the lawn in about an hour?

You're on. Bring drinks.

He sent a thumbs-up, and Lori set the phone aside and returned to her laptop, this time smiling. If she hustled, she could get the rest of these reports done before they arrived.

With five minutes to spare, she uploaded the last of the reports and did a victory dance in her chair. Fuck yeah, efficiency. By the time she got out to the lawn outside the library, the sun was dipping behind the tallest buildings on the horizon, and her stomach was *growling*. She found a spot near the pond to stretch out and sent a message to Patrick with her location. Then she folded her arms behind her head and closed her eyes, listening to the evening birds.

"How bucolic."

Geoff's voice made Lori open her eyes, blinking up at the two of them leaning over her, silhouetted against the sky. "Hey." She sniffed the air. "I smell food."

Geoff held up a large paper bag. As Lori sat up and brushed grass out of her hair, he said, "I had to take the bag from Patrick so he didn't eat all the cornbread in the car."

Patrick put his hand on his chest. "It took a superhuman amount of restraint, let me tell you."

"You had *no* restraint," Geoff corrected, pulling the bag

farther away as Patrick reached for it. "He was going to tell you they ran out."

Lori looked aghast at Patrick. "I'm starting to think you can't be trusted."

Patrick held up a blanket. "I brought this, though, so you have to give me some credit." He spread it out on the grass.

Geoff handed out paper plates, disposable utensils, and a roll of paper towels before unloading a ridiculous number of food containers. As he set each one out, Patrick began pulling them open and making obscene noises of pleasure. Geoff paused after the third one. "Do you mind not fucking our dinner?"

"That would be a waste of this amazing food." Patrick sighed in contentment. "I haven't been back to this place since last summer, and I've been craving it. But their special is way too much food for two people and we always have a ton of leftovers."

"Surprising, the way you eat." Geoff poked his husband with a plastic fork.

"Love me, love my appetite." Patrick began spooning mashed sweet potatoes onto his plate.

The breeze kept the bugs mostly away, and Lori was able to really enjoy herself as they sat and chatted through dinner. They shared about their days, with a bit of work talk before Patrick brought them around to discussing some new Netflix show he and Geoff had started watching that Lori had already seen. Conversation flowed easily, and between that and the congenial atmosphere, Lori was more comfortable than she'd been in weeks.

"You know, I don't do this much," she said, tossing another empty rib into their trash bag.

"Eat barbecue?" Geoff offered.

Lori shook her head and reached for another rib. "Picnic."

The campus was a lot prettier than she realized, now that she was taking time to sit by the pond and look around. She'd been here for years, and it was easy to forget that this world-renowned research university sat in one of the most picturesque parts of the state. In some ways, one of the most picturesque parts of the country. The trees surrounding the pond had come to full summer foliage now, weeping willows trailing long tendrils over the still water, green oak leaves gleaming in the fading light. Another breeze carried the scent of honeysuckle to mingle with their takeout barbecue.

"I'm gonna miss this place," Lori said out loud.

Geoff shifted, looking quickly to Patrick before glancing away.

Patrick was studying Geoff with his eyebrows drawn together, a thin line of concentration between them. But he directed his question to Lori. "Where are you going?"

Oh. She'd hoped that telling Geoff would mean he'd tell Patrick, but apparently that was not the situation here. "I'm applying for jobs in New York. Boston, too, but mostly New York. I'm hoping to move into the city, where I can do more work as a therapist and educator in my field."

Patrick's expression shifted to something politely neutral. "Well, that's exciting. Good luck. New York is a great place. I..." He paused, a moment of sadness passing so quickly over his expression that she would have missed it if she had blinked at the wrong time. "I really liked it there." His laugh sounded genuine, though. "I don't miss the housing, I'll tell you that. Apartments like closets. I think one of my sublets actually *was* a closet, come to think of it."

"Yeah, I mean, it's all up in the air." She was qualifying her plans, and she shouldn't be, but the words kept coming like she was trying to soften some blow. "I applied weeks ago for a bunch of positions and I haven't heard anything. A few 'thanks, we got your resume' auto-responses, and that was it. So, who knows?" She shrugged. "Maybe I'll still be in Mapleton for a while longer."

Patrick seemed fine with the news, and that relief settled on Lori like a balm. Geoff, maybe feeling guilty, spoke up. "She told me Friday night when we were texting. I meant to tell you." That was all. He didn't say that he forgot, just that he meant to tell Patrick. And didn't.

"It's all right," Patrick said, then changed the subject. "Lori, you're still coming to game night on Friday, right?"

"That's the plan." She used one of the many Wet-Naps to clean her hands. "What can I expect?"

"There's one couple who usually joins us," Geoff answered. "Trey and Porter, who live in the condo downstairs from us. Plus Maddy and Russell from NPT, and Liam from the history department. Do you know Liam O'Reilly? White guy, wears a lot of plaid...looks kind of like Jack Black but with glasses?"

"Oh, yeah!" Lori nodded. "I see him around the campus coffee shop. What do you all play?"

"There are themes. This time it's words. We've got Scrabble, Boggle, Quiddler, Balderdash, a few others." Geoff counted them off on his fingers. "We do teams. We can teach you how to play any you don't know."

"Are you bringing me in because I'm a ringer?" Lori asked. "You know I have an English degree."

"It can't hurt." Patrick grimaced. "Our team's lost the last three game nights, so we keep having to buy the pizza."

"You should know going into this that I'm a competitive asshole." She grinned. "Just ask my crew team at Smith."

Patrick groaned in mock horror. "Oh no, not another of you. Geoff is ready to draw blood every week."

Lori laughed while Geoff shoved his husband. "I am not," he protested. "I just have a healthy respect for the pleasures of winning."

"That's it, hmm?" she teased, leaning closer to him. "The pleasures of winning?"

"*All* pleasures, in fact." Geoff winked at her, and she couldn't deny the way her stomach fluttered.

Patrick reached between them for the last piece of cornbread, deliberately getting in their way. "Excuse me, but if you're done having a *moment,* there's perfectly good cornbread going to waste here." He took a bite and chewed thoughtfully, then patted his stomach. "And now it's just going to *waist.*"

Geoff and Lori rolled their eyes at the same time, caught each other doing so, and all three broke apart in laughter. "You're ridiculous." Geoff said.

"Thanks, babe." Patrick smiled and took another bite of cornbread.

They were cute, and it was sweet, and yet this interaction reminded Lori that she was an outsider. This was their marriage that she was invited into for these moments of friendship, and maybe for some physical intimacy, but the true heart of their relationship lay beyond her. Which was fine, obviously. That would make leaving easier.

"You have more work to do?" Geoff asked Lori.

"Finished." She patted the canvas satchel. "Got it all done after I heard dinner was arriving."

"Congrats." Geoff looked to Patrick, who shrugged one shoulder and then nodded in agreement for…something. "We're thinking about going up to the U-Bar. You want to come?"

Lori hesitated. Yeah, it would be fun to have a drink with these guys, but she had to rein in her immediate desire to say yes. They had been spending increasing amounts of time together, and she should probably take a little break. "I think I'm gonna just go home," she said. "I've got a bunch of laundry I've been letting pile up since the trip."

"Oh, okay." Geoff's smile faded a bit. "This was nice, though."

"It was. Definitely." She made sure her own smile was big enough to convey that this was fine; everything was fine. "What do I owe you for dinner?"

Patrick waved her away. "It's on us. You can help with the pizza Friday night."

"Want me to bring beer?"

Patrick scoffed. "Of *course*."

They were all getting to their feet now, cleaning up trash, folding the blanket, and Lori suddenly found herself right next to Patrick. *Right next* to him, face-to-face, looking up at him, and he seemed as surprised to be so close as she was. And his gaze went directly to her mouth.

His expression, unguarded and longing, unlocked something inside Lori. She leaned in and kissed him. *This is fine, this is fine,* she told herself as he parted her lips with his, deepening the kiss, one of his hands pressing between her shoulder blades. She steadied herself with her hands on his biceps and leaned into this moment, reminding herself they'd kissed before, they'd kissed after ice cream; this was not new ground, even as every kiss between them felt a bit like something new and deep and unexplored.

She stepped back, breaking the kiss through sheer force of will. Geoff was watching, lips parted and breathing heavily like he'd been the one she was kissing. Lori was suddenly too hot all over. "Is it greedy to kiss you too?"

Geoff's lips twitched—a ghost of a smile. "I'm okay with greedy." He moved in close, took her by the hips, and claimed her mouth.

Lori should not get this consumed by a simple kiss, but nothing about the way Geoff kissed was simple. When she finally drew back, her unsteady legs threatened not to support her. "Yeah," she said, breathless, to no one in particular. "Friday."

Heart thumping, she gathered up her bag. Before anything else could happen, Lori turned and headed toward her office building, ignoring the currents of longing racing through her blood.

14

Whatever apprehensions Geoff had had about Lori fitting in with the game night group proved unfounded, as not only was she her normal direct, funny self, but she also kicked ass at every game they played. Luckily for Geoff, she was on their team.

"Fucking finally!" Patrick crowed, raising a fist in triumph as Maddy announced the evening's score totals at the end of the night. "I thought I was never gonna stop paying for our pizza. *You* all get it next time."

"Yeah, yeah." Russell threw a balled-up napkin at him. "But you all bring the beer. That's the trade."

"You're just lucky you brought your girlfriend here to rescue you," Trey said.

Ugh. Trey. One half of Trey and Porter, the couple from downstairs. He accompanied his words with a world-class smirk. Over the years, Geoff had learned to ignore his douchebag comments. They were fun to invite over for game night, but comments like that kept them all from hanging out more often. Patrick rolled his eyes, but something clenched up inside Geoff, a tight fist of irritation he had to work to suppress.

Lori didn't seem bothered, raising her beer. "Don't be a sore loser, Trey. I just met you."

Porter, Trey's husband, gave him a nudge. "If you were better at spelling, you might not have tanked so bad."

"Fuck you, bitch." Trey laughed, and everyone laughed, and the knot eased in Geoff's gut. Trey was always shooting his mouth off about something. He didn't mean anything by it.

"Let's set a date for the next game night." Maddy pulled out her phone. "What's everybody up to two weekends from now? We're not playing anything that weekend."

"Can't do it." Patrick shook his head. "We're heading out to P-town. Annual vacation." He squeezed Geoff's hand.

Geoff almost forgot about their upcoming trip, with the hubbub surrounding Lori. Provincetown was one of their favorite places. "Gaycationland," as many people called it, lay at the very tip of Cape Cod, a queer-centric haven of shops and beaches. They tried to visit every year, usually as soon as Geoff finished his summer work.

"We should probably just wait until you come back." Russell had his phone out as well. "And I'm open to doing something midweek if the timing lines up right."

"The joys of scheduling get-togethers as an adult, right?" Liam sighed, and then that sigh turned into a yawn. "Ugh. I'm sorry. I'm wiped out. Think I'm gonna call it a night."

Liam's departure triggered a series of other goodbyes, people gathering their belongings and games. Lori walked with them, as though she were leaving, even though her overnight bag was still sitting in the breakfast nook. As the doors slid open, Maddy gestured for her to precede them. "You want to come with?"

Lori shook her head. "I want to talk a few things over with Geoff before I head out. It was nice meeting you, though."

The rest of them piled into the elevator, and the doors slid shut on the group.

"A few things to talk over with me?" Geoff asked.

"Nah." Lori grinned. "But I didn't want everybody knowing I was sticking around. Not sure how you feel about *rumors.*"

Geoff hadn't considered it. "I suppose that's worth keeping in mind."

"What are people gonna say? That we're all fucking?" Patrick sat on the couch and crossed his ankle over his knee. "They wouldn't be wrong."

"Trey talks shit sometimes." Geoff didn't want to admit it, but Trey's occasional quips about him and Patrick not being "queer enough," for whatever reason Trey had cooked up that week, were annoying.

Patrick waved his hand. "Trey's full of shit all the time. He doesn't mean anything by it, though. Porter keeps him in line."

"What kinds of things does he say?" Lori went into the kitchen and came out with another beer, then sat on the armchair as Geoff settled in beside Patrick.

Geoff tried to put his finger on anything specific, but it was harder than he thought. "I don't think he likes bi guys much. He's always saying things like tonight, when he called you our girlfriend, or Patrick's girlfriend, whatever. Hinting that we're not committed to each other or something."

"There was one time," Patrick said, shifting on the couch, "when Geoff first brought Liam to the group, and Trey said something like I should watch out because Geoff was bringing other men home." He shrugged. "I've never really thought much about it." He put one hand lightly on Geoff's shoulder. "I didn't realize it bothered you. You want me to talk to him?"

"Thanks, but I can say something directly if it matters to me." Geoff didn't need someone fighting battles for him. "I think that sort of thing gets in my head, though. Stereotypes about bi guys being likely to cheat, or unable to be with just one person." He hesitated, but they were here, so he might as well go all-in. "It's one of my hang-ups about polyamory, I think."

"That came up in my research a fair amount." Lori crossed her legs, and suddenly she had shifted into the attitude of the professional. "Bisexuals and pansexuals across the gender spectrum often expressed fears that polyamory was fulfilling the worst stereotypes about themselves. That was compounded for many people of color, especially Black people, with the way we are assumed to be hypersexual."

"I know it shouldn't matter," Geoff said. "I generally don't care what others think of me, but this feels different. It could be because I came into my sexuality so late in life. Or maybe because of the hypersexualization stereotypes you mention. Or because I already feel like an outsider, not having grown up around many other queer Black men."

Lori leaned forward in her chair. "It is also possible," she began, with great dramatic emphasis, "that your friend Trey is a dick."

Geoff and Patrick both laughed, and whatever tension had arisen melted away. "Trey's shit at word games too," Patrick added. "He's always rude when he's losing."

"You guys are lucky you had me tonight." Lori gave them a mischievous smile. "I really saved your asses."

"Not *completely*," Geoff said, at the same time that Patrick said, "Yup." Geoff looked at his husband. "You think we're hopeless without her?"

"I think she's better than both of us, yeah." Patrick raised his eyebrows. "You don't?"

Geoff hesitated, having fun with this and not yet ready to acquiesce. "I think I can hold my own."

Lori cleared her throat, and they both looked over at her. "Care to put it to the test?"

Patrick stroked his beard. "What do you have in mind?"

Lori walked over to the pile of games still on the table and slid Scrabble out, then held it up.

Geoff and Patrick looked at each other.

"We can make it interesting." She moved the game back and forth in a little shimmy. "Strip Scrabble. Every round, whoever has the lowest point word has to take off a piece of clothing."

"Strip. Scrabble." Geoff could not be hearing this right. He adjusted his glasses.

Next to him, Patrick was grinning. "I'm here for this. Come on." He moved the coffee table out of the way, clearing a spot on the floor. "You have to play strip games on the floor. The table is too formal."

"All right. Floor it is." Lori sat opposite Patrick, and then they both turned to Geoff. "What do you think?"

He started to laugh. This was ridiculous, but he could use a little ridiculous. "Sure. Fine. Whatever you want."

That's how he ended up half-naked, sitting grumpily on the floor in just his boxers next to Patrick in the same state of undress while a nearly fully clothed Lori cackled and put down *another* word across a double-word score space.

"Christ, Lori!" Patrick shook his head. "This isn't fair."

Lori, who had removed her bra beneath her shirt but no other clothing, twirled the garment around her finger. "From where I'm sitting, it looks pretty fair to me." She hummed at the paper where she was keeping score. "Patrick, you're at the bottom again."

"Well." Patrick shrugged, playing with the waistband on his boxers. "It's not a bad place to be." He waggled his eyebrows and took off his last piece of clothing.

Lori glanced between naked Patrick and Geoff, who was practically naked himself, and then slid the Scrabble board out of the way. Before Geoff could ask what was happening, or what she was doing, she crawled across the empty space and kissed Patrick on the mouth.

When they'd begun this "sleeping with Lori" experiment, Geoff hadn't realized how much he would like watching. Sitting here, he could focus on the way Lori slid into Patrick's lap, bringing a hand up to cup the side of his face. Patrick was smiling while he kissed her. He smiled like that while kissing Geoff sometimes too, when he was really into it. He couldn't ignore a small coil of jealousy, but the larger emotion bubbling up inside him was pleasure mixed with lust.

Lori turned his head away from the kiss and looked at Geoff. "It's your turn."

Geoff blinked, looking down at his letters, and at the Scrabble board shoved out of the way. "What? We're not still playing, are we?"

Lori laughed, the sound throaty and dark, and then reached across the space between them to tug at his boxers. "Take them off."

Geoff caught on and paused, lifting his chin and returning her smile. "I didn't lose this round. I'm not sure I should take them off yet."

"You were gonna lose the next, I bet." Her expression was teasing, fingers working up to the waistband, all while she straddled Patrick's bare hips.

Patrick nodded, his expression serious, although his lips twitched. "She's right, Geoff. Besides, it's obviously much more fun if you're naked."

"I'll trade you." Lori pulled her T-shirt off, revealing a rich brown expanse of skin and her beautiful, soft breasts. Her nipples tightened in the cooler air, and god, he wanted his mouth on them again. The sight drove him right back into his memories, the way she felt all around his cock, the press of her body against his. He pulled off his boxers.

"There we go," Lori purred. She leaned over to him and lightly brushed fingers across his cock, and it stiffened, the sensation traveling throughout his groin. One hand still teasing Geoff, she turned to face Patrick again, who was trapped beneath her. "How about we take this to the bedroom?"

Patrick didn't say yes, though; he looked over at Geoff to check in, despite Geoff's impatience for more. His blood thrummed with that low-grade, intense desire that muddled his thoughts and pushed him into action.

"Come on." Geoff leaned across them and kissed his husband. "She's right."

ON AN INTELLECTUAL LEVEL, Lori had known she was coming over for sex, but the knowledge felt different than the raw, consuming desire curling through her blood when Patrick *tossed* her onto the bed. He'd carried her into the bedroom, literally carried her as though she weighed nothing, and her heart rate ratcheted up to another echelon as he stripped her jeans and underwear off in one fluid movement.

Whatever hesitation they had allowed last time, it was gone, and Geoff moved like a man who knew exactly what he was doing as he leaned half over her and captured her mouth with his. His low moan vibrated through her body like a physical touch. And as she kissed him, other hands moved her legs, parting them, air brushing suddenly cold against the heat between her thighs.

That cold disappeared instead as a hot mouth closed over her clit and sucked. *Holy shit.* Lori's cry was swallowed by Geoff's insistent kisses. She couldn't see beyond Geoff, but strong, firm hands held her thighs apart, and a coarse beard tickled her inner thighs as Patrick worked some seriously incredible magic over her tender flesh. Geoff kept her pinned here while Patrick ate her out, and she definitely had no intention of trying to escape. They were both amazing with their tongues. She squirmed, body quickly growing overwhelmed by the pleasure building between her legs.

Lori finally broke the kiss, gasping in a long breath of air, and looked down the length of her body to see Patrick working her over. He was gorgeous; they were both gorgeous, and whatever plans she'd had to stay playful and flirtatious melted away like hot wax in her increasingly desperate desire for more. There was nothing like seeing a man's face between her thighs, and when Patrick lifted one of her legs up over her shoulder for better leverage, good god, she might explode.

Geoff dragged her gaze back to his with a hand on her chin, his thumb skimming her kiss-swollen lips. The delicate touch contrasted with Patrick's tongue pressing hard over her bud: light and heavy, soft and intense, a myriad of sensations igniting a slow burn beneath her skin. While watching her face, Geoff began to roll one nipple between his fingers, firm and just this side of too rough. She opened her mouth in a gasp that turned into a moan as her pussy suddenly stretched around something thick and hard. Patrick's mouth hadn't left, working her clit like he could do this all night, his fingers teasing the sensitive places inside her.

"Fuck." It came out like a prayer on her lips. "I can't...I'm gonna come."

"Yeah." Geoff kissed her again, teasing her mouth open, swallowing her gasp as he switched to twisting her other nipple. "Do it. I want to see you."

He lifted his head just as the pressure inside her built to the breaking point. She couldn't move away, couldn't escape as it was nearly too much, her body taut like a bowstring and pulsing beneath the insistent pressure of Patrick's lips and tongue. Reaching out for something, anything, she gripped Geoff's biceps, fingers digging into the solid flesh, and hung on as she teetered on the knife-edge between pleasure and pain. She hovered there, breathless, in the impossibly long moment, and then her world shattered. Climax ripped through her, blossoming outward from her clit through her body, pulsing waves of pleasure sending her clenching endlessly on Patrick's fingers. It was never going to stop. She didn't want it to stop. Her body moved of its own volition, thrusting, quaking, and Geoff was her anchor, holding her and watching with his lips parted in lust as she came in his arms.

Patrick wasn't moving away. Instead, he kept going. He sucked more gently at her clit, lapping it with his tongue, curling his fingers inside her, and milked her through her climax and oh, holy hell, up to another one. She hadn't even come down from the first when she was making that climb again, her breaths turning into hoarse cries that scraped against her throat. Her fingernails dug half-moons into Geoff's biceps and she clenched Patrick's head between her thighs as yes, oh, *oh*, she was coming again, and everything was light and color and sound and the unending firing of nerves.

Patrick finally released her clit, and she released Geoff and collapsed down to the bed, her body going boneless, muscles weak. The world had softened somehow, the edges blurring, and she still pulsed with the aftershocks.

"I'm dead," she said weakly, smiling through her own words. "God, I'm dead."

"Patrick, you killed her." Geoff grabbed his husband and pulled him up the length of the bed, pulling his mouth downward into a kiss. "You taste like her." He slanted his head to the side and deepened the kiss. That made Lori long for another round, even as she had to catch her breath to recover. Yeah, okay, these guys might be the death of her, and it wasn't a bad way to go.

Patrick finished kissing his husband and moved over to kiss Lori, as if this was the most natural progression, and she brushed her tongue against his. He did taste like her, and it sated some deep-seated desire to claim him and mark him as hers.

But he isn't yours. Her desire to claim was misplaced; she was drawn to him by sex, yes, by this postorgasmic glow, by oxytocin and the cocktail of hormones coursing through her veins. He wasn't hers, and Geoff wasn't hers, and she should be satisfied with friendship and some damn amazing sex.

She was pulled out of her thoughts by touch: fingers were moving between her legs, brushing over the swollen, soaking bud, and she shivered from head to toe.

She broke the kiss to roll back onto her back, letting her

legs fall open. Geoff knelt between them, gently brushing fingers over her clit, watching her response. She smiled at him. "Whatcha doin' down there?"

"Testing." He returned her smile. "How do you feel? Are you all done?"

Lori laughed. It felt good, her body relaxed and loose. "Am I done? Hell no, I'm not done. I thought there was some talk about getting to fuck both of you, and right now, *nobody's* fucking me."

Stretched out next to her, Patrick laughed. Geoff looked at her with mischief in those dark eyes. "Yeah? You want to get fucked?"

She was about to make another joke when Geoff suddenly slid fingers inside her, two or maybe three, stretching her so wide, she gasped. Damn, she was wet and relaxed, and he penetrated her with no effort at all, filling her with those beautiful fingers. The laughter died in her throat, replaced by a moan. She hadn't realized she'd closed her eyes until Geoff asked, "Look at me, beautiful," and she blinked them open, the endearment taking her by surprise. Geoff was intent on her as he worked his fingers in and out of her tight sheath, repeating his question. "You want to get fucked?"

Lori nodded. "Yeah. Holy hell, yeah." Her muscles clenched around him greedily, like she hadn't already come twice. But she wanted more. Right now, body lax and open, was the perfect time to get exactly what she wanted…except it wasn't just about her. "Patrick?" She couldn't move, with Geoff still fingering her, stealing her breath, but she could reach over and interlace her fingers with the man beside her. "Tell me what you want."

"I want you both to be happy."

Lori reached down to Geoff's hand, gently encouraging

him to remove his fingers, and then she could turn to face Patrick fully. "Nope. Tell me what *you* want."

Patrick looked up at her, dazed, like nobody ever asked him what he wanted before. But that wasn't like Geoff; Geoff was a thoughtful man and clearly a generous lover. Maybe Patrick just never told thought about his own needs as separate from his partner's. "I…" He looked at Geoff, then back at Lori. "I want to be inside you. With Geoff."

There, that was an answer. Lori nodded. "Condoms."

She took a moment, in the hubbub of reaching for protection, to fondle Patrick's cock. Moderate length and girth, he fit beautifully in her hand, the rose-colored tip slick with his arousal. She slid her fingertips across the sensitive head, watching his dick twitch. He finally reached down to put a hand over hers to still it. "Have mercy, please."

"This is mercy." She took a condom and unrolled it over his length. Then, without preamble, without wanting to wait a moment longer, she straddled him and slid onto his cock.

"Oh, *fuck*." Patrick swore like the words were torn out of him, hands steadying Lori's hips.

She'd rushed this, wanting to feel him in her, and his cock filled her pussy deeper and more thoroughly than she'd expected. She stayed motionless, their hips flush against each other, her hands braced on his chest. Inside her, his dick pulsed with his heartbeat. Fuck, he seemed so much bigger inside her, and her bravado faded with this pure, primal instinct begging her to move.

Lori stayed still, though, as Geoff moved into position behind her. Geoff gently pressed on the middle of her back, encouraging her to bend over. She did, lying flat on Patrick's chest with her knees drawn up on either side. This position stretched her differently around him, pressing against other erogenous zones inside her. She didn't want to move, frozen in position as the enormity of what she was about to undertake washed over her.

Geoff's slick fingers circled her ass, gently, but firmly, confidently, until he began working one slender digit inside. Lori relaxed as much as she could. She was already so full, and they were going to stretch her to the breaking point. She wanted it, lust and longing and fear mingling inside her, and Geoff added another finger with a slow, slick stretch. He had done this before, of course, knew exactly how to open her up, how to press gently inside, sliding two fingers deep into her tight ass as she breathed through the unusual sensation.

Beneath her, Patrick made a strangled noise. "Fuck, I can feel that," he said breathlessly. "Oh my god."

Geoff added more lube, and then he was stretching her more, the pressure nearly uncomfortable but still good, still not too much. "You okay?" he asked, somehow sounding impossibly calm, even as Lori was ready to jump out of her skin with tension.

"Yeah." She didn't sound okay, even to her own ears, but she was, *ohh*, she was. "It's so good. It's…so much." Lying on Patrick like this, his heartbeat thundering in her ear, she felt small and fragile and delicate and *fuck*, she wanted them to push her limits and was terrified at the same time. "Go slow," she heard herself say, vulnerability slipping out.

Patrick smoothed a hand down her back. "It's gonna feel so good. You're gonna feel so good, sweetheart."

She wasn't his sweetheart, wasn't anyone's sweetheart, but the endearment washed over her like a balm, softening the raw intensity of this moment. Geoff was still moving his fingers inside her, and she was going to scream if she didn't get more right now.

"Please," she begged. "Please, I need you."

He slid his fingers free, gently, leaving her empty and yet still so full, and then there were the sounds of a condom wrapper and a lube bottle. Soon, his slick, blunt cock nudged against her entrance. This was it. She had to let go, to give herself over, to trust. She closed her eyes, mouth falling open, and yielded.

A strangled noise came from her throat as Geoff's thick cock head pushed inside. He stopped, his hands on her hips, somehow steady and grounding. "Tell me when."

"More." Lori squeezed her eyes tightly shut, needing to focus on this overwhelming sensation. She needed more. She needed all of this, needed to be caught between them. Geoff put a hand on her ass, right above where his cock was splitting her open, holding her in place as he gently began to move forward.

"Fuck." Patrick's voice had jumped an octave. "Fuck, I can feel that. I can...oh, *oh my god.*"

Geoff was silent, but his breath rasped loudly in the air, or maybe it was Lori's breathing, or Patrick's, his chest rising and falling beneath her ear. She couldn't keep her thoughts straight. The world narrowed down to the sensations between her legs. Slick, slow, Geoff kept penetrating her ass with his cock, millimeter by millimeter. She relaxed, her body opening for him. He went on forever, like this would never end, and she was making the most abandoned, helpless whimpers that she was powerless to stop. Beneath her, Patrick's breathing had become low, soft moans. Behind her, Geoff was silent.

The last inch, and his hips pressed flush against her ass, filling her completely. Lori's breath caught. Geoff smoothed a hand over her lower back. "Look at you," he murmured, his voice low and filthy and rough. "You should see yourself, stretched around our cocks like this. You're so beautiful."

There it was again, another compliment, more praise, and Lori's defenses were down. She blinked her eyes open, but the world was a blur. Patrick had one hand tracing up and down her back, slowly, his breathing regulating as he grew used to the tightness, soothing her with his touch. Lori couldn't think straight. In some deep animal part of her brain, she was only a collection of nerve endings, and this double-stretched feeling flayed her open like sex never did. She was naked, and vulnerable, and helpless in the face of this intensity.

Before she could fully relax—she might never relax, might never come down from this high—Patrick began to thrust. They were just gentle rocking movements of his hips, maybe an inch or so, in and out, but each movement rubbed hard over her G-spot and stole her breath.

"There we go." Geoff moved his hands back to her hips once more and began to move as well. Their cocks slid against each other inside her, separated by only the thinnest of walls, and Lori mewled and dropped her forehead back to Patrick's chest.

This wasn't who she was. She was confident and outspoken and playful in bed; she wasn't one to lose herself in the emotional openness of sex. Sex was fun. It brought her joy. This kind of sex, though, stripped her defenses and left her operating on pure instinct. She didn't move at all, paralyzed by her need and her overwhelmed senses.

"Lori. Sweetheart." Patrick's voice brought her back to herself, made her lift her head and look down at him. His face was flushed, lips swollen, eyes dark with lust. He looked as destroyed as she felt. "Tell me you're okay."

They had stopped moving, and she blinked, focusing.

"Yeah." She kissed him, the barest brushing of lips, all she could manage in her blissed-out state. "Don't stop."

She let the men inside her guide her movements, let them control the bend and flex of her body, and held on for the ride. Pressure built, her muscles tensed, and her pleasure escalated. She floated on the current as it carried her, helpless to do anything but feel, until her body reached that impossibly high peak.

She hovered, hovered, and crashed over the edge.

Through the haze of pleasure-pain, the sharp razor of unbearable intensity, she felt them still moving inside her, heard Geoff cry out and thrust once more, heard Patrick chase him over the edge. Stuffed full like this, she could feel their cocks pulsing in release. God, she was going to die like this. There was no way for her to survive this much pleasure, and that was her last thought before everything went white and soft and she drifted away.

Her muscles weren't working properly. She could barely lift her head, and she lay limply across Patrick's chest as they each disentangled themselves from her. Then, Patrick gently rolled her to the side, and the noises of cleanup and soft conversation reached her ears before they slid into bed with her again and held her, one on each side. Geoff was the one in front, now, and he brushed a curl away from her forehead. "Hey." He leaned in to kiss her, and the kiss tasted salty. She blinked.

"Am I crying?" Regaining some muscle control, she brushed her hand over her cheek. "Shit." She never cried after sex.

Patrick's voice rumbled behind her. "We were worried we broke you."

"You did." She laughed, because laughing was easier than

confronting this open vulnerability inside her. Something had shifted, and she couldn't define it, but this connection to Geoff and Patrick seemed solid where it had once felt breakable. Now, the only thing feeling breakable was her. She swallowed. "I'm broken." And yeah, as she sat up, her body protested in some distinctly broken ways. "I think I need a shower."

"You want company?" Geoff asked, and Lori smiled, putting a hand flat on his chest.

"Not this time, bud." She leaned in to kiss him, though, so he'd know there were no hard feelings. "Maybe after."

On wobbly legs, she got up to grab her overnight bag.

15

Geoff was the kind of guy to fall asleep at a moment's notice, so it didn't surprise Patrick that by the time he got out of his shower, his husband was conked out in bed. He looked so sweet, stretched out on his side of the bed, bare-chested and lightly snoring. Patrick had expected to find Lori snuggled up with him, but she wasn't in the bedroom. Hopefully, she hadn't left. Tonight had been intense, and he wouldn't blame her if she'd slipped out rather than stayed to deal with the aftermath.

He found her standing out on the balcony with her arms crossed on the railing, looking out at the night. She wore a purple silk nightgown that flowed down to her knees, and she'd wrapped her curls up in a silk scarf to spill out at the crown of her head. She looked over her shoulder to smile at him as he joined her on the balcony.

"Thought I'd find you in bed." It was so easy to casually touch her now, lightly rubbing between her shoulder blades.

"I'm too amped up to sleep." She leaned on her folded arms. "It's quiet out here."

"Generally, yeah. It's not New York." Immediately as the words left his mouth, he wished he could snatch them back in. Geoff hadn't told him about Lori's plans to move away, and Patrick still wasn't sure why, but he had been circling around the idea all week now. The thought of her leaving unsettled something inside him that he couldn't articulate.

Lori made a soft "hmm" noise and looked down to the river. Although it wasn't visible in the darkness, the sounds of water rushing over rocks rose up to him through the blackness. "I'll miss Mapleton. I'll miss places like this."

"I'll miss you."

The words slipped out without him consciously deciding to say them. Lori smiled, a sad smile in the moonlight. "You barely know me."

"I know you enough to know I'll miss you."

He leaned on the railing beside her. In the darkness, without having to look at her face, it was easy to make these declarations. He was only telling the truth, but maybe the truth didn't have a place in this empty, quiet space between them.

"New York's not far." She turned her head away from him, looking off into the distance. Her hair cut a curled silhouette against the star-filled sky. "Do you miss it?"

His instinct was to respond the way he always did when people asked, to say, *I don't miss the traffic,* or *New York's so expensive, I'm better off here,* but those responses were always incomplete. "It's complicated."

She looked back toward him. "I've got time."

The light coming in from the glass doors behind them illuminated the curve of her cheekbone, the shadow of her lashes. She was beautiful, and he wanted to kiss her. The desire settled on him differently, not like the urgent intensity of sex, but like the soft swell of emotion in its aftermath. Was this all right? He and Geoff had discussed this briefly, the idea of kissing her when they were alone. Although they had said it was fine, neither had done so yet. So, even as he wanted to step in and press his lips to hers, he didn't.

"Leaving New York meant I could take care of my mom until she died, and I'll never regret that. I met Geoff here, and I'll never regret that either." Those parts were easy, the positives he'd earned for staying here. "Geoff's job means I can pursue my career as a musician without having to worry about money. I'm lucky. Most artists don't have that freedom." He looked down at his hands curled together, his elbows resting on the metal railing, and then out at the shadow of water far below them. "I don't know what my life would have been like if I'd gone back to Juilliard after my mom died instead of staying in Massachusetts. I don't like to think about it."

"Because you'd have lost Geoff?"

"That's part of it." Patrick paused. He didn't share this part of himself with anyone but Geoff, and then, only in the quiet times between them, when Geoff let him open up and pour out his confusion and longings into the empty space. "Most musicians don't make it in New York. Artists, actors, singers, musicians, writers, all the creatives, New York chews them up and spits them out again. It's an expensive place to live when you aren't making any money. I don't want to be gigging my whole life. I don't want to live with five roommates in a fourth-floor walk-up in Queens, eating ramen and waiting tables and hoping each new audition will net me something great."

He hesitated, and Lori stepped gently into that hesitation. "But some part of you *does* want that. Right?"

Patrick laughed bitterly, hanging his head, the tumult of

emotions bubbling up inside him. "Fuck, Lori, I'm a thirty-five-year-old man. I'm too old to be living like that anymore." He closed his eyes. She had to know what he wasn't saying, so he might as well just say it. "But, yes. I wonder all the time. What if I could have done something great? What if I could have actually *made* it?" He stood upright, no longer leaning over, and gripped the iron railing. The rough edges pressed into the soft skin of his palms, the metal still warm from the heat of the day. "I know I'm good, Lori. I don't know if I'm 'New York' good, but I know I'm good, and I wonder all the time what could have been."

She let his words settle, standing as well, so they were shoulder to shoulder on the small porch. "What's your dream role? Symphony?"

"Pit orchestra, actually. I love live performances. Theater, the ballet, all of it." He'd gone to so many shows while living in the city, spending most of his available cash on rush and standee tickets to consume as much theater as possible.

"You ever think about giving it another try?"

"I try not to think about it anymore." He had entertained thoughts of it in the early days of his relationship with Geoff, back before Geoff had settled into his current job, before they'd bought the condo, before he settled into a routine with Nine Possum Thursday and started giving violin lessons and developed new rhythms to his life. "Geoff's going to get tenure at the university. He's shaped his life around his academics He's worked for this his *whole life*. I would never ask him to give that up, not when he's already supporting me the way he is. It's not fair." He tried to smile, but his face felt too tight. "I can't say I don't envy you. Going after what you want. Nothing holding you back." He winced at the words. "I don't mean that. Geoff's not holding me back."

"I know what you mean." She exhaled fast and shook her head, curls bouncing above the scarf. "It's scary, but I can't second-guess myself. I can't spend the rest of my life wondering what might have been." She blanched, pulling back visibly. "I'm sorry. I didn't mean…"

"It's okay. It's fair. I've made my choices."

"Does Geoff know?"

She didn't specify what she was asking about—his feelings, his regrets, his former hopes—but Patrick could fill in the blanks and knew she probably meant all of it.

"I don't know. Probably. He's practically a genius. But if you're asking if we talk about it, no, not anymore." They'd had enough of those conversations at the beginning, and again when Patrick had proposed, and there wasn't a reason to revisit them now.

"How have you two been since we all started sleeping together? Everything okay?"

Patrick laughed. "Great time to ask, after we slept together again."

Lori hung her head and echoed his laughter. "Sorry. I'm not on my game tonight."

"I dunno. You seemed pretty on your game earlier." He nudged her with his elbow.

Lori leaned over and bit him on the shoulder, gently, affectionately. "Shut up."

"Did you just bite me?"

"I bite all the people I care about. Answer the question."

Even offhanded, her comment that she cared about him made something warm settle in Patrick's heart. "Yeah, we're good. Better than good. It's rejuvenated us."

"New things can be like that." Lori nodded, her posture

and expression slipping into the mode of Lori Clark, PhD. She probably didn't realize it. "It's new relationship energy."

"I know. I read all the polyamory books back in the day." Patrick smiled, so she'd know he wasn't making fun of her. "It doesn't usually last that long."

"It's true. And in our case, we won't even have time for that. With me leaving and all." Her voice dropped on the last few words, even though her expression stayed neutral. "But I'm having fun. As long as you're both having fun too, I don't see why this can't continue."

"We should go out this week."

"We've been going out."

"But like...like actually *go out*."

Lori raised an eyebrow. "Like on a date?"

"Yeah. Like on a motherfucking *date*."

"All three of us?"

"Why not?"

Lori tipped her head to the side and studied him, like she was trying to figure him out. "How is this different than what we've been doing?"

"I don't know. Maybe we've already been dating. It's been a long time since I've dated anybody. But I want to be dating you." He paused. "And I'm pretty confident I speak for Geoff too."

"Hmm." She turned her attention back to the night. "Tell me about this date."

"Dinner and a movie."

"Classic, classic." She nodded. "Just one date?"

Patrick laughed. "You want to get together more than once?"

"My nights are pretty free lately." She shrugged. "I know

you've got the band on Wednesday, but we could work around it."

"Or you could go out with Geoff without me."

Lori raised an eyebrow. "Like on a date?"

Patrick had to laugh. "You're killing me. Yeah, like on a date. I like when he's off having fun when I can't be home."

"So many dates, we might have to make a schedule." She nudged him with her elbow.

"We've got that shared Google Calendar," Patrick suggested. "You could actually start putting things on it. And we should probably start a group text."

Lori's smile faltered.

"No on the group text?" Patrick rubbed his beard. He hadn't thought it was a big deal.

"Group text makes sense. It's just..." She shook her head. "Never mind. It's just something Hannah said. Text me up." Then she covered a yawn with her free hand. "Is there really room for me in that bed? I can sleep on the couch."

Patrick gave her other hand a squeeze. "There's room."

16

Lori frowned at her phone again, for what was probably the fifth time tonight. *We're going to a bar,* Geoff had typed in the group text. *Be ready at nine.* And then he hadn't specified anything else.

A bar? A bar didn't exactly seem like the kind of adventure she'd come to expect after this week. They'd been on dates every night. On Monday, she'd done dinner and a movie with both of them. On Tuesday, they'd driven to the top of Mt. Williams and had a picnic. *Another picnic,* just because she'd liked the barbecue picnic on the campus lawn. On Wednesday, when Patrick was at practice, she and Geoff had gone to a gallery to see one of the new exhibits. Yesterday, the three of them had spent the evening hitting local bookstores. And tonight, apparently, it was…a bar.

The doorbell rang at precisely nine, which was no surprise. Geoff was terrifyingly punctual. She opened the door to see them both standing there, and damn. *Damn.* Geoff wore a slim-fitting teal button-down shirt with the top few buttons undone and a pair of sleek gray trousers. Patrick wore a white oxford shirt with the sleeves rolled up above the elbows and a pair of navy-blue jeans, and he had on suspenders.

"Holy shit," she said out loud, because they needed to know. "You guys look amazing."

"You too." Geoff took her by the shoulders to look her up and down. Lori had worn a white dress that clung to all her curves and barely reached her knees, the kind of dress she'd wear when she wanted to find some hot guy to take her home. She'd hoped to wow them, but she hadn't expected how much she'd be wowed in return.

"What kind of bar is this?" Lori asked. "You're dressed really nicely."

"I'll tell you on the way."

Lori frowned. "I don't like the sound of that." But she trusted them—which was surprising in itself—and thus got in the car anyway. Patrick had given her the front seat in a gentlemanly gesture, and she'd taken it.

"Tokens," Geoff finally answered, steering them onto the highway out of town. "We're going to Tokens. The barcade. It's karaoke night."

"What?" Lori made a face. "I don't sing in front of people."

"You don't have to," Patrick explained, leaning forward from the front seat. "Geoff and I can sing enough for the three of us."

"You're serious." She turned in her seat so she could look at both of them. "You guys sing karaoke?"

"Patrick sings karaoke," Geoff corrected. "What I do is some kind of horrible wailing that deafens small children and brings fear to the hearts of men."

"Oh, come on." Patrick nudged his husband's shoulder from the back seat. "You're not that bad."

"Not that bad," Geoff repeated, with a meaningful look at

Lori. "This is the most favorable compliment he can think to give me."

This was nowhere near what Lori had expected for the night, but she was more excited than anything. Even if she didn't like singing in front of groups, she could at least enjoy the guys singing, and probably some video games as well. "I can't wait," she said, and meant it.

Patrick really knew what he was doing. He had a stage presence, of course, and even though the evening had barely kicked off, he had the bar singing along with "Pour Some Sugar on Me" in only one verse. Lori couldn't help joining in, especially when he *got up on a table* and started fiddling with the buttons on his shirt.

"Who is this guy?" Lori asked Geoff, grinning.

Geoff was staring up at Patrick with the most ridiculous, enamored smile on his face, like Patrick was the only guy in the world. Watching the two of them together, Lori felt warm all over. She wasn't just on the outside looking in. She was part of this, somehow, and the thought was sobering and comforting at once.

"You want to do a duet with me?" Geoff asked. "I swear, I'm a good partner."

Lori raised an eyebrow, then shook her head and turned back to her drink. "Ask me when I've had, like, three more of these." She held up her glass and drank more. "And I'll tell you no again."

Patrick had energized the whole room, and the next few singers did similarly upbeat pieces before it was Geoff's turn. He strode to the front of the room with casual gravitas, the way he probably walked up to the front of his classroom: like he owned the place.

The song started, a familiar guitar riff that Lori would

know anywhere. She had to laugh as Geoff struck a pose and began loudly, enthusiastically singing "What's Up" by 4 Non Blondes. By the time he got to the refrain, the "hey yeah yeah yeah" part, everybody was singing along with him.

She leaned over to Patrick, who was sitting beside her, speaking loudly to be heard over the crowd. "I thought you said he couldn't sing! He's really good." Just as she finished speaking, Geoff hit a sour note and just kept going. "Okay, he's *pretty* good," she amended, and Patrick laughed.

"We have fun." Patrick tossed back the last of his drink. "Isn't that what it's all about?"

They passed the evening with cabinet arcade games in between Patrick and Geoff's repeated trips to the front of the bar to sing karaoke. Lori died endlessly playing *Galaga* but found her groove in *Ms. Pac-Man*, enough to make it to the leaderboard by the time she lost her last life.

"You're too young for this game." Geoff watched her enter her initials into the "Top Ten" screen. "How are you so good at it?"

"The laundromat near Smith has one of these." Lori finished and stepped back with a flourish. "When I was in undergrad, I spent as many quarters on this baby as I did on the wash."

"A woman of many talents." Geoff gestured to the front of the room. "You sure singing's not one of them? I won't ask again."

"Don't ask again." She waved him off. "Go on, have fun."

He and Patrick finished the evening just past midnight with a surprisingly touching duet of "Islands in the Stream" that brought the room to applause. Most of the people were more than halfway to drunk, except Geoff, who was driving them home that night. By the time they staggered out into the

Tokens parking lot a little after midnight, Lori was a giggly mess and Patrick had taken to singing songs he didn't know all the words to and making up alternatives.

"Geoff!" Patrick interrupted himself midsong, leaning on the car door. "Come here and let me kiss you."

Geoff went willingly.

"And you." Patrick dragged her into the embrace. Surprised, Lori let him pull her up against the two of them, and when he kissed her—lazy and sweet, a sleepy drunk kiss —she kissed back. They hadn't kissed this week, hadn't slept together, and her body thrummed with the desire for something. Turning to the side, she switched from kissing Patrick to Geoff, and then back again, relishing the press of lips and tongue and the overwhelming confusion of not knowing who was who with her eyes closed.

A catcall from behind her made them break the kiss.

"Get a room!" somebody shouted.

"Eat shit!" Patrick called back, but he was grinning in such a way that Lori couldn't help but grin back. They stared at one another like three fools, and she couldn't be happier. Or maybe that was just the booze talking.

Geoff broke the silence. "Come to P-town with us next weekend."

Lori blinked. She wasn't sober enough for this conversation. "What?"

"Provincetown. Last weekend you said you've never been. We've got a king suite at a B and B within walking distance of Commercial Street. Let us take you there."

Lori looked over to Patrick. "Did you know he was gonna ask me this?"

Patrick shrugged, the movement slower than normal. "We

talked about it last night. I think it's a good idea. We both love having you around."

Her impulse was to say yes, immediately, but she forced that impulse back. She was drunk, and she'd spent five glorious days in a row with these guys, and she wasn't in the best place to make a decision. "Let me think about it."

"Think about it." Geoff touched his forehead to hers lightly, a gesture so intimate, it took her breath away.

The moment passed. They disentangled limbs and piled into the car, Lori in the back seat this time. Patrick kept trying to get handsy with Geoff while he drove, which they all found supremely hilarious because Geoff kept rebuffing him.

"Ask him about the time I blew him in the car after ice cream," Patrick announced.

"What?" Lori leaned forward. "Geoff, is this true? But road safety!"

Geoff gave a long-suffering sigh. "I plead the Fifth."

The stars outside shone brightly in the clear night, and with the windows down, the wind whipped Lori's curls around her face. She was with Geoff and Patrick. She'd had a pretty damn good week. And maybe next weekend she'd go to Provincetown.

Whatever the future might hold, tonight everything was all right.

LORI STARED at the mountain of odds and ends piled up in Hannah's basement with her hands on her hips. "This is a lot of shit."

"I know." Hannah brushed the back of her hand over her

forehead. "I told myself I'd finish decluttering before we move, but I've been waiting to pack up boxes until today."

"I am uncertain exactly what you expect me to do, and why you expect me to do it with no pizza."

"Pizza's coming. Help me pack this shit up. It's all getting donated." Hannah waved her arm at the expanse of basement. Items were piled up in stacks like stalagmites. Lori grimaced at the pile closest to her. At least she'd put her hair up for this. She should have brought a bonnet too.

"Don't give me that look." Hannah gave her friend a gentle shove. "I'll be doing the same thing for you when you move."

"*If* I move, you mean." Lori took a tape gun and set up one of the boxes for packing. "It's been weeks, and nobody's written back."

"Did you follow up?"

"Sure did. On the phone like an adult. Got a few nos. Two places told me they were on a hiring freeze because of budget cuts, and the others said they were still considering and to wait." She sighed. "It's not all bad. I've been having fun here in Mapleton in the meantime."

Hannah nodded knowingly, filling her own box. "Is this why you've been so bad about returning my texts this week? All that dick you've been getting?"

Lori snorted. "I have not gotten any dick this week, thank you very much." She paused. "We've been going on dates."

"Dates, really?" Hannah smiled. "That's cute, actually."

"It is. A few nights ago, they took me to sing karaoke."

Hannah paused. "But you don't sing karaoke."

"I know, but they do." Lori shrugged. "And look at you. Finally getting ready to move in with Ben and Mitchell."

Hannah bit her lip. "I wasn't sure how I'd feel about it, but as the months passed, it seemed like the next logical step."

"Who brought it up?"

"Mitchell, of course." Out of the two men Hannah was dating, Mitchell was the most practical one. "He pointed out homes in the area and calculated how easy they'd be to afford. He even mapped it out: one shared bedroom, and two spares for work or for days when we want to sleep apart. He'd done a spreadsheet of contributing factors." Hannah got a distant look in her eyes when she was talking about her partners, complete with a dopey smile on her face. "I love that man."

Lori could hardly believe that within a year, Hannah had gone from uncertainty about a polyamorous relationship to planning on buying a house with two men. "I'm happy for you."

Hannah came back to reality. "Thanks. It's still a bit strange to think about."

"How'd your parents take it?"

"Surprisingly well." Hannah finished filling one box and taped it up. "They're both pretty liberal hippies, so that's a plus." She tossed the tape gun to Lori. "So, all that dating. Things getting serious with your guys?"

"They're not my guys." Lori aggressively taped up the box. "They're each other's guys who happen to be spending time with me as well."

"A lot of time with you," Hannah corrected.

Lori moved onto another box. "They invited me to go with them to Provincetown this weekend."

"Ooh, they've got a great sex shop out in P-town." Hannah perked up immediately. "You should check it out for me. See how they're merchandizing product."

"I didn't say I was going."

"Well, what did you say?"

"I told them I'd think about it."

"And?"

"And I've been thinking about it. I've never been, and it sounds fun. Time away, swimming in the ocean, fresh lobster…" She kept her attention on the box so she wouldn't have to see Hannah's expression. When Hannah didn't say anything, though, Lori looked up. Hannah had this sweet, endearing smile on her face that was fairly disgusting. "Don't give me that look." Lori tossed the tape gun back.

Hannah spoke slowly, like she was carefully choosing her words. "Are you sure you want to move to New York?"

Lori busied herself in the work of loading boxes, because it was something do with her hands, and nervous energy had begun to spark all throughout her body. "I don't know," she said at last. "If I don't get offered any of these jobs, maybe I'll stick around for another year or so. Take on more clients at Relationship Therapy Associates." The idea brought up mixed feelings as she said it out loud. "It's not what I want to be doing, but I figure, another year and I'll have a better idea where things stand. Maybe less. Maybe six months." She didn't have to say, *By then I'll know if they're sick of sharing their marriage with me.*

"Sure." Hannah sounded encouraging. "Lots can change in a short period of time."

Lori nodded. Lots of things already *had* changed, and she wasn't sure how to feel about that.

17

"I can't believe the dunes."

Geoff looked in the rearview mirror at Lori's exclamation, smiling at the sight of her nearly pressed against the car window. "They're huge, right?"

"I wish you could see the ocean past them. Can you see it if you climb them?" She shifted to look back up front, practically bouncing.

In the passenger seat, Patrick snorted. "Yes, you can. Our first year here, Geoff made me climb one. They are giant and sandy and exhausting."

"I'd still hike one with you, if you wanted to see," Geoff offered. "But we usually drive out to the ocean instead."

Lori's excitement was palpable, and it made Geoff smile. She'd seemed unsure about this trip, and he was glad she was here. Who knew what the future held, anyway, and they might as well enjoy all the time together they could. It wasn't like this was going to be a repeat thing. Besides, everybody in Massachusetts should experience Provincetown in high summer at some point in their lives.

Geoff couldn't help seeing the landmarks for the first time, through Lori's eyes, as they drove down the ever-narrowing stretch of Route 6 out to the very tip of the Cape. The colorful houses with salt-blasted shingles lining the bay side of the road, the marshy expanses in between breathtaking rolling dunes, the displays of buoys and lobster traps on rooftops—everything was so quintessentially Cape Cod.

"You've never been to the Cape at all, or just never been to P-town?" Geoff asked. It was unfathomable that she'd lived in Massachusetts for so long without ever going to the Cape at all, unless she hated the ocean.

"Just P-Town. I've been to other parts, but never this far. I forget how big the Cape is. You guys come here every year?"

"We try to," Patrick answered. "We went the first summer we were dating, and ever since then, it's been a tradition. It's the same every year, but that's kind of the charm."

Lori nodded, and in the rearview mirror, her expression was wistful. "Never had a place like that. Just...always on the move."

She exclaimed over an egret flying over the marshes, and Geoff let her happy comments fill the silence as they approached their turnoff into Provincetown.

The king suite at their B and B had begun to feel like a home away from home after all these yearly visits. They'd loved it on the first stay and kept coming back. Geoff's nostalgia threatened to overwhelm him as he stepped into the room and inhaled the scent of clean linens and salt air. The balcony doors were open, and from their vantage point, they could see the faintest hint of water out beyond the town.

Lori dropped her bag and went to the balcony immediately, while Patrick busied himself pulling out the sofa bed. Not that Geoff could imagine they'd use it much. Having Lori cuddled in bed between him and Patrick had been an unexpected pleasure of her sleepover last game night. She was all soft skin and sweet smell, and while she slept, she made these adorable noises of contentment. Geoff had woken up in the middle of the night and stayed awake just to listen. Having that again, all weekend, felt like an undeserved luxury.

Lori spun to face them through the balcony French doors. "What should we do? Do we go to the beach, go shopping, what?"

Patrick neatly laid the extra pillow out on the sofa bed and stood to admire his handiwork. "We can do whatever you want. You're the new one here."

"And you're the experts. Tell me what you usually do while you're here." Lori bypassed the sofa bed and flopped down on the giant king-sized bed.

He wanted to show her everything, all at once. "I think we have to do Commercial Street first. Do you like lobster? We can get lobster."

"I love all fish and shellfish."

"And then tomorrow, maybe the beach?" Geoff looked to Patrick. "What do you think? Think we can get a burning permit?"

"If we get there early enough, sure." Patrick was looking between the two of them, his expression soft. Geoff could *see* the tender thoughts behind those eyes. That was dangerous; if they let tender thoughts overtake them, the end of this would break their hearts.

"Come on." Geoff grabbed Lori's hand and tugged her off the bed. "Don't get settled. There's so much to see."

She smiled at his enthusiasm and let him drag her to her feet. "Okay, okay. Let me grab my wallet."

Commercial Street wound through downtown Provincetown, framed by touristy T-shirt shops, restaurants, art galleries, bars, and clubs, and Geoff knew the history of everything. He'd learned it little by little, picking up details on each visit, and he pointed out what he knew as they walked along toward the Lobster Pot restaurant. He was halfway through a story about the origins of the invasive rugosa rose shrub when he noticed Patrick laughing, right past Lori's shoulder.

Puzzled, Geoff stopped. "What?"

Patrick shook his head. "You. I didn't realize how much you knew about P-town."

Another person might feel self-conscious, but Geoff would never feel self-conscious about his depth of knowledge. "I'm a history professor, Patrick. Even if this isn't my area of expertise."

"I love it." Lori looked up at him, fondness in her dark eyes. She wasn't humoring him either; she really seemed to love his stories, and his heart unfolded like a flower inside his chest.

Geoff took her hand, and on her other side, Patrick did the same. They walked along like that, side by side on the sidewalk, maneuvering around other passersby, and Lori prompted him to continue his story.

The Lobster Pot, as always, delivered on delicious food in a beautiful ambiance overlooking the harbor. Lori proclaimed that she'd never had a meal that good, and that she couldn't possibly eat anything else, but then dragged them to an ice cream shop for dessert anyway. They walked through the Whaler's Wharf, an open-air market that led right down to the shore, and sat on benches to watch seagulls winging their way across the sky in the gathering twilight.

"I'm starting to think ice cream might be a thing with us."

Lori drew her tongue around another loop of soft-serve, and Geoff forgot what he was going to say for a minute.

"A thing? Do we have things now?" Patrick leaned over to Geoff. "Did you hear this, Geoff? We've got a thing."

"I like things." Geoff turned back to his own ice cream, crunching into the cone. The three of them had this comfortable rhythm together, and it was both peaceful and *easy*. Was it supposed to be this easy? He could sidestep effortlessly into this new pattern, fit Lori into his routine like she was meant to be there. For a moment, he closed his eyes and imagined her coming home to them, or settling into bed between them, or reading in the breakfast nook while Patrick practiced violin and he whipped up some new baked good in the kitchen.

The voice in the back of his head reminded him that she was leaving, this was impermanent, and besides, he didn't *want* to complicate his life. This weekend, though, he could pretend.

"—the sex shop."

Geoff perked up at that. Lori and Patrick had been talking, and he'd somehow tuned them out.

"The one down at the end of the street, near the pizza shop?" Patrick nodded. "It's nice. You want to go in there?"

"Hell yes, I do." Lori licked another bit of ice cream. "I promised Hannah I'd do research into how they were merchandising."

"Is she going to be jealous if you cheat on her shop with another?" Patrick stroked his beard, looking comically serious. "It's important to negotiate these boundaries ahead of time."

Lori laughed. "Out of everything she had to say about me coming on this trip with you two, shopping for competing sex toys was *not* a problem."

Geoff shifted on the hard bench, his ice cream temporarily forgotten. "What did she have to say?"

"Oh, you know." Lori waved a hand, but she wasn't making eye contact. She looked out at the beach instead. "She just wants me to be happy."

Lori didn't elaborate further. She instead worked on finishing her ice cream with focused precision, and Geoff got distracted again by the methodical swipes of her tongue. Eventually, she got up and walked out on the sand, leaving an empty space on the bench between them. Geoff scooted closer to Patrick as he watched her approach the shore, the setting sun in the distance illuminating her silhouette against the water.

"You all right?" Patrick asked.

"Hmm?" Geoff tore his gaze away from Lori. "Yeah. I'm fine. Why?"

"You've got your deep-thinking face on." Patrick nudged him with an elbow, then leaned over to kiss Geoff's shoulder. "I just wanted to check in."

"I'm not doing any deep thinking." Geoff smiled. "Or trying not to, anyway. I'm trying to just be here, now."

Patrick's fingers skimmed the back of his neck, gentle and light. "I love you."

Geoff rested his hand on Patrick's knee. "I love you too."

"This is okay, right? Lori being here?" Patrick's expression showed that he knew this had been his idea, along with his fears about pushing Geoff into something. "I thought it would be fun."

"It's fun. Don't worry about it." Geoff gave Patrick's knee a squeeze. "Speaking of fun, looks like we're headed to the sex shop tonight." He waggled his eyebrows, making Patrick laugh.

"We'll have to pick up something new to try while we're here." Patrick's attention shifted to Geoff's mouth. Okay, Geoff could let himself get distracted this way, and leaned in to kiss Patrick deep and slow.

"Enough of that, you two." Lori's voice pulled Geoff out of the moment. She stood over them, beaming. "Sex toy shopping awaits."

Geoff rolled his eyes and let Lori pull him and Patrick to their feet.

18

Patrick hadn't intended on spending much money at the sex shop, but it was hard to resist the newest and shiniest, and he ended up buying a new prostate massager and a beautiful leather cock ring that Geoff had helpfully suggested for him. Geoff didn't buy anything, and Lori disappeared off into her own corners to chat with sales staff and, eventually, left with a bag. Patrick didn't know what she'd bought, but she kept giving them both cheeky smiles on the walk back to their B and B.

As soon as they got back into the room, Lori sprawled out on her back in the middle of the king-sized bed, her various bags spread out beside her. In addition to her sex shop purchases, she had also bought a P-town hoodie, a conch shell, and a bag of saltwater taffy that she insisted was for Hannah, Ben, and Mitchell even though she kept eating it.

Geoff sat next to Lori on the bed while Patrick slipped out of his shoes. "You tired?"

"Nah." She smiled at him. "I was hoping to try out some of

our new toys tonight." Propping herself up on her elbows, she nodded to Patrick. "At least, I'd love to see some of yours."

Patrick looked to his bag over on the desk. "Now?"

Lori shrugged. "If you want." Her impish smile indicated that she wanted it right now. "Unless *you're* too tired."

Patrick laughed. Like hell he'd turn down whatever was about to happen, no matter how tired he was. Fortunately, he was still pretty awake. "I think we should be talking about an even exchange. I have no idea what *you* bought."

Lori pursed her lips, thinking. "I guess that's fair. Geoff, what do you think?" She eyed him next to her.

"Seems fair to me."

Lori scooted up on the bed, leaving her bags piled there, and instead went over to the desk where Patrick had set his bag.

"Hey!" he protested as she went to open it up.

Lori paused. "Do you not want me to look?"

"No, you can look." Why was he getting embarrassed? After everything they'd done together so far, this shouldn't even register on the scale. Something about the intensity of her expression, though, was pushing some definite buttons inside him. He'd seen hints of Lori's dominance, the same traits of Geoff's that dropped him into his needy, submissive state, but she hadn't unleashed much of it in their previous encounters. This dangerous look, though, had him wondering if that was about to change.

She rummaged around and pulled out the leather cock ring first. They had helpfully already cut the tags off it at the store. It was black leather, handcrafted, with snaps for straps to go around his balls as well as his cock. Lori's tongue poked out of her mouth in focus as she examined it. Seeing the toy in her hands had blood rushing into Patrick's dick without him really being ready for it.

"Your husband here has some subby tendencies, huh?" Lori directed the question to Geoff.

"A few, yeah." Geoff smiled. "You've picked up on that?"

"Mmm." Lori was looking at Patrick again, and that look had his heart racing. Shit, nobody looked at him like that, except maybe Geoff. She was still holding the cock ring when she walked over to him, reached up, and took hold of a thick handful of his hair. He was several inches taller than her, but when she tugged him downward, he dropped to his knees automatically, and the moan slipping out of his throat was completely involuntary.

Lori wore a light sundress that swirled around her knees, and as he knelt there, she inched the hem up, revealing sheer blue panties that made his mouth water. He was at eye level with her pussy, dark curls barely visible through the sheer fabric, and god, he could *smell* her.

"Be a good boy, Patrick," she whispered.

Oh, fuck. His hands trembled as he reached up to bring her panties down, revealing her bare skin. This was different than before, the power dynamic clearly shifted, and he should be frightened by how much he wanted her in this moment. Specifically, how much he wanted to *obey*. She stepped out of the panties and then spread her legs apart, still holding up the hem of her dress. Her soft folds glistened, and he leaned in to bury his face between her legs.

He felt rather than heard her gasp, all senses muffled but the salty-sweet tang of her against his tongue and the scent of her arousal filling his nose. She tasted so good, and he reached up to cup her ass in his hands to bring her closer.

Immediately, she slapped his hands away, and he drew back in surprise to look up at her.

"No hands. Don't touch me, don't touch yourself. Hands palm-up on your thighs." She stared down at him, a playful, wicked grin on her lips, and fuck, he could fall in love with this woman.

The thought came and dissolved just as fast, and he scooted forward on his knees to devour her once more. Kneeling in this position, his hands resting palm-up on his thighs, helplessness coursed through him alongside adrenaline. Geoff was surely watching from the bed, and that had him throbbing hard in his pants. Fuck, he wished he was naked. He tried to focus on his task, on teasing her clit with his tongue, trying to get leverage to suck. The cold drag of leather against his cheek made him jump. She was sliding the cock ring over his face, teasing him with it, promising more, and it shouldn't be possible for him to be this hard with no one touching him.

Lori began to rock her hips against his face, riding him, and Patrick could stay like this forever. He wanted to please her, to make her come, and he couldn't do as much as he wanted in this helpless position even as the helplessness was turning him on further.

When she stepped back, releasing his head, he lost his balance and had to steady himself. He gulped in breaths of fresh air. Lori wasn't smiling anymore, her eyes heavy-lidded, mouth parted with ragged breaths. She let the hem of her dress drop and stepped back on wobbly legs.

"He's good," she said, not to Patrick, but to Geoff. Geoff looked as intense as he usually got when they were fooling around. Shit. The two of them giving off the same dominant energy might kill him. He might have gotten in over his head here.

Lori brushed Patrick's hair off his forehead. "Get naked," she commanded him. "You can stand."

He hurried to obey, his legs tense from kneeling for so long, and he had to steady himself on the wall as he got to his feet. While he was undressing, Lori went to Geoff, and she sat next to him to kiss him. They were murmuring to each other, whispering words he couldn't hear, and Geoff began to smile. Fuck, he knew that smile. Lori was still playing with the cock ring, leather straps wrapped around her fingers...until she handed the ring to Geoff. Then she grabbed her bags off the bed and headed toward the bathroom.

Confused, half-naked, Patrick paused in his undressing to raise an eyebrow at Geoff. Geoff gave him the same controlling stare. "I think she told you to get naked."

"Are you on her side now?"

Geoff tipped his head to the side. "Are you *against* the two of us having our way with you?"

Patrick let out all the air in his lungs with a huff, and he was probably blushing with his entire body now. Also, he couldn't get rid of the silly smile on his face as he stripped out of the rest of his clothes and stood naked before Geoff.

Geoff took Patrick's dick in hand with practiced ease, giving him a long, steady stroke from root to tip. Geoff knew just how to touch him, to twist lightly at the head, spreading his leaking slickness over the tight flushed skin. Patrick couldn't help thrusting his hips into Geoff's grip as he kept stroking, playing, teasing, and fuck, *fuck*, he wasn't going to be able to take much more of this.

Geoff, who knew him better than anyone, chose that minute to let him go. Patrick's cock bobbed once. "Here you go." Geoff held up the cock ring by one strap. "Your new outfit for the evening."

Patrick licked his suddenly dry lips and took the leather in hand. Its tight squeeze around the base of his cock felt... Well, it felt fucking *incredible*, a little snugger than he might like, but perfect for the discomfort that snugness caused. Geoff watched, breathing heavily, as Patrick wrapped the other strap around the base of his balls, and the final strap carefully up between them. Shit, that was tight, like a vise squeezing him, and he let out a choked moan as Geoff stroked the tightly stretched skin of his balls.

"That's damn sexy," Geoff breathed. "How does it feel?"

"It's a lot." Patrick was trying not to pant, and failing, his chest heaving. "It's like you're touching me all the time."

"And if I actually do touch you?" Geoff palmed the head of his cock again, and Patrick gasped. His balls tried to draw up, and couldn't, and the resulting pleasure-pain stole his breath away.

"Perfect." Geoff let go of his dick and brushed the hair off Patrick's forehead, leaning in to kiss him softly on the mouth. "You tell me if it's too much, okay?"

"Yeah. Okay." Patrick nodded frantically, although it would take a *lot* for him to want this to stop anytime soon.

"You think you can fuck me in that?"

Patrick's cock pulsed with the mere thought of it, and he nodded. "Maybe not as deep, but...I think so."

Geoff looked off toward the bathroom, into which Lori had disappeared, and then started undressing. "Good. Because I really want you to fuck me." He pulled Patrick in for a filthy openmouthed kiss, gripping the back of his neck. "You taste like Lori," he said against Patrick's mouth. "I like it."

Geoff stretched out on the bed and palmed his half-hard

cock, moving in long, slow strokes. He put one foot flat on the bed, bending his knee up, exposing the tender skin between his legs. "Lube's on the nightstand. Come get me ready."

Patrick loved this. He loved kneeling between Geoff's legs, his own cock throbbing and wrapped in leather, slicking his fingers with lube to press against Geoff's tight hole. His husband was still stroking his cock, watching Patrick's movements. When Patrick slid one finger inside, Geoff sighed.

The door to the bathroom creaked open, and Patrick froze at the sight of Lori. Holy fuck. She was completely naked, miles of beautiful golden-brown skin, and she wore a purple leather harness buckled around her hips. Protruding from that harness was a large, thick, baby blue silicone cock, and she was stroking it as if it were real.

"Jesus." Patrick's swear slipped from his lips, and he forgot what he was doing for a moment at the sight of her and the realization of everything yet to come. She was going to fuck him, wasn't she? She was going to fuck him while he fucked Geoff, while he wore this leather cock ring, and Patrick had to bite his lip to keep from whimpering.

When he looked back at Geoff, his husband was smiling. "Don't stop." Geoff kept stroking his cock. "We're gonna make this so good for you, babe."

Lori sauntered over to where they lay together on the bed, Patrick working another finger into Geoff's slick hole while trying to catch his breath. Patrick wanted to look at both of them, couldn't, and instead focused his attention on Geoff while Lori's gaze pressed against him like a touch. In his peripheral vision, she kept stroking the cock, *her* cock, easy and slow. It was so hot, he might combust right here.

"You all right there?" Lori's voice teased him. "You seem a little worked up."

"I'm going to have a heart attack, yeah." Patrick laughed, and it sounded punched out of him. "But I'm good." So far, anyway, while this was all theoretical, while the anticipation skittered under his skin.

"You want to take my cock?" she asked.

"God, yes." He couldn't look away. "That looks so good on you."

Geoff was smiling beneath him, working his dick steadily but not too fast. Patrick chose that moment to add a third finger, and Geoff moaned on the exhale. "That's so good."

Patrick probed gently, opening him up, the motions easy and familiar, until Geoff nodded. "I'm ready."

Patrick wiped his lube-slicked hands on a tissue, heart still pounding in his ribs. Geoff sat up.

"Lori," Geoff said, "I'm gonna open him up for you."

Lori nodded, pausing like she was deciding something. "Patrick, while he opens you up, come here and suck my cock."

That was…unexpectedly sexy and a little humiliating, but in the good way, and Patrick shuffled over on his hands and knees to where she stood next to the bed. This was twice he'd been putting his mouth on her, or near her, and wow, she knew just what got him. He opened his mouth and began to suck on the thick silicone dildo. She slid her fingers through the short hair at the back of his head, her touch soothing even as she fucked gently into his face.

Patrick moaned around the fake cock as Geoff's slick fingers began to press into him. Geoff wasn't taking his time; he knew exactly what Patrick could take, knew how desperate Patrick might be, and he was working him open quick and dirty, just how he liked. His cock throbbed in its leather wrappings. Each time his erection flagged a bit, the tightness of the leather made him hard all over again, a reminder of what he was doing here. And, yeah, he loved sex, he loved experimenting, but this was *way* above anything he'd done before, and he was already trying not to fall apart at the seams.

"Such a good boy." Lori's crooning words pressed buttons deep in his gut. Something low and hot curled there, desire and need and lust that threatened to overwhelm him, make him sob and beg. He might be able to come like this. Geoff was pressing three fingers against his prostate, rubbing over it with each slick thrust of his hand, and if anyone touched his cock, he could possibly come all over this bed. The silicone in his mouth muffled most of his noises, which was incredible as well, and damn, maybe he was kinkier than he'd thought.

Geoff slid his fingers carefully out, and Lori withdrew, and Patrick was left empty from both ends and reeling at the sudden loss of sensation.

"Here we go." Lori pressed two fingers into his mouth, and oh, that was *another* kink he hadn't known about. "You're gonna be so good for us, aren't you?" She slid her fingers out.

Patrick nodded, not trusting his voice to speak. He looked between Geoff and Lori and forced the words out. "How do... how do you want me?"

Geoff stretched out on his back with two pillows beneath his hips. "I want to watch you as she fucks you." He grabbed the lube again and handed it to Patrick. "Come here."

Patrick positioned himself between Geoff's legs, the cock ring still pressing too tight against his tender skin, and yeah, they were gonna leave it on him, the pressure probably the only thing staving off his imminent need to come. Even so, he had to move slowly as he lined up his cock and carefully pressed into Geoff's ass. God, the tightness gripped around him, slick and wet and ready. He could only go a bit more than halfway before the ring stopped him, but it was enough for now. He caught his breath, propped up on hands and knees, his legs spread, and held himself trembling right there.

"So good." Geoff brushed a hand over Patrick's cheek, tender, soft. "I can't wait to watch you take her cock."

Patrick swallowed, anticipation and anxiousness and excitement tangling up inside him. Had he ever taken a cock that size before? Maybe, maybe not; certainly not recently. It was bigger than Geoff, bigger than him, and he might be ready for it, but he still trembled. The bed dipped behind him as Lori climbed up, and then her lube-slicked fingers teased around his already-wet hole.

"I'll go slow," she murmured, one hand lightly on his hip. "I've never done this before."

Patrick laughed, as much as he could laugh with this tension building in his body. "That makes all of us."

He tried to stay relaxed as she pressed against him, slippery and absolutely huge, and then suddenly, his body yielded all at once and the head was inside. It was *enormous*, and he cried out in reflex but not in pain.

"Are you all right?" Lori asked.

"Yeah." He sounded strangled, but he wasn't lying; the pleasure building in him was just too much for words. Geoff moved beneath him, withdrawing and then pushing back, fucking his ass onto Patrick's cock. They'd barely started, and Patrick felt like he was going to explode. "More," he gasped.

He could hear Lori's smile in her words. "Ask nicely."

Oh, fuck. "Please go deeper."

She did, the next slide easier, giving him another few inches that opened him right up. His body tried to clench around her, tried to close up, and couldn't, and that was... breathtaking. Beneath him, Geoff started moving again, short thrusts that rubbed the sensitive swollen head of Patrick's cock. Lori wasn't fully in, and he wanted more, and knew he had to ask.

"Please," he repeated. "Please, fill me all the way."

Lori smoothed a hand over his back, slow circles, before gripping his hips with both hands and pressing the whole cock inside him in one long, steady stroke.

Patrick cried out, louder and harsher, and if it weren't for the cock ring, he'd have come right then. "Oh, god," he sobbed, and he might have been crying.

"Are you all right?" Geoff asked, concerned.

Patrick nodded frantically; he was better than all right, he was *incandescent*, he was beyond words. "Fuck, I need to move. I need to *move*."

"Here." Geoff's hands fumbled between them, around the base of Patrick's cock, and then suddenly, the leather came away, and blood surged into his cock as his balls drew up snug with his body. Holy shit, holy fuck, holy everything, Patrick began to thrust into Geoff with long, uncontrollable movements. Every shift of his hips moved Lori's large cock in and out of him, until she was fucking him as well, and he was filling Geoff while also being filled up, and he couldn't find words for the pressure inside his body. It wasn't like the way an orgasm usually built, spreading outward from his groin; his entire body seemed to be burning up at once. He was making noises, crying out and moaning and gasping, and he couldn't stop, as the burning finally took him over and his senses whited out at once.

Everything fell away, and he was lost.

He didn't feel what happened next, but when he opened his eyes, he was lying on his side, spent, empty, and Lori and Geoff were both cuddled up to him. Lori had slipped out of the harness, left it lying off on the floor, and she was stroking his hair while Geoff held him. Geoff was still hard, pressed against his stomach, and despite how much he wanted to do so, Patrick didn't really have time to reciprocate in the intensity of that moment.

"Holy hell," Patrick said, and Geoff laughed.

"Thank god. I thought we might have lost you there."

"I might be permanently altered." Patrick flopped over onto his back. "I'm a mess."

"We're all messes." Lori smiled.

Patrick nodded. "Can I..." He was too wiped out to do anything else, but that didn't mean the night was over. "Can I watch you two fuck?"

Geoff and Lori looked at each other, both smiling, and each shrugged at the same time. "I'd like that," Lori said, after a pause. "I mean, I could also put the strap-on back on, if you want."

Geoff laughed. "Maybe next time." He paused, the smile slipping, and oh. There might not be a next time. Patrick hadn't thought of that. Now, though, with the aftermath of emotions crashing through him, the possibility loomed over them all. He had to put it aside.

Geoff fumbled for a condom on the nightstand as Lori climbed over to him, and suddenly they were kissing, devouring each other, and Patrick lay there watching. They moved fast. They had to be as turned-on as he had been. He was able to lie there and enjoy as Lori helped Geoff with the condom, slicking it down over his cock, and then climbed gracefully on top of him to take him all the way into her pussy. They moved together, breathing together, moaning and gasping in unison. Patrick reached down carefully below Lori, below Geoff's leg, and found the wet slick of Geoff's hole. He traced the outer lip, swollen from their sex, and Geoff whimpered and grasped the sheets beneath him with one hand while the other found Lori's clit.

Lori came first, seizing up and crying out, and Geoff followed soon after, groaning as he emptied himself into the condom. Fuck, Patrick wanted to watch this over and over again. Afterward, they would need to clean up, to shower and change and come down from this ridiculous high, but right now, all Patrick could think was that he did not want this to be the last time.

19

"There we go!"

Patrick's triumphant cry pulled Lori's attention away from the horizon, where she'd been slowly watching the sun sink below the waves. Patrick sat back on his heels and gestured proudly at the fire he'd built on the beach. "Look!"

"Very nice." Lori was more entertained by the way Patrick nudged Geoff to get his praise too. Geoff put his phone in his pocket and gave Patrick the appropriate accolades, although Patrick rolled his eyes.

"You two are no fun."

"We are *very* fun." Lori scooted closer to the fire as the flames licked into the dry wood. They'd purchased a few bundles after Geoff secured the burning permit that morning, enough wood to keep the fire going into the night. Now, with the last traces of sun slipping below the horizon, the first twinkling stars came into view in the blue-gray sky overhead. Lori lay back on the beach blanket they'd stretched beside the fire.

She could see the appeal of P-town, or at least the appeal of visiting it with Patrick and Geoff. They knew all the best places to eat and shop, the can't-miss stuff, and they didn't drag her out of bed in the single digits. Even Patrick, who was the earliest riser out of all of them, had snuck out on his own this morning and came back with breakfast sandwiches, pastry, and coffee from the Provincetown Portuguese Bakery just as Lori was waking up. They'd eaten it sitting on the big king-sized bed in their pajamas, sunlight and fresh air streaming in from the porch. Today, after a day of shopping and eating, they'd come to the beach for a sunset bonfire.

Flames crackled, the heat radiating into the soles of Lori's feet. She wiggled her toes and sighed.

Geoff stretched out next to her. "Nice, right?"

"So nice." She closed her eyes. "I could sleep right here."

"The tide might come in and wash you away." Patrick's voice made her open her eyes. He was settling into the space on Geoff's other side. "I think we're high enough, but it's hard to tell."

"I never come to the ocean." Lori pushed up onto her elbows to look out past the fire at the waves lapping the shore. "I should swim. Or at least put my feet in the water."

Without waiting for them, Lori shimmied out of her shorts and tank top to the bikini underneath and ran into the ocean. The water was breathtakingly cold. It was too early in the season for swimming, probably, and she paused with the water lapping her knees, ready to turn around and go back. Behind her, their laughter echoed across the sand.

"Cold?" Patrick called.

Lori glanced back over her shoulder, where they'd both sat up to watch her. "It's freezing!"

"You want to come back by the fire?" Geoff asked.

She paused, braced herself, and then ran full-tilt into the waves. "Fuck, fuck, fuck," she chanted under her breath before diving beneath the freezing cold water. All the air escaped her lungs in a huff, and she popped back up again, water sheeting off her. On the shore, Geoff and Patrick were cheering and laughing. She dipped back down beneath the surface once more. This time, the water didn't take her breath away quite as much. It was still cold, but she could tolerate it. She surfaced and floated onto her back, putting her feet up in front of her, toes peeking out of the water. The waves carried her up and down like being rocked to sleep.

She could get used to this. Vacation with the guys, swimming in the ocean, good food and good company. For the first time since she'd applied for those jobs in New York, the thought came to mind that maybe it wouldn't be the worst thing in the world if they didn't respond.

When the sky grew darker, and the inky-black waters blended with the sand, Lori emerged from the ocean into the cool night. The fire provided welcome warmth as she wrapped herself in a towel and huddled down at her corner of the blanket. Patrick stacked a few more logs onto the pile, and one of the burned pieces cracked, sending a shower of sparks up into the sky.

Geoff pressed his hand to Lori's leg. "You're freezing."

"I'll warm up." She held her hands up to the fire, letting the heat soak into her skin, rubbing her palms together. When that wasn't enough warmth, she pulled her baggy sweatshirt down over her head and removed her wet bikini top from underneath it. "There. That's better." She sighed, finally warming up, finally relaxing again.

Patrick pointed out constellations as they appeared in the growing darkness, tossing out some astronomy facts, and

Geoff filled in the gaps with explaining some of the mythology behind them, and even though Lori already knew some of this, she didn't mind listening to the two of them. She let their words fade into a low background hum of banter before the conversation died down, leaving them all in contemplative silence staring at the fire or back up at the stars.

"Thanks," Lori said into the quiet.

Geoff and Patrick both looked over at her, the firelight illuminating half their faces, casting shadows across the rest.

"For inviting me along. For having me on your trip." She hadn't really said it before now, and it needed to be said aloud. "I know this is something you two usually just do together. Inviting me into that…it means a lot."

They had to know she wasn't just talking about the weekend.

Geoff spoke slowly, like he did when he was thinking deeply about something. "It's nice having you here. You add something new."

Lori looked into the fire. "I've been told I do that."

"It's not just because of the sex." Geoff was getting direct, now, and he put his hand on her bare knee. "It's because it's you."

Lori ducked her head, unable to keep the smile from her lips. "Come on, stop it. You're killing me."

"He's not wrong," Patrick said, and Lori glanced over. "We wouldn't have you here with us if we didn't want you here. It's special. You're special."

The direct comments had her squirming. She didn't want to do this here on the beach; she didn't want to feel this tumult of emotions. "Thanks. But can we just not get sappy?"

Geoff leaned in to kiss her cheek. "What's wrong with sappy?"

Lori blew a raspberry at him, making Patrick laugh and Geoff wipe his face. It was a deflection, sure, but she wasn't ready to face this kind of emotion. She wasn't ready to confront anything other than the happy times together. Wasn't that enough? Why did they have to go and bring feelings into it?

Even though this wasn't their fault. She couldn't deny how easily she fell into step with them, emotionally and physically; her interests overlapped theirs, and having the two of them together seemed like a perfect blend of everything she wanted from a relationship.

Relationship. The word settled into her mind like a stone. Obviously, technically, every ongoing series of interactions with someone was a relationship, in the strictest application of the term. But she had somehow gotten herself mixed up in a capital-R relationship, and as more than an accessory, to boot. The therapist in her pushed for the most helpful solutions: *Clear the air. Establish some new ground rules. Give all of you some distance.* But the sappy romantic inside her resisted, because right now, they were sitting at the tip of the Cape around a beach bonfire, and she was happy. She didn't want to ruin the moment.

Tomorrow, when they headed home, she would bring them firmly back to reality.

Tonight, though?

Tonight, reality could wait.

BACK IN THEIR ROOM, Patrick was the one to bring up the idea that their night didn't have to be over.

"A nightclub?" Lori was still wrapped in a towel, sand

gritty between her toes. "I'll pass. I have to wash my hair, and I have a long date with that hot shower." At their mutual hesitation, she waved them off. "Go without me! Seriously. You don't need me to have fun. Go have a date, just the two of you. You've been only dating *me* for weeks now."

Geoff protested a bit, but Patrick eventually convinced him, and they changed into nicer clothes and left Lori alone in the B and B room. She took a steaming hot shower and deep conditioned her hair, and then in the quiet of the empty room, carefully tended her curls. The process soothed her jangle of nerves and calmed the restless part of her thinking of their triad and insisting, *You could have this.*

Afterward, Lori sat on the balcony with her phone and a wine cooler from the fridge and listened to the nightlife sounds of Provincetown. Music echoed up to her from a few streets away. Did Patrick and Geoff have a club they always went to, or did they try someplace new all the time? Probably one regular place. They seemed to fall into familiar patterns everywhere they went. She was the disruptor, shaking up those patterns.

The sweet, cold wine soothed like the cool night air, and Lori savored both for another minute before checking her phone. She had avoided it today, wanting to be in the present, but she couldn't deny she was also pretending the outside world didn't exist. Now, with the place to herself for a few hours, she scrolled through her email.

The sender caught her attention first, then the subject line: *Scheduling interview.* She speed-read the email, then read it again, more slowly, making sure she understood everything. Excitement and dismay warred inside her, which made no sense. This should be just excitement. She'd had her sights on one job above all else, one organization in particular, and they wanted to meet with her in person because she "seemed like she would be a great fit."

Lori sat with the phone in her lap for so long that the screen went to sleep, and she didn't wake it up again. Someone was laughing down the block, the sound echoing up to her on the balcony. No, not one person. Two people laughing together. A couple. Their words were distorted, and she couldn't understand them, but whatever they were saying was making them both laugh even harder. Lori closed her eyes. The breeze blew past her face, colder than she expected.

She unlocked her phone and turned her attention back to the screen. Thumbs sliding over the tiny keyboard, she composed a reply.

GEOFF WAS cozy and did not want to get out of this bed, especially with the rain lashing the windows, but something felt...off. He blinked heavy eyelids against the light—gray with the storm, but still bright enough to make him squint—and reached out to feel only empty sheets. Last night came flooding back to him, coming home in the wee hours, still a little drunk, and finding Lori asleep in the pull-out sofa bed instead of the king-sized expanse they'd shared the night before. He'd slept with Patrick, of course, but now Patrick was gone wherever he went in the morning, and the bed was empty. Geoff reached over to the nightstand for his phone, fumbling with sleep-numb fingers, and read the text Patrick had sent from twenty minutes ago. *Breakfast*, it said. Damn, who would even willingly go out in this rain? Patrick, apparently. Geoff loved the hell out of that man, but they were quite different people, weren't they?

Geoff propped himself up on his elbows and peered over at Lori, curled up under the thin blanket on the sofa bed. She had her back to him, body curved like a parenthesis into the empty space between herself and the glass doors. For a moment, his heart pressed against his ribs like it was just too big for the space.

"Lori," he said aloud into the quiet room.

She grunted once but didn't move, and he repeated her name. This time, she rolled over, the bedsprings creaking, and gave him an annoyed glare from beneath the ridge of her hair bonnet. He beckoned, and her frown deepened.

"Come here." He patted the empty bed beside him. "It's lonely."

Lori pursed her lips. She seemed to be making up her mind, her expression uncertain and grumpy from being woken up, and he didn't know why he wasn't holding her in his arms right now. Finally, she slid out of the bed, her expression still surly, and padded over to slide into the bed. "This is a bad idea," she said, but she curled up into him anyway, backing herself up against his chest.

"Why is this a bad idea?" Geoff couldn't fathom any reason why she shouldn't be right here, pressed snugly against him. Her skin smelled sweet, and he nuzzled into her neck, breathing her in.

"It just is." She didn't give him more of an answer than that, but she let herself be held, eventually relaxing into his embrace. With her warm body against him, Geoff's eyelids grew heavy, and before he could form another complete thought, he slipped back into sleep.

He woke some time later with a warm hand rubbing his back. "I've got breakfast," Patrick said, voice low and soothing, like Geoff was a skittish animal.

Geoff opened his eyes. The light was brighter now, but still gray, and the rain continued lashing down outside. He rolled away from Lori, who was lightly snoring in his arms, to see his husband kneeling on the bed with an unbearably tender expression on his face. Patrick's hair and beard were wet, but he must have changed since coming back to the room, since the rest of him was dry.

"I got lonely," Geoff explained, but Patrick shook his head and smiled.

"It's fine. You're fine. You want some breakfast?"

Geoff nodded, rubbing sleepily at his eyes. He reluctantly left Lori snoozing and joined Patrick at the table in the corner for egg sandwiches that were somehow still hot. "Why did you go out in that rain?"

"I told you. Breakfast." Patrick smiled. His smile cracked open all the uncertain parts inside Geoff, and god, he loved this man, and he said it out loud.

"I love you too," Patrick replied, his words easy and simple, and maybe it could be like this. This easy, simple thing, like hot breakfast on a rainy morning, like a beautiful woman sleeping in their bed, like the way he and Patrick continued to come back together as though they were inexorably bound.

"I'm sad we have to go back today." Geoff hated the end of this weekend, hated it more for the way this thing between the three of them would have to end now. Provincetown was a blissful escape from whatever else the world had in store for them. Going home didn't usually feel this painful.

"You won't be happy to go back to your own bed?" Patrick asked.

Geoff took a bite of his sandwich, chewed and swallowed. "I guess." He looked out at the rain.

"You ever think about moving?" Patrick asked.

"What, like to Provincetown?" Geoff shook his head. "We'd never be able to afford it."

Patrick frowned, but didn't comment.

Geoff took another bite of sandwich. "Thank you for breakfast. This is delicious."

Patrick looked over at Lori, still asleep. "I should wake her up. She'll want a hot sandwich."

Geoff watched as Patrick climbed into bed with Lori, carefully easing himself down behind her. He kissed her cheek, like this was the most natural, intimate connection, and Geoff didn't feel sad or lost or lonely at all. This was *right*, somehow. How could something this complicated be right? And after today, it would end, and he couldn't pretend to play house anymore.

Lori took half of an egg sandwich and almost a full cup of coffee to wake all the way up enough to speak, and then it was to thank Patrick for going out in the rain for breakfast. She was adorable like this, even morning-grumpy and barely verbal, and Geoff couldn't keep from sneaking glances at her as she ate.

"Seriously, though." She gestured to the glass doors. "What is this shit? And why would you go out in it?"

"I like the rain," Patrick said. "Geoff does too. He goes running in the rain all the time."

"You're both ridiculous." She unfolded the foil from more of her sandwich and took another bite. "Not looking forward to heading back to reality today." Almost as an afterthought, she added, "I've got an interview in New York this week."

Geoff paused, and then realized he was frozen and forced himself to take a sip of coffee. "One of the organizations you applied to?"

"My first choice." She wasn't making eye contact with them, looking instead out the windows at the rain. "It's still a long shot. I don't know. But I guess it's progress."

"Good for you," Patrick said, with the same cheerful tone he used when he was trying to persuade Geoff to snap out of some funk. "That's exciting."

Exciting, really? Geoff tried to read if Patrick meant it, but he seemed so sincere. *Of course, he's sincere.* Geoff chided his inner voice. Patrick was happy for Lori, and Geoff should be too.

"Yeah," Geoff echoed. "It's what you want, right?"

"I think so." She finished her sandwich, and they all sat in silence for a few minutes.

I think so, she'd said. Not *yes, definitely,* but *I think so.* Geoff shouldn't be happy about the spark of hope blossoming in his chest at that. Hope for what? There was nothing to hope for.

Lori finished her sandwich and stood up immediately, tossing the foil into the trash. "My stuff is everywhere. If we're going to check out of here by noon, I have to start packing." She hauled her suitcase out of the corner. "Packing's the worst, isn't it? All these signs that things are ending."

Geoff had nothing to add to that, so he gave her a few words of agreement, and grabbed his clothes to go get dressed where he wouldn't have to watch her pack and wouldn't have to avoid Patrick's too-sympathetic eyes.

20

L ori sat on one of the benches in Bryant Park, the sun filtering through the shade trees overhead and dappling her legs and the sidewalk in mottled patterns. Today was beautiful. It was the perfect day, as far as New York perfect days went: warm but not hot, with a light breeze that felt more like a Mapleton spring than being in the heart of the city. To her left, the back of the New York Public Library rose up against the blue sky. She was going to read so many books here. No matter how stressed she got, she could soothe herself in a library. After she moved, she was going to find the best nooks in the NYPL to sit and read. When she was reading, she wouldn't be lonely.

She had been putting off this phone call for a while, but she shouldn't put it off any longer. She pushed the name on her contacts list and the ringer echoed in her ear.

"Lori?"

"Hi, Ma." Something eased out of Lori at her mom's voice, warm and gentle and so close in her ear. "How are you?"

"Oh, you know. The usual. Damn Beverly used up all the

data on the shared plan because she forgot to turn on Wi-Fi watching her shows, and she's being stubborn about paying for it. Irene keeps leaving her bras hanging up in the shower even though all of us have to use it, and I'm tired of moving her lacy bits around…"

Lori smiled at her mom's rant about the three "aunts," closing her eyes for a moment so she could pretend her mom was next to her on this bench, bitching about the women she loved and lived with. Women who had become her mom's family. Women who had cared for her and supported her beyond the way any individual relationship would. Lori made appropriate noises of surprise, disgust, and approval at the right pauses in the story, and waited for her mom to wind down.

"And what about you? It's been a long time, Lori. I was starting to think you'd never call."

"It's been barely a week, and you can call me too, you know."

Her mom made a "tsk" noise. "What's the news? What are the updates?"

"Ma, can I ask you something?" Lori hadn't meant to ask, and the question just slipped out.

"Of course, honey, you can ask me anything. Are you all right?" Suddenly, her mom was all concern. "Do you need help?"

"No, I'm fine, I'm fine. I just…" Shit, she hadn't really conceived of how to phrase this question. "You know about my dissertation and my research. You know all the things I've been studying all these years."

A long pause. "Of course, I do, hon."

This was difficult to talk about. They never brought it up,

the hidden secret that she *knew* without anyone addressing. "How'd you make it work, all these years? With...my aunts."

"Why are you asking this now? You're done your research. Thought you'd bring it up back when you were first studying all this, but you've got your degree, and now you're asking?"

Her mom didn't sound angry, just confused, and Lori didn't want to get too deep into it. She played with the hem of her dress, rubbing the lacy edge between her fingers. "I didn't want to pry. But now...it's something I've been wondering."

Her mom sighed. Lori could picture her sighing, pushing her glasses up the bridge of her nose with one finger, giving a long-suffering look to the heavens. "They're family, Lori, as much as you and your brother. I don't know how we make it work. We just do. We love each other, and we sacrifice for each other, and we support each other. And when I want someone to turn to, one of them is here for me. And I'm here for them. That's what a relationship is. It's what a marriage should be. Just because we're not like other families, doesn't mean it's not real."

Lori let out a breath. "Do you think it's ridiculous, getting involved with more than one person?"

"Lori, baby, do you want to give me some specifics, or are we just going to live in this land of hypotheticals?"

She should have known she couldn't keep dancing around the actual facts forever without being called on it. "I'm trying to make some decisions. I'm not ready to talk about all of it yet. But I promise, when I do, I'll let you know."

"All right, all right. Anything you can tell me at all?"

"I'm in New York right now. They offered me the job."

"What?" Her mom's exclamation, loud and surprised, made Lori pull the phone away from her ear. "You bury news like that, asking all this cryptic shit? Honey, that's incredible! Good for you. You must be so excited."

"I am. I am. It's just…it's big. I'd be moving, uprooting everything. I guess I'm a little nervous." She hated admitting it out loud. "I've been chasing this down for so long, it feels strange to be hesitant about it."

Another pause at the other end of the line. "You're worried about leaving some people behind?"

That was one way of putting it. "Yeah."

"Does leaving mean leaving them for good? Distance doesn't mean endings, you know. Distance might just mean a challenge."

Lori had thought about that, about what her life might look like if she tried to keep this going from New York. It wasn't across the globe, after all. When she pictured Geoff and Patrick together at home, though, and her living hours away, it seemed like endless heartache.

"I don't want to do a distance thing."

"These people you're worried about leaving behind, how do they feel about you going?"

This was getting into a dangerous borderline of specificity. "I think they probably want me to stay."

"Yup, sounds about right." Her mom sighed. "Sweetheart, I'm not going to tell you what to do. You're grown. But you know I'll support you no matter what. Whatever you decide, I'm here. I've made some decisions in my lifetime that other people didn't agree with, and I know what it's like. Sometimes there's no good choice."

"Thanks." Even those words made her feel a little better.

"Did you accept the job yet?"

"I told them I need to think about it. There's a lot to figure out. Even if I take it, I'll need time to pack, to find an apartment, to actually move…" She trailed off. *Even if I take it.* It wasn't a done deal. She could just walk away from this and stay in Mapleton. Sure, it wasn't her dream, but it wasn't *terrible.*

Were Geoff and Patrick enough to override the baseline of "not terrible"?

"Keep me up to date, all right?" her mom asked. "I want to be in the loop."

"I'll keep you in the loop." Lori smiled. "Promise."

GEOFF HADN'T BEEN the same since they got back from Provincetown last weekend, and even if Patrick hadn't been able to tell by his general mopey demeanor, tonight's dinner at the Mapleton Pub was enough to signal it loud and clear.

"This is nice, isn't it?" Geoff asked, again, like he hadn't asked it twice before during this very same dinner.

"It is." Patrick smiled. "Are you having a nice time too?"

"I am." Geoff nodded, then paused. "Did I already say all this?"

"Twice."

Geoff sighed, noisy and dramatic, the way he could be sometimes that still made Patrick smile with fondness. "I don't know where my mind is tonight. I'm all over the place."

"It's summer vacation, Geoff. Maybe you're just struggling to transition into it." They both knew that wasn't the reason, but Patrick didn't need to make Geoff confront any of his feelings tonight. He would do it enough on his own, given the time.

Geoff, though, wasn't having it, and he adjusted his glasses with a frown. "Patrick, I have a PhD in two things:

African history and your bullshit. Please don't patronize me."

Patrick ducked his head. "Sorry. I didn't want you to have to go through your feelings right now."

"It's silly, right?" Geoff set his knife and fork down. "I'm so happy with the two of us. Why do I keep missing Lori?"

"It's okay to miss Lori. I miss her too." They all knew her putting some distance between them was healthy, especially after Provincetown, but that didn't mean he particularly liked it. And Geoff was broadcasting his dislike loudly enough that she could probably *hear* it. "But this gives us some time to focus on us. And that's probably good."

"I guess so." Geoff took a drink of water, then a much larger drink of beer. "I read the books she loaned me, and I know all about new relationship energy and that sort of thing. I know these confusing feelings are normal. But they suck."

Patrick laughed. He couldn't help it; Geoff didn't usually use imprecise words like that. Geoff knew he wasn't being laughed at, and he smiled in response as well. Patrick reached across the table and took Geoff's free hand. "I agree. But can we just focus on us for now? You and me. We're still at the core of this." That center relationship was his rock.

"You've still got your gig tomorrow night, right?" Geoff asked. "I'm looking forward to it."

"Yeah. I'm glad you're coming." Patrick's mood turned a degree south. He wished Geoff hadn't brought up the band. The band made him think of music, made him think of New York, made him think of Lori. He changed the subject. "What's on tap for you next week?"

Geoff stared off into the middle distance, thinking. "I haven't scheduled anything, honestly."

"No summer plans? Geoff, that's not like you." Patrick

kept his tone light, teasing, but this was *very* out of character for Geoff, who liked to have multiple irons in the fire at any given time.

"I know. I thought I might do some research, try to get something out for peer review before the fall semester starts. But nothing else has really been calling me lately. I need...a new challenge." Geoff seemed to want to say something else, his mouth opening, but he closed it just as fast, and Patrick didn't push.

"New game?" He hadn't seen Geoff playing anything lately.

"Maybe. There's tons of stuff out now, plus the Steam Summer Sale. Maybe I'll pick up something new." Geoff reached for his beer glass, paused, and then held it up. "But for now, it's us. And that's nice. Right?"

Patrick clinked his beer glass with Geoff's. "Of course."

NINE POSSUM THURSDAY'S set was nearly half over before Geoff spotted Lori in the crowd. There were so many people here, and his eyes were mostly focused on Patrick, as usual, but Lori's electric energy caught his attention at some point, and then he couldn't look away. She'd come to watch Patrick play. She really did like his music, or she liked him; Geoff wasn't sure which it was and also didn't know that it mattered. And she must have known that Geoff would be here too, but she hadn't come over to him. So Geoff let her have her space.

Near the end of the set, though, a warm hand pressed against his arm, and he turned to look right into her dark, sparkling eyes. "Hi." Her smile seemed reserved.

"Hi," he replied.

He hadn't seen her all week, and their texts had been pretty sparse as well. He knew she had gone to New York for the interview, but he hadn't asked how it went and she hadn't told.

He looked over to where she'd been standing. "I saw you over there a little while ago. Figured you might want your space."

She shrugged. "I thought so too, but it turns out I don't. Want to dance?"

Maybe they should talk, but he didn't want to, so he simply nodded and took her in his arms as the next song began. He could get absorbed in this kind of movement, whirling around, dipping her and spinning her out on his arm. Laughter bubbled up naturally, and some of the tensions inside him dissolved away. He hadn't realized he'd been carrying those tensions this week.

The band switched to a slower ballad. Lori moved into his arms without hesitation, taking his hand in hers. He wrapped one arm around her waist to hold her close against him. Maddy was singing something about a sailor lost, but Geoff wasn't listening. The scent of Lori's hair filled his nose, the softness of her breasts against his chest, the heat of her wherever they touched. It had only been days, but he missed this. *Oh*, how he missed this.

She tipped her head back to look at him, and he didn't think, didn't hesitate; he leaned down and kissed her.

Fuck, the taste of her. His hand tightened on hers, reflexively, and the fingernails on her other hand pressed sharp points into his shoulder blade. Her lips parted beneath his, softening, and his tongue swept against hers. It was as if they were alone in this room. No one else existed beyond this kiss, this moment, this driving need that swelled up in his blood and consumed him. The need to fuck her, yes, but something more, something deep and profound, a yearning that scared the shit out of him.

He pulled away, tearing his lips from hers, and the effort *hurt*. "Stay." He spoke before he could think not to.

Her eyes closed, and she exhaled slowly, shakily before opening them again. "I care about you." He read the words on her lips, even though she was speaking so quietly, he could barely hear her over the music. Then she stepped back, glancing once at the stage where Patrick was still playing. Her hand fell from Geoff's grip. "I shouldn't have come," she said, louder this time. "It's too soon." And she turned and shoved through the crowd toward the door.

Geoff inhaled, exhaled, and there wasn't enough air in this room. It was too tight, too warm, too close. The song ended, people had begun to clap, and the band took up an encore. This song was a raucous, rowdy folk tune that half the room seemed to know the words to, but Geoff didn't hear anything beyond the low, echoing beat of his heart.

After the show, the lights came up and the people filtered out, and Geoff found Patrick in the green room packing up with the band. Whatever look Geoff was giving, it had Patrick setting his things down immediately to lead Geoff out back into the alley behind the venue, the door slamming shut behind them.

"Hey." Patrick touched Geoff's shoulders. "What's going on? Are you okay?"

Geoff nodded, even though his blood was thrumming with heat and need and frustration.

"Really?"

Geoff paused, stopped nodding, and shook his head. "I'm

not—I need something. I need you." He dragged Patrick in, pulling him in for a kiss, harsh and scorching and with too much teeth. Patrick was here, he was solid, he wasn't leaving, and Geoff could use this to forget.

Patrick kissed him back, rough and hungry, and Geoff spun him around and slammed him up against the brick wall. He *needed*, and he wanted to *take*.

"Easy." Patrick put his hands on Geoff's chest, steadying him, breaking their kiss. In the dim light filtering over the fence into their alleyway, his eyes were wide. "Take it easy. I'm here." He licked his lips, already plump and soft from their kisses. "Is this about Lori? I saw you two together."

Patrick's tone wasn't accusing, but Geoff's stab of guilt made him pause, loosening his grip on the lapels of Patrick's shirt. He had kissed her without Patrick. And even though they'd said it was fine, even though Patrick had kissed her before, this was a first for him, and he was all mixed up in so many ways.

"It's okay," Patrick said. "I don't mind. How was she? Is she all right? We haven't—"

"It's out of hand." Geoff shook his head. "I asked her to stay. I want her to stay."

Patrick tipped his head, expression going soft. "Oh, hon."

"I know," Geoff cut him off. "I know she's not going to stay. I know I need some space from her, for a while. I feel... lost, and shaken, and I don't like this, Patrick. I need—" What? What did he need? He'd come here to find Patrick, to get this grounding.

"You need to forget for a little while?" Patrick asked, his voice soft. He was pressed up against this brick wall, his face all angles and shadows, and Geoff was still holding his lapels. When Geoff didn't answer, Patrick grabbed him behind the neck and pulled him in for another harsh, brutal kiss.

Geoff needed *this*, and he stepped in to press Patrick more aggressively into the wall, crushing him against it. He was hard, so hard, and it didn't make *sense* for him to be so fucking turned on, confused and lost and wanting more than he could have. But Patrick was right there, sweetly yielding.

Patrick touched Geoff's cock through his jeans, and Geoff jumped and pulled back. "What?" he mouthed, looking around them at the deserted alley, realizing again where they were and what they were doing.

Patrick palmed his length, gripping him through the fabric, and Geoff closed his eyes. "I can't do that," Geoff said, even though he wanted so much to keep going. "I can't use you like that. I love you."

"Shh." Patrick tugged open Geoff's button-fly jeans, buttons sliding free one by one. "Put me on my knees, sweetheart."

Patrick's sweet, hot mouth around Geoff's cock made him sob, a harsh, broken sound, and he pressed his knuckles into his mouth to stop it. He slammed a hand forward against the brick wall to support himself, eyes falling closed. Maybe this was wrong, but he didn't have to think, didn't have to feel, could focus on the bone-deep lust consuming him. Patrick knew just what to do, how to stroke all of Geoff's hot spots to get him off in no time, and Geoff was barely able to catch a few breaths before the need spiraling up inside him crested and took him over in a sharp-edged climax. It was pleasure, yes, but also relief, the temporary absence of thought. Patrick swallowed around him, mouth soft and wet and perfect and exactly what Geoff needed right now. Geoff looked down, saw Patrick's hand moving fast over his own length, stroking himself to the edge before he tensed up with a muffled moan and came over his fist and the ground.

"God, Patrick." Geoff stepped back, still reeling, his emotions tumbling down to something like equilibrium. Patrick still knelt there at his feet, so good, so perfect. Geoff didn't deserve this man. He pulled Patrick up, laving the back of Patrick's hand with his tongue, licking him clean of his own mess. "I'm sorry," Geoff said, and they kissed, messy and slick and full of too much emotion for the moment to contain. "I'm a mess. We're a mess."

"It's okay." Patrick kissed his knuckles. "Let's go home."

MIDWAY THROUGH GEOFF'S third attempt at an apology that night, Patrick finally put his hand over his husband's mouth. "Geoff. Stop."

Geoff had the sense to look abashed this time. "I can't help it," he said, words muffled against Patrick's palm.

Patrick released him. They'd come home and showered, and now that they were cozied up together on the couch, Geoff wanted to keep going back to apologizing for his actions. "I don't want to hear it. Besides, you and I both know I'm apparently a filthy cock slut."

Geoff smiled at the words, but it was a sad smile. "It's probably pointless to admit that I think I'm in over my head here. I just wanted sex, and I've caught feelings somewhere along the way."

"It's normal."

"Was it like this for you, back when you were seeing multiple people?" Geoff asked. "So many complicated feelings?"

"I've been trying to remember, honestly." Patrick had combed through his memories quite a bit and couldn't remember the same intensity he was feeling now. "I know it was different. But I'm pretty sure it's because I wasn't in love with any of them. Not like now, not like the way I love you."

Geoff laced his fingers with Patrick's. "And Lori?"

Patrick stroked his beard, tugging the coarse hairs into alignment. The sensation helped him stay present while his heartbeat sped up. "I don't know, Geoff." Saying it out loud, that was scary, too scary. "It's so soon. It's not like with us, where we had months, years to figure it out."

"I knew I was going to fall in love with you after our first date."

Geoff's expression was so earnest, so sincere, that Patrick's heart ached. He was right too; he'd known he was in love with Geoff within weeks. "We didn't say it right away."

"We weren't fools." Geoff looked down at their entwined fingers. "Maybe we're fools now."

"I've always been a fool for you," Patrick teased, making Geoff smile.

"I don't know what happens if I say it out loud." Geoff stared off into the middle distance. "I could fall in love with Lori." As soon as the words were out, he closed his eyes. "That's a lot to say out loud."

Geoff was being honest, and Patrick wasn't ready. Geoff probably knew. "What if we just walk away?" Patrick asked. "We've got our marriage. Each other. We're happy."

"We could do that." Geoff swallowed. "We have to do that, right? What's the alternative? We beg her to stay?"

"We can't beg her to stay." Patrick shook his head. "Even if we want her to." *I want her to.* He thought the words but didn't say them. Geoff had already done enough tonight.

"We could do a long-distance thing. It isn't even that far." Geoff seemed to try out the words, but then frowned. "It's not the same."

"If we're going to be with her, I want to *be with her*. Not three trains and a car ride away." Patrick sighed. "Maybe that's selfish, but I can't give that relationship the time it deserves without being with her."

"And we can't leave." Geoff said it with certainty. "Our life is here." He hesitated, then, his eyes going wide and vulnerable as a realization seemed to occur to him. "*My* life is here."

"Don't." Patrick shook his head.

"But you lived there. You want to go back, I *know* you want to go back. You could—"

"*Don't*," Patrick insisted, covering Geoff's mouth with his hand. It was all he could say. If Geoff asked him to swear that he didn't want to go to New York, he would have to lie, and he didn't want to lie. He wasn't going to leave Geoff for anything, not for Lori, not for New York, not even for Lori in New York, but being asked to say it out loud or even reassure Geoff right now was going to break him apart. He pressed his palm firmly against Geoff's lips and begged, silently, that Geoff would not ask this of him.

Geoff's gaze softened, tender and understanding. He knew, he had to know, and he wouldn't ask. After a moment, Patrick took his hand away, and they interlaced their fingers and were silent together.

Geoff finally broke the silence. "So, we walk away."

Patrick nodded. "We walk away."

Geoff hung his head. "I hate this."

Patrick squeezed his hand. "At least we've got each other." It was a comfort, sure, but it rang hollow. They might have each other, but they didn't have her.

21

L   ori couldn't stop looking chagrined as she opened the door to her apartment and invited Hannah in. "Thanks for coming."

Hannah rolled her eyes and thrust the bottle of tequila into Lori's hands. "It's too much perfect symmetry for me to miss it. Plus, this is what friends are for. Drinks and comfort on a Monday night." She let herself in and flopped down on the couch. "You gave me enough shit last year, I feel like it's fair to give you some back."

"It's fair." Lori cradled the bottle of tequila. "Thank you for this."

"Crack it open. I don't have to be at the shop until noon tomorrow." Hannah put her feet up. "And bring snacks."

Lori returned to the living room with snacks and the tequila. "This is really not a good look for me."

"Because you're not a perfect therapist with perfect answers for every situation? Yeah, I know." Hannah grabbed the bag of chips and tore it open. "It's got to be killing you to be in this pickle when it's literally the thing you advise people about. Have you talked to *your* therapist about everything?"

"I filled her in." Lori grabbed a handful of chips. "It was helpful to talk it out, but I'm still no closer to a solution. And it's not her job to provide solutions. She gave me some stuff to think over, but I don't know. It seems like I'm in a lose-lose situation."

"Put it in words." Hannah beckoned. "Tell me what you're thinking."

"I have two key options here." Lori held up one finger. "One: I leave Mapleton for good and take my dream job in Manhattan. I move to the city and work as a relationship therapist and outreach coordinator at an amazing center that does fantastic work making people's lives better." She held up a second finger. "Or two: I stay here in Mapleton and play third wheel for a couple of married guys who already have each other and probably will get over me within a few weeks."

"Ouch." Hannah winced. "That's a pretty cold way of putting it."

"Yeah, but listen to what happens if I spin it this way." Lori tucked her leg up beneath her on the couch to get a better vantage point, and went back to holding up one finger. "One: I risk everything for love, embodying the polyamorous principles on which I based my entire research career to pursue a relationship with not one but two men I care deeply about." Second finger. "Or, two: I move away for a job opportunity."

"Fucking yikes." Hannah sipped her tequila. "You're right. It's all about the spin. And you've ruled out a long-distance relationship?"

Lori made a face. "I can't do that, not in a closed triad. I'd be too lonely trying to sustain it. If I choose New York, I'd need to make a clean break."

"When do you need to tell the job people?"

"I told them last week that I needed a week to decide." Lori winced. "That week is up tomorrow."

"Then this really is the eleventh hour."

"Practically, if not literally." Lori sighed. "I even tried flipping a coin. I felt weird about every possible outcome." She shoved some chips into her mouth and crunched them noisily. "This isn't like me, Hannah." Lori gestured to herself. "I make decisions. I pursue things. That's my whole gig: I decide what I want and then go after it. But now, I feel like that's wrong. I feel like, if I leave now, I'm leaving behind this one big chance at love." She closed her eyes, the *L* word too heavy to look at head-on. "I don't even know if Geoff and Patrick feel the same way about me. They already have each other. It feels selfish to even ask."

"What if they do love you?" Hannah asked.

Lori opened her eyes this time, because she had to face this. "How can I know? Am I supposed to just go over there and *ask?* And what then? Do I risk everything in the hopes that our relationship lasts? It's been such a short time. Months. I may never get another opportunity like this in my field again. And yet…" She hesitated, and her face felt hot. "I don't know if I'm going to feel like this about anyone else, ever again."

Hannah reached out and took her hand, the one that wasn't clutching the glass of tequila. "I wish I knew what to tell you. There isn't a good answer here."

"What would you do, if you were me?"

Hannah's eyes went wide, and she adjusted her glasses. "Me? In your shoes? Lori, I'm not like you."

"But…if you were." She just needed this perspective, even if it wasn't the right one.

Hannah hesitated. "If it were me? I'd..." She swallowed, like the words were stuck in her throat. "I'd go to New York."

Lori raised her eyebrows. She thought for sure that Hannah would recommend she stay with the guys, especially when Hannah herself was about to buy a house with the men she loved. "Really?"

"Really. Lori, it's what you've wanted your whole academic career. This is your *dream.* I could never recommend you give it up for anyone, even for love. If it's love, if it's really love, maybe it'll work out some other way."

Lori nodded slowly, realization settling inside her stomach like a heavy weight. She put her untouched glass of tequila down on the table. "I need to go talk to them."

"What, now? Tonight?" Hannah gaped. "I just got here."

"I know. I'm sorry." Lori put her hands on her head. "I need to know for sure."

"Okay." Hannah set her own glass down. "You need a ride?"

"No, I didn't have anything to drink." Lori hesitated. "You want to stay here tonight? I'm not going to stay—I mean, I'll be coming back here."

Hannah smiled tenderly. "Sure. I'll stay. I told the guys I wasn't coming home tonight anyway. Figured this whole thing might take a lot longer."

Lori laughed, but it came out shaky. "Thanks. Save me the tequila for after. I'll definitely need it."

GEOFF HAD BEEN DOZING on Patrick's shoulder, the two of them falling asleep in front of some Food Network marathon, when the downstairs buzzer jolted them awake.

"What the hell?" Geoff rubbed a hand across his eyes, and then grabbed his glasses off the coffee table. "It's ten thirty on a Monday night."

Frowning, Patrick went to activate the security camera for the elevator lobby. "It's Lori." He looked back at Geoff, then at the tiny screen. "Lori?" he asked into the mic, as if they didn't very well know it was her.

"Hey." Her voice came through the speaker tinny and overly loud. "I'm sorry. I know it's late. Can I come up?"

Patrick looked over at Geoff. "Should I? I know you said...a couple of days ago, you said you wanted space."

That was true, but right now, his heart was pounding, and he wanted nothing more than to see her. "Invite her up. If...if you're okay with it."

Patrick invited her up and pushed the access code to call the elevator.

"I hope she's okay," Patrick said. Geoff hadn't even considered that possibility, that she'd come over unannounced because something was wrong. He checked his phone, but there were no missed texts or calls.

The elevator dinged, the doors slid open, and Lori walked out into their living room with wide eyes and her hair already wrapped up in its evening scarf.

"I'm sorry to just barge in without texting or calling. I had to see you both." She looked like she was going to go hug Patrick, but she paused, hands twitching before she shoved them in the pockets of her pajama pants. Glancing down at herself, she bit her lip as though realizing for the first time she was in pajamas. "I...didn't really think this through."

"Are you okay?" Patrick bridged the distance between them, and he hugged her. Geoff's heart filled his throat. Patrick was always so good at these things, the easy embraces, the casual physical contact. Lori relaxed in his embrace, wrapping her arms around his midsection.

"I'm okay." She stepped back, clearing her throat and putting space between them, and looked between Geoff and Patrick before her eyes settled on Geoff. "Sorry I ran out on you the other night."

"It's okay." He didn't know what to do with his hands. "I probably shouldn't have pushed things."

"Do you love me?"

Lori's words echoed in the condo, too loud for the night and the quiet of the space, and Geoff's stomach dropped out from under him. He swallowed, then swallowed again, and the lump in his throat wouldn't go away. She locked eyes with him and wouldn't let him look elsewhere, her gaze burning into his.

He could deflect. He could ask her the same question, or ask her why she needed to know, or even look to Patrick for help. But she'd asked him directly, and she deserved a direct answer, even if putting the word into his mouth was terrifying.

"Yes."

The word came out quietly, without the fanfare it probably deserved, but Geoff had barely admitted this to himself and now had to admit it to the room. "It's probably too soon," he admitted. "And I know I'm not supposed to. And it probably doesn't matter in the long run. But yes. I...do love you."

Lori closed her eyes. She nodded slowly before rounding on Patrick. "What about you?"

Patrick took a small step backward, away from her. "It's soon."

"I know it's soon. Do you love me?"

Patrick laughed, a wry chuckle that Geoff had heard before

when Patrick was overwhelmed. "Yeah. For whatever the fuck it means, or whatever good it is, yeah. I do love you." He looked to Geoff and shrugged helplessly.

Lori sagged, and it was hard to tell whether she sagged with relief or exhaustion. "I love both of you fools. So, what the hell am I supposed to do now?"

"What?" Geoff got to his feet. "What do you mean?"

"I'm taking the job." She looked between the two of them, the three of them forming the points of a triangle across the living room. "The organization I really want to work for offered me a position. I'm gonna take it. I'm moving to New York."

Anger welled up in Geoff, his body burning hot from the inside. "Why'd you ask, then? Why'd you make us say it out loud, if you're just going to turn and leave?"

"Because I had to know!" Lori was nearly shouting back. "I had to know what I was losing before I threw it away." She balled up her hands into fists and... Oh, she was crying. Tears welled at the corners of her eyes, spilling over her cheekbones, and Geoff had to move forward and take her into his arms. She pounded her fists into his back, but she pressed her face into his chest at the same time, and he held her. Geoff looked over her head at Patrick, who was standing with his hands limp at his sides, helpless in the face of this. Geoff gestured him closer, and Patrick moved into the embrace as well, curling his body around Lori's and holding both of them.

"I'm sorry," Geoff said. He wasn't even sure what he was apologizing for. For loving her? For putting her in this mess? For inviting her into their bed in the first place? No, not that third one. He could never be sorry for that. His heart might be tearing itself up inside him, but he couldn't be sorry for having this small taste of something bigger and more wonderful than he could have imagined.

"At least you'll have each other." Lori's words were muffled in Geoff's chest.

"It won't be the same," Patrick said into her curls. He looked at Geoff, and his eyes were soft with unspoken emotions. "It's not the same."

Lori pushed back gently, disentangling herself from them, her eyes still wet. "Look at me, like a fool." She wiped the back of her hand across her face, clearing the tears, and Geoff wordlessly handed her a tissue from the coffee table. "Thanks."

"When will you leave?"

"A couple of weeks. I have to find a place to stay, and get everything packed up, but I don't have much." Her voice had stopped trembling, and Geoff could already see her starting over, picking up her life and rebuilding it someplace new. "You know, it's not that far. Maybe you guys could come visit sometime, after I get settled. After…things settle."

Geoff could imagine the thought behind her words. *After it wouldn't hurt so bad.* "Maybe," he offered.

"And who knows what'll happen down the road, right?" Lori spread her arms wide. She was already stepping back, already creating distance. "Nine Possum Thursday picks up, or some other university's got a tenure-track position, maybe you'll end up in New York again. Wouldn't that be something?" Her smile didn't reach her eyes. "All of us, same big city? Stranger things have happened."

Geoff froze, a jolt like electricity sizzling down his spine. His thoughts raced ahead of his ability to process them, tumbling over one another like they did when he was deep into research, unlocking and compiling new ideas. He barely heard Patrick repeat the same word he'd said to Lori just a few days ago.

"Stay," Patrick said quietly. "Stay with us tonight."

"I can't." Lori shook her head. "I don't want to make this harder than it already is. I just...I just need to go." She inhaled and exhaled, and without another word, got into the elevator and let the door slide shut.

Patrick sank onto the sofa, but Geoff was rooted to the spot where he'd been standing. Ideas were still coming to him, a possibility he hadn't really considered before this moment.

"Babe?" Patrick said, touching his hand, pulling Geoff out of the moment. "Are you okay?"

"I'm okay." Geoff nodded. "I need to work through some things."

"Me too." Patrick squeezed his hand. "You want some time alone?"

Geoff pushed his glasses up his nose. "I think...I want some time...with the computer."

22

Geoff had said he'd wanted alone time with the computer, and Patrick didn't press. He hadn't pressed for the past five days, when Geoff had spent most of his free time frowning at the screen while Patrick was left to fend for himself. Geoff surfaced for meals, but otherwise it was like living with a zombie. Now, as the week ended, he was starting to wonder if he needed to shake Geoff out of his funk. Maybe they should go out together. Maybe Geoff needed a distraction.

He was surprised, then, when Geoff stepped between him and the television. Even backlit, the determined set of Geoff's jaw was noticeable. "Can we talk?"

Patrick flicked off the TV. "Always."

"Come outside with me."

Geoff didn't usually invite Patrick out to his thinking spot. Patrick followed as they walked through the parking lot, the gravel crunching beneath his feet, and resisted the impulse to press Geoff for conversation. If there was anything he knew about his husband, it was that Geoff would talk when he was ready.

Geoff made room for Patrick on his thinking rock, the one that protruded out over the river rushing below. It was dusk, and the evening chorus of birdsong echoed down the river. They hung their feet over the edge and looked down at the water below.

"I used to be scared of the water," Geoff said quietly.

Patrick nodded. He knew this about his husband; Geoff had told him about enduring swimming lessons, about his childhood fears of drowning.

"You got over it." Patrick brushed his fingers across the back of Geoff's hand.

"I never told you how." Geoff turned his hand palm-up, letting Patrick interlace their fingers. "I was about…eleven or twelve, I think. We were on vacation in the Adirondacks. We had this cabin right on the edge of the deepest, darkest lake. There was a dock that stuck out into the water. For days, I wouldn't even go on the dock. I would sit on shore, terrified, even though I was perfectly capable of swimming. I was so mad that the lake was *there*, like it was taunting me or something." He smiled wistfully. "One night, I realized I wasn't mad at the lake. I was mad at myself for being scared. I was mad that my fear was controlling me."

Patrick could picture it, Geoff with his oversized glasses, having a reckoning with himself in a cabin.

"I went out, in the middle of the night. The moon was so bright, it was like daylight. I took off all my clothes, and I walked out to the end of that dock, and I jumped in the water."

Patrick squeezed Geoff's hand, but didn't interrupt.

Geoff shook his head. "I was terrified. But I made myself

stay in the water anyway. Treading water in the dark, trying to stop being scared."

"And it worked?" he asked.

"Eventually." Geoff looked at their interlaced fingers. "Or I got used to the fear. I'm not sure which."

They sat in silence for a few minutes, with the water rushing beneath them, and then Geoff started speaking again. "I'm afraid of a lot of things, Patrick. I'm afraid of everything in my life I can't control. I'm afraid of making the wrong decisions. But most of all, I'm afraid that I'm going to look back and regret what I didn't do. I don't want to avoid the lake. I want to jump in."

Patrick knew what Geoff was going to say next before he said it, but it didn't make sense. Geoff wouldn't offer this, wouldn't make this kind of sacrifice, when he'd worked his whole life to get this far.

"Babe," he began, but Geoff interrupted him.

"Did you know," Geoff said over the start of his objection, "that if you're a highly regarded professor with an extensive publication history, sometimes another university will offer you a tenure-track position?"

Patrick stared. Was Geoff saying what he thought he was saying?

Geoff smiled. "I think we should move to New York."

"You've been researching jobs?" The past week suddenly made a lot more sense.

Geoff nodded. "I've been making calls. Apparently, my CV is...notable. I have a couple of interviews scheduled next week. I can call and cancel, or I can go through with them."

"It's not a sure thing, though."

"I'm not concerned with the time frame. I'm willing to keep looking until I find something that gives me the same opportunities I have here." Geoff took Patrick's other hand and held it close, so they were looking into each other's eyes, hands locked together. "You could be a pit musician. You could go after that again."

Patrick swallowed. "I don't know if I'm good enough." The words scraped out of his throat, and he hated saying them.

"You'll never know unless you try. But if we stay here, you'll never go after your dream. I know this is still your dream."

Patrick watched the water rushing beneath them, the steady flow of water moving ever onward. The river never stopped. "You think we should move for Lori."

"Yes." Geoff had no uncertainty in his voice. "And I think we should move for us."

Patrick had to let go of Geoff's hands. He turned away, emotion bubbling up inside him. "It might not work out."

"I know."

Patrick ran through the possibilities in his mind. The risks. The terrifying prospect of really chasing after his dream at the same time that they chased a nontraditional relationship.

"We both love her," Geoff reminded him, like Patrick needed reminding, like Patrick hadn't spent the last week thinking of her. She'd been on his mind every moment: He'd thought of her cuddling between him and Geoff in their king-sized bed, thought of her smile and her laugh and her playful comments. He'd thought of what his life would look like without her in it.

"You really think it's worth the risk?" Patrick asked.

"I do." Geoff nodded. "But if you're not on board, I'll let it go. I love you, and I won't push you past your limits. And you don't have to decide right now. I've been thinking about it all week. If you want time, we can—"

"I don't need time." Patrick felt like he'd spent years of his life waiting. "I'm in. Let's jump in this lake."

Geoff gripped the back of Patrick's neck and pulled him in for a kiss, their mouths colliding like a force of nature. Patrick found Geoff's shoulders, his arms, and held him in place. He loved this man. Whatever life had in store for them, they could face it together.

Geoff broke the kiss and pressed his forehead to Patrick's, both of them breathing heavily.

"When you say jump in the lake," Geoff frowned slightly, "I just want to confirm…"

"Metaphorical lake. Let's move to New York." The words sent a flood of emotion through Patrick's body. "Fuck. Let's move to New York."

LORI SCANNED the array of boxes scattered around the living room, overwhelmed. Packing was terrible, even for a minimalist like her who culled and decluttered every month or so. This felt final in a different manner than her previous moves, each box like packing away a piece of her emotions. After days of crying and moping, now she just felt wrung-out and empty. Maybe she'd made the right decision; maybe she hadn't. She might never be sure.

The only thing she could do was pick up and move forward with whatever her life had become and make the best of her new future. In the city, she could pursue the career she'd been chasing since her undergraduate days. She could do so much good for so many people. Each night, she'd tried to comfort herself with those thoughts while ignoring the hollowed-out loneliness inside. It was Saturday night, and she was packing boxes.

The doorbell rang, and then rang again, and then a third time. What the hell? She set down the books she'd been packing and peered through the peephole. In astonishment, she swung open the door to Geoff and Patrick. Her heart raced at the sight of them, that lonely, empty feeling inside her immediately crying out for her to run to them, throw herself in their arms, and ask to never be separated again. Instead, she stayed rooted to the spot. "What are you doing here?"

Geoff looked past her and then pushed his glasses up on his nose. "Can we come in?"

She stepped aside to let them pass. A dozen scenarios were running through her mind. She wasn't counting on needing to say goodbye to them again. A clean break would have been easier, and now things were just going to be messy. But if they wanted one last fling, a small part of her wasn't sure she'd be able to resist. Maybe she could have one final amazing night to remember them by.

They stood in her living room, side by side, and Lori faced them with her arms crossed. She was going to need all her emotional armor to see this through.

Geoff swallowed before he spoke. "Last night, Patrick and I sat down to talk. About a lot of things." He hesitated, and then continued. "I told him this story about a lake…" He trailed off, and then looked to Patrick, who shook his head and smiled with affection at his husband.

"We should have rehearsed this." Patrick ran a hand through his hair and took a deep, shuddering breath. "Look. Let's get right to the point. We want to move to New York."

Lori stared at them. She couldn't have heard that correctly, right? Her brain ground to a halt, frozen by the words on his lips.

"I've been running away from my own goals and dreams since my mom died," Patrick continued. "I love the band, and I love giving music lessons, but what I really want to do is be a pit musician in the city. I miss New York, and I miss doing what I love."

Geoff jumped into the conversation. "There are a lot of colleges and universities in New York. Tenure is an option at several of them. I don't know if I'm going to get something right away, but I'm going to keep trying."

"But it's not about careers. Not really." Patrick held Geoff's hand, like they were trying to give each other strength, and Lori's heart cracked open a tiny bit even while her brain struggled to process everything they were saying. "We're going to move to the city because we want to be with you."

Lori closed her eyes. She hadn't wanted to hope for this. She hadn't wanted to ask, hadn't felt like she *deserved* to ask. With her eyes still squeezed tight against the hope in their faces, she choked out her question. "What if it doesn't work out?"

"We can't live with ourselves unless we try." Geoff's voice sounded as wrecked with emotion as she felt. "Neither of us. We can't stay here and watch you move away and never know what might have been."

Lori blinked her eyes open, and they were filled with tears that she fought back. She would not cry, not over this, not over what she wanted so badly. She clenched her fists by her side, holding back the emotion, fingernails digging into her own palms.

"You would do this for me?" she asked. "You would uproot

your whole lives and move somewhere brand-new...to be with me?"

Geoff nodded, and Patrick looked disbelieving. "Of course," Patrick said. "We love you."

She threw herself into their arms.

Patrick and Geoff wrapped her in a hug, and there were too many arms, and it was ridiculous and overwhelming and just perfect. "There's so much to figure out." Her voice came out muffled, buried into Geoff's chest.

"We talked about some things yesterday, when we made the decision." Patrick stroked her back, fingertips trailing lightly up and down.

Lori tipped her head back to look at him in disbelief. "You made the decision yesterday, but you didn't come over until today?"

"We wanted to be sure," Geoff said. "And figure out logistics, possible timelines, where we might live...we made a spreadsheet."

Lori rested her forehead against Geoff's chest. "You made a spreadsheet. Of course, you did." She loved these dorks.

Still smiling, she pulled Geoff's mouth down for a kiss. Then, she kissed Patrick, because they were both here, and she loved both of them, and she suddenly remembered the gorgeous, messy kisses in the parking lot of Tokens after karaoke and her body lit up from the inside. *I could have this*, she thought.

I can have this.

I have this.

It was too much, kissing them in the living room, surrounded by boxes.

"Bed." She pulled away and grabbed each of them by the hand.

"Now?" Patrick laughed but followed, as did Geoff.

"Yes. Now. It's been forever, and I want you *now*." She had shut down this part of her brain, trying desperately not to want this anymore once she said her goodbyes. Now, with the ocean of possibility stretched out before her, her desires came roaring back with a force that left her breathless. "Any objections?"

Both men shook their heads, and Geoff answered, "Hell no."

GEOFF HADN'T EXPECTED the day to end up here, in Lori's bed, tumbling down against her onto the soft surface... but he'd be lying if he said he hadn't hoped. His body thrummed with need. He and Patrick hadn't been intimate since that night outside the club, when he was desperate and strung out, and Patrick was so beautiful and willing. Now, with Lori stripping out of her clothing, desire surged hot through his veins.

"Wait." He stilled her hands as she was about to unfasten her jeans. "Let me."

Lori shivered as Geoff slid her jeans down her hips, and sucked in a quiet breath when Patrick joined him, unfastening her bra. They stripped her of her clothing with slow delibera-tion, and Geoff had to drop to his knees and press his mouth to the skin he uncovered: her belly, her hip bone, the downy patch of hair at the juncture of her thighs. She smelled amaz-ing, like sex and the ocean, and he dipped his tongue deeper into her folds, longing to taste.

Lori dug her fingernails into his scalp, thighs suddenly trembling. Geoff sat back on his heels and looked up at her and Patrick above him. Patrick stood behind her, mouthing the tender skin of her neck, hands cupping her full breasts. Lori had her eyes closed and head thrown back. Geoff got to his feet and kissed Lori again, then Patrick, and he slid his hands beneath Patrick's shirt to the warm skin beneath.

Lori sucked in a breath watching them. Her eyes had gone dark, liquid, needy. He could get used to seeing her like this. He wanted to see her like this over and over, and god, now he got to.

Lori helped strip Patrick the same way they'd undressed her, if a little rougher, tugging off his jeans while Geoff pulled off his shirt. Patrick ended up tangled in his pants and shoes and fell to the bed, laughing, and then it was all kissing and touching and the last clothes—Geoff's—carelessly tossed aside.

"Wait, my clothes will wrinkle," Patrick protested, only half-serious, and Geoff got up off the bed.

"I'll fold your clothes," Geoff said. "I know you can't focus if they're not in a pile."

Lori watched him do so, looking between him and Patrick, and her eyes sparkled with affection when she leaned down to kiss Patrick once more. "It's a good thing you've got your husband to indulge your weirdness, because I'm not having it."

Patrick laughed. "Fair enough."

Lori and Patrick were adorable and sweet, and watching them laugh made something beautiful ache inside Geoff. How could he have ever worried he'd be jealous? Just the thought of the two of them together had him filled with affection...and achingly hard. The juxtaposition made him dizzy.

"I want to watch you together," Geoff said breathlessly. He hadn't gotten to see Patrick with Lori, not without being involved himself, and he wanted that more than he wanted to participate.

"Will you warm me up?" Lori asked Geoff, smiling.

She was so wet when he slid his fingers between her legs, he had to take a moment to catch his breath. He could watch her forever, stretched out on her back, rocking her hips up to meet Geoff's touches as he steadily rubbed her clit. She bit her lip, stifling a moan as Patrick began to roll her nipples between his fingers.

"Fuck," she gasped when Geoff slid two fingers inside her. She was so wet, so snug, so perfect, and he curled his fingers inside her the way she'd taught him while his thumb pressed small circles into her clit. When her muscles tensed, Geoff pulled away, withdrawing his hand despite her protests.

"I want to watch you come on Patrick's cock," he whispered.

Lori didn't question, instead moving quickly to grab a condom from her purse.

Watching this process—Lori rolling a condom over Patrick's erection, Patrick pulling her face down for another hot, desperate kiss, Lori rolling onto her back and Patrick settling between her thighs—Geoff couldn't imagine wanting to be anywhere else than beside them, lightly stroking his cock. He would have his own turn with each of them, with both of them. Maybe tonight, maybe tomorrow, maybe each day and maybe, just maybe, for the rest of his life.

But right now, the two people he cared about most held each other close, and he could bear witness to each movement, each shift, each hitching breath and moan.

Lori arched up to meet Patrick's thrust as he filled her, her body taking him in. She curled her toes into the sheets and bit her lip. Patrick rested his head down on hers, foreheads touching, as he caught his breath. He slid his hands beneath her shoulders, palm-up, cupping her for leverage as he took his weight on his forearms and began to move.

They were beautiful. Patrick's long torso, his lines of muscle, his peach skin flushing with arousal and heat. Beneath him, Lori raised her hips to meet him, her brown skin gleaming with sweat, hair spread out on the pillow. With each press of Patrick's hips, each time he slid inside her, she made a soft noise of pleasure.

"Look at you," Geoff murmured, stroking his erection. He didn't want to come yet, but the sight of them was as hot as taking part. He couldn't bear *not* to rub his thumb over his leaking slit, pleasure sparking inside him.

"Fuck." Patrick sounded raw and open. He kissed Lori, their lips pressing, breath mingling. "You're gorgeous," he told her. And then he looked over at Geoff, wordless, the ghost of a smile hovering around his mouth. "You like watching?"

Geoff smiled back. It was obvious with how hard he was, but Patrick needed to hear it, and he wanted to say it. "I love watching. I love watching you fill her up with your cock. Does he feel good, Lori? Is he doing a good job fucking you?"

"Mmm." She smiled, glancing over at him, her expression blissful. "So good. He's so good."

"Is he gonna make you come?"

"Yeah." Her voice was breathless, and she slid a hand carefully between them, searching out her clit. "I want to come on his cock."

Patrick let out another choked moan. Dirty talk really did it for him, and Geoff was all too happy to oblige.

"Does she feel good, sweetheart?" Geoff asked. "All snug and wet around you?"

"*So* good." Patrick was thrusting harder now, hips snapping forward, driving into her.

Geoff turned to Lori, who was fingering her clit, breathing heavily. "You want him to slow down? You want me to make him wait with his dick all the way in you, holding it there while you rub your clit?"

Lori smiled as Patrick gasped. "That seems so cruel." She reached her free hand up to brush some hair from Patrick's forehead. "Do it. Stay still for me."

Patrick groaned, broken and desperate, and his hips shuddered to a halt. Lori began to move, agonizingly slowly, rocking her hips against Patrick while he trembled and tried to hold himself still. Geoff watched her fingers dance over her clit, rubbing back and forth dizzyingly fast even as her hips moved so slowly.

"*Please.*" Patrick choked out the word.

"Please what?" Lori reached one leg up to wrap around his hips, dragging him in deeper and then holding him there.

"Please let me move."

"But you make such a good toy," she teased. She was good at this, devastatingly good, and Geoff was stroking himself faster at the sight of it. "I'm gonna get myself right...right to the edge." Her words were coming out shakier as she brought herself to that peak. "And then, I'm gonna let you fuck me over it."

Patrick nodded furiously. He was shaking all over with the effort of holding still, and damn, Geoff wanted him, wanted to kiss him, to fuck him.

"You're so good," Geoff crooned. "You look perfect like this."

Patrick smiled, the praise probably going right to his erection. "I'm going to explode."

"Not yet you're not," Lori responded, and then she threw her head back, hips pushing up into him like she couldn't bear not to have every millimeter of his cock filling her up. And then she cried out, pulling her hand from between them. "Now," she gasped. "Fuck me. Make me *come*." Her voice broke on the last word, and Patrick's body shuddered into action.

He thrust into her over and over like a man possessed, his hips a blur of movement. Lori arched up, both hands going around his shoulders, and cried out wordlessly. Her body spasmed, rocked with pleasure, and Patrick groaned as he continued to piston in and out. Finally, Lori sagged, her hands slipping to the bed, and Patrick buried himself all the way into her and shuddered through his release.

Geoff caught his breath. He was shaking like it was him, either the one being fucked or the one fucking, and his dick throbbed as he watched them come down from their high.

Lori kissed Patrick, pulling his face gently to hers, whispering words to him that only they could hear. This was their moment. That was all right. But then Lori reached for Geoff, cupping his head in her hand, and brought his mouth down for a kiss. Her lips were swollen and soft, her kisses languid with postorgasm relaxation, and Geoff could kiss her all day.

Lori smiled up at him and then turned to Patrick, who was recovering, rolling away to take care of the condom. "You all right, there, hon?"

Patrick looked up at the pet name, and his answering smile was sheepish. "I'm great."

Geoff was still hard, body thrumming with need, but the need only went as far as the physical. Emotionally, he could be happy like this. He was happy for them. He was happy for all of them.

"Don't give me that look." Lori rolled her eyes. "You look like a sap."

Geoff laughed. "I am a sap. I'm happy."

Lori reached over to the nightstand and grabbed another condom, tossing it to him. "Here."

Geoff looked down, frowning in confusion.

Lori spread her legs apart and cocked an eyebrow. "You think I'm done? I told you boys the very first night we spent together. I am a *repeat* kind of girl."

Geoff's erection pulsed. "I thought...you two were done..."

"I'm done," Patrick explained, stretching out on the bed.

Lori licked her lips. "And I'm not. So. Hurry up."

Geoff laughed. He was already slicking the condom down, hands shaking a bit, although he tried to still them. "I'm not going to last long. That was...something else."

Lori pushed him down onto his back in the middle of the bed and climbed on top of him, straddling his hips. "Then I'd better take control of this."

Geoff's eyes rolled back into his head as she guided him inside her. She was so wet and soft and open from her first orgasm, body yielding perfectly to his, and he couldn't resist thrusting up the rest of the way. She rode him hard and fast, taking his cock without hesitation and driving him to the edge so quickly, he could barely think. He couldn't control the moans and gasps slipping from his lips. This was heaven, as close to heaven as he could imagine. Lori began to rub her clit again, chasing her second climax.

Pleasure built inside Geoff, pooling low in his belly, flowing heavy and hot through his veins, rushing to overtake him until he could barely think from the need to come, to come, to *come*. Patrick leaned in, cupped the side of his face, and kissed him.

"Go on," Patrick whispered against his mouth. "Come for us."

Geoff broke. The orgasm crashed through him, and he cried out into Patrick's mouth, fisting the sheets below him, his cock pulsing with release. Lori was still moving, still rocking her hips, until she, too, went motionless above him. Her muscles rippled all along his length, her climax milking out the last of his pleasure, until Geoff sagged back onto the bed.

Afterward, when they were cleaned up and curled together, Geoff pressed a kiss to the back of Lori's neck. She was sandwiched between them, her body a warm, soft expanse that Geoff could not stop touching.

"I can't believe I get to have this," he said out loud, and she smiled.

"All of us," Lori said, and she pressed a kiss to Patrick's nose. "We all get to have this."

Patrick kissed her softly, and over her hip, he took Geoff's hand in his.

EPILOGUE

December

"Careful! Don't knock the needles off!" Lori helped guide Patrick past the doorway of the apartment, wincing as he hit the doorframe with the branches of their Christmas tree.

Geoff managed the other end of the tree, which was just clearing the door. "Are you sure this is going to fit?" he asked again. "It's a big tree."

"I measured," Patrick insisted.

"And you took into account the height of the stand?"

Patrick rolled his eyes. "This isn't the first time I've done this, you know."

"But it's your first time without lofted ceilings," Geoff pointed out.

Lori was perfectly capable of helping, but it was more fun at this point to stand back and watch Geoff and Patrick put the tree up on their own. *Their* tree. In their apartment. Their very own two-bedroom place, that they'd moved into just last month after a few months of separate flats in the city. Now, this was home, the place where they were going to spend their very own first Christmas together next week.

She put on a kettle for tea as the two guys got the tree upright. They didn't have many nights off together, now that Patrick was working as a substitute violinist for multiple shows, including the Rockettes' *Christmas Spectacular* with its ridiculous performance schedule. Fortunately, they really only had to plan around Patrick's schedule; her work with the Center was mostly during the day, and Geoff was on winter break from teaching at the university. But tonight, they'd eked out an evening together to get their tree and share some pre-holiday festivities.

Geoff insisted on doing the lights, because Patrick apparently didn't understand "the proper ratio" for lighting a Christmas tree, which let Patrick and Lori sit together on the couch with their tea while watching Geoff meticulously drape multicolored bulbs around the branches.

Lori patted Patrick on the leg. "I finally heard back from Hannah and the guys."

Geoff poked his head out from behind the tree. "What's the verdict? Are they going to come?"

"Day after Christmas." Lori nodded. "Giant Friendsmas here in the city."

"And your mom's still visiting on Christmas Eve?" Patrick asked.

"Yup. Christmas Eve here before heading out to see my brother." Lori sighed. "It's a busy holiday season."

Patrick nodded. "And you're all still fine with me doing the evening show on Christmas day?"

"Even better. We're going to see it. Lori got us tickets." Geoff bent to plug in the strand of lights, and their tree burst into color.

Patrick squeezed Lori's hand, and then called Geoff over for a kiss. "It's beautiful, babe."

"Don't rest now. We've got ornaments to put up." Geoff rubbed his hands together, then frowned as his palms peeled apart. "I'm covered in sap. I'd better wash up."

"Fresh tree means sap." Patrick dropped a kiss on Lori's cheek. "Come on. Everybody does ornaments. We're a family now."

Lori groaned dramatically, but it was all for show. She couldn't help but smile as Patrick and Geoff started opening up boxes of ornaments, their own from Christmases past, now mixed in with the ones she'd brought with her when she moved.

Family.

This might not have been the family she envisioned a year ago, but life was an unpredictable, terrifying, beautiful ride. She wouldn't trade this for anything.

Still smiling, she joined them in decorating their tree.

ACKNOWLEDGMENTS

This book, like all my books, came into existence in no small part thanks to my incredible support network. My agent, the geektacular Saritza Hernandez, stayed by my side as I wrestled with the different possibilities for this book and helped me stay true to my vision, even though that meant some big scary steps forward. She is a tremendous advocate for her authors and I'm lucky to work with her.

It feels perfect to me that the amazing Tera Cuskaden edited this final book of the *Comes in Threes* series, since she has supported this series since the beginning. Her willingness to dig into late-night brainstorming helped bring this dream to fruition. Her honesty and passion for this project inspired me whenever my confidence waned. A special thanks goes to the duo of Christa Desir and Manuela Velasco for super helpful copy edits. Also, Zoe York made this gorgeous cover, and I'm so grateful for her enthusiasm for the project and her prodigious skill.

I had a whole passel of friends offering love, tough love, and valuable distractions throughout this process. A good portion of this book was written in productivity sprints with Felicia "Ray" Davin at a number of western Massachusetts coffee shops. Her presence made absurd writing deadlines seem civilized and even enjoyable. Amanda's long-distance cheering kept me going when I couldn't see the end in sight. Laura provided baked goods, commiseration, and calm advice when I had to be emotionally scraped off the ceiling. Crystal is always available to kick my ass or hold my hand, and knows which one I need. Chris is here for all my highs and lows with the unending confidence of someone who believes in me even when I don't believe in myself.

Finally, to you, the readers. In the months leading up to the RITA™ ceremony this past summer, I was awe-struck and humbled by the Romancelandia community for their support. You folks are talented, passionate, daring, persistent, and brilliant. You make me want to be a better writer, and I'm grateful every day that you choose to read my work. Thank you.

ABOUT THE AUTHOR

RITA™ Award-winning author Elia Winters is a fat, tattooed, polyamorous bisexual who loves petting cats and fighting the patriarchy. She holds a Master's degree in English Literature and teaches at a small rural high school, where she also runs the drama club. In her spare time, she is equally likely to be found playing tabletop games, kneading bread, cross-stitching, or binge-watching Marie Kondo. A sex educator and kink-positive feminist, Elia reviews sex toys, speaks at kink conventions, and writes geeky, kinky, cozy erotic romance. She currently lives in western Massachusetts with her loving husband and their weird pets.

ALSO BY ELIA WINTERS

Comes In Threes

Three-Way Split

Just Past Two

Slices of Pi

Even Odds

Tied Score

Single Player

Other Titles

Purely Professional

Playing Knotty

Stay informed about Elia Winters! Receive bonus content and subscriber-only specials, plus info on new releases and personal appearances. eliawinters.com/newsletter